Project Boing;)

Brian W. Robinson

ISBN: 979-8-218-24330-2

CONTENTS

ANALYSIS

I looked around the circle, into the eyes of a dozen people, stopping at Stefan, a computer programmer in his midtwenties who had a tattoo of the Twitter Fail Whale on the underside of his left wrist. I asked, "How did you get the coke?" I was curious; I was moving the conversation along. But I also was collecting information, signals, data points, dots. "I mean, how did you afford it? A 'brick' sounds like an expensive amount."

Stefan rubbed the Fail Whale with the top of his right wrist, as if he were polishing it. His folding chair squeaked in rhythm with his rubbing. "From the VCs, man. They were throwing money at our startup, even before the app, even when we were in stealth mode. I shit you not. Money just appeared in our First Republic account. Our credit limits kept magically increasing. We got invited to go rock climbing with President Obama's Tech Czar. Hot chicks showed up unannounced at my grandma's garage where we ate, slept, and coded."

The rest of us expressed a mixture of awe and admiration through our head nods, eye rolls, and mutterings. Collectively, we were like dots that connected to form a circle. A particular type of circle—a Decision Hour Circle.

I like to think of every group conversation as a sort of data collection opportunity that allows me to connect the dots into a coherent picture. In this case, the group conversation was conducted by a professional moderator, a middle-aged woman who smelled like lavender and insisted we call her Ma'am, apparently as both a title and a name. She was an employee of Washboard Acres, and we were temporary inhabitants of the institution, where incarceration-worthy but nonviolent citizens paid a civic debt. Her key qualification for leading this weekly Decision Hour Circle, where each of us was expected to make a life-affirming decision, was that she was a recovering drug addict, like the other dots in this circle—except for me.

Ma'am probed deeper. "How your parents feel 'bout all that, Stefan?"

"My dad had his own startups in the nineties, during the dot-com bubble, so he seemed to know what I was going through without hearing the details. My mom I kept in the dark 'til I got arrested. But she could tell shit was happening. Moms know."

Ma'am clicked her tongue. "Damn straight, moms know."

I'd been connecting my own dots about Stefan, dots I collected during this particular group session, dots I collected during conversations Stefan and I had while sharing a doorless room over the previous three weeks, and dots I collected from being a contributing member of the tech industry, from the beginning of my career at the dusk of the last millennium, until today in the year 2012, at the dawn of a new millennium that's only 1% finished, living and working in Silicon Valley (aka The Valley), where important pioneering companies utilized silicon-based computer circuitry in their products. This territory, which just a few generations ago was made up of small towns, fruit orchards, and a sleepy university called Stanford, has been overrun by high-tech business development, exorbitant housing prices, electric-car traffic jams, mediocre Indian food, and epic, multifront Quora wars over the impact cloud computing will have on humanity.

Stefan continued, "I majored in computer science, but I took a lot of classes outside my major. The hardest one, the one that most blew my mind, was called The Philosophy of Ethical Decision Making. I knew I was doing the wrong thing by buying that brick of coke. I knew it intellectually, from my ethics class. But I also knew it in my bones, man. Know what I mean?"

"We hear you, bro," said Bo, a large man who had a daily habit of persuading the rest of us to keep the television in the break area tuned to Comcast SportsNet, for coverage of the San Jose Sharks during the Stanley Cup playoffs, via good-natured threats of physical violence, like, "Touch that remote, and I'll pound your head. Just kidding." Otherwise, Washboard Acres functioned like a meritocracy, a society that rewards and elevates citizens based on their abilities and accomplishments. Bo made a reference to the currently-popular cable television show *Breaking Bad.* "Let me guess. You ordered a pizza to throw on your roof, *amirite*?"

Stefan chuckled, and so did a few of the others. "Yeah, part of me thought I was going to become some kind of drug kingpin. But I kept the brick in my trunk for weeks. I couldn't bring myself to do anything with it. Just having it made me feel like I had gas in the tank, money in the bank."

When you *connect the dots*, you make sense out of signals that might, at first glance, appear to be unrelated. When a child learning her numbers connects a sequence of numbered dots with a pencil, a picture emerges—for example, of a clown, an elephant, or a carousel. Typically, some aspect of the picture is drawn already—the clown's nose, the elephant's eye, the flag atop the carousel. In real life, no aspect of the picture is already drawn, and the dots aren't numbered, and when you connect the dots, there's no guarantee the correct picture will emerge. But in this case, the dots coalesced into a clear picture of Stefan.

He was born and raised in Palo Alto, the only child of two Stanford professors of Economics. After graduating from California State University, East Bay, with a degree in computer science, he founded a mobile app startup with three college friends. They created Cocky Roach, a gaming app where you controlled an animated cockroach's journey through a fast-food restaurant by tapping your smartphone screen to avoid being stepped on by various animated shoes. It was devilishly difficult to get beyond the second or third shoe; most games ended within four seconds. Even so, the app became a viral hit, with more than 20 million people downloading it to their iPhones in the first month after it launched. The app was free to download and play, so they received no revenue from it. However, as everyone in the Valley knows, *revenue follows eyeballs*; if you have users, it's only a matter of time before you'll figure out how to monetize them. Stefan and his friends pulled in more than seven million dollars from venture capital companies who wanted a stake in their company before it started to monetize. They accepted the money and did what many young men in their position have done: they spent it on drugs and sports cars.

Then, as a result of a lawsuit from another mobile gaming company that claimed Stefan and his friends violated one of their patents, Cocky Roach was removed from the iPhone app store. They spent the next few months working on a photo messaging app when, high on VC-funded hashish, Stefan was caught stealing burritos from a Sunnyvale 7-11 while carrying a distributable amount of cocaine in the trunk of his Fusion Red Tesla Roadster. His arrest and arbitration settlement with the state government resulted in his nine-month stay at Washboard Acres, where I met him halfway through his incarceration. I initially judged him to be a sociopathic, potentially violent drug addict, but eventually I came to the conclusion that he was a smart and talented young man, with a fluid sense of morality, whose personal brand was heavily and adversely shaped by a combination of peer pressure, popular culture, and the libertarian-fueled sense of entitlement that pervades the Valley.

I know what you're thinking: fluid morality, status obsessed, pervasive sense of entitlement—I just described a sociopath. Perhaps. But I found Stefan to be a kinder, gentler type of sociopath than I originally judged him to be. The best thing about collecting and analyzing information is that we can learn from it to better understand the world around us.

I raised my hand to get Stefan's attention. "Let me get this right. When you were arrested, you didn't have any users?"

"I think they were all users, professor." Bo had taken to calling me professor.

Stefan and I were the only members of the Decision Hour Circle who worked in the tech industry, so it was easy to understand Bo's confusion. "By users, I mean people who utilized Stefan's product. In our industry, we refer to an individual person who uses a digital product as a unique user."

Ma'am explained to me, like I was five, "Every drug user is unique. We all drug addicts, right? We all unique." The others nodded.

I shrugged; I wasn't a drug addict. "Yes, Ma'am. But in this case, a unique user means a customer who visits a website or uses a mobile application. For example, a person could play Cocky Roach on his iPhone, and he could play Cocky Roach on his iPad, his PC, and his Xbox—"

"It was only available on iOS," interrupted Stefan.

"I'm talking theoretically."

"Gotcha. We had those other platforms on our roadmap. It was going to happen." Stefan *Got It*, even though none of the others did.

"This person playing Cocky Roach on multiple platforms is just one person. Mathematicians have developed formulas for counting him once, uniquely, across devices, to determine whether the audience is growing, shrinking, or staying the same. Advertisers pay publishers, such as Stefan, to put ads on their websites and apps, and they want to know how many unique, individual people are seeing their ads."

Bo inhaled as if he'd been holding his breath. "Wow, you know a lot of stuff, professor. Maybe you can help me get this monkey off my back." As I'd just experienced with the confusion over the word "user," sometimes terms and phrases mean different things to different people. This was another of those times.

"I just might be able to help you there. I once got a monkey off my back with a ripe avocado." Everyone around the circle laughed, each in his or her own way, from a giggle to a guffaw. But as I continued talking, they all became aggressively silent. "It was during a photo shoot for my company's brand campaign. The photos would feature a monkey with a mohawk hairstyle that was supposed to visually represent the personalization our products offered to our users. We were ready to take the photos, but the monkey had climbed on my back and wouldn't get off. I don't know why he was so enamored with my back. I offered him a banana, but he smooshed it into my neck. I tried placing another banana on a table a short distance away, hoping he'd hop off to retrieve it. But he only clung tighter, scratching me deeply. Eventually, after his trainer tried coaxing him away with various fruits, meats, deserts, and vegetables, he climbed off me for the avocado. So that's what I recommend for getting a monkey off your back: avocado."

Stefan looked me in the eyes while slowly shaking his head and rubbing his Fail Whale tattoo. Bo stared sadly into his lap. Ma'am appeared to be looking up and to the left of me, disgustedly. The rest of the group seemed either depressed or angry. Ma'am explained, "Having a monkey on your back means you got a drug habit you're trying to kick. You ever had a drug habit, Glenn?"

"No. I've only literally had a monkey on my back."

"You shouldn't joke about having a monkey on your back, professor." Bo looked like he wanted to pound my head. Several others grumbled in agreement.

Stefan tried to help. "Hey, guys, Glenn's just a victim of his white-collar privilege. He doesn't understand gritty, real-life experience."

"Please, I'm not a victim of anything except my own ignorance. I apologize. In my meetings at work, everyone knows what I'm talking about. In fact, I have a reputation for having a big impact and moving the needle."

Bo jumped to his feet. "Moving the needle! What the hell's that supposed to mean, professor?" Three others jumped up to hold him back.

I didn't know what to say or do. I did what I normally do in such situations: I paused, awaiting further information. Ma'am provided it, after removing her palm from her face. "How many of you in this room have abused heroin?" Ten people raised their hands, including Bo and Ma'am. Ten of thirteen = 77%. "We used needles, Glenn, to destroy careers, our families, and ourselves."

I sighed and nodded. Bo and the others sat down. I took another approach. "I admire the power of metaphors, like having a monkey on your back or moving the needle or blocking & tackling. But they only work if used with the right audience, in the right context." Then I did something show-offy that I regret. I shifted the collar of my shirt to reveal a one-inch scar on the base of my neck that I got from the monkey digging his fingernails into me. "Here's where the monkey scratched me."

A roar of indignation filled the room as the dozen other people showed off multiple dozens of more impressive scars resulting from knife wounds, gunshots, bites, gruesome accidents, and amateur surgeries. A Filipino man removed his shirt to show a pattern of lashes on his back, emanating from his spine outward, like reddened angel wings, that he created himself while participating in an annual Good Friday flagellation ritual in his home country. "That's a real scar, bitch!"

I agreed.

As everyone settled down, Ma'am turned to me. "This is Decision Hour, Glenn. What's your decision?"

I arrived with a decision in mind—exercise three to four times per week so I can fit into my grad school clothes again—but as I was about to express it, multiple thoughts fought for primacy in my mind, rendering me temporarily mute. My stay at Washboard Acres had been challenging. Never before had I had such difficulty connecting dots into meaningful pictures. Never before had I been surrounded by so many people who didn't Get It. I had no access to the digital media and technology that helped me ground myself in relevant information. I felt disoriented, bewildered, untethered. The only way I kept steady was by regularly reminding myself of a useful asset I'd brought with me: my professional motto. My motto kept me oriented even when the environment around me was disorienting. It had become an essential part of me since I'd launched it several months earlier at work. The moment I first said it out loud in front of my work colleagues was an important dot connecting my previous life's work to my stay at Washboard Acres. So rather than express the decision I'd prepared for this meeting, I changed it up. "I'm glad I created a personal motto. I don't regret it, despite how things turned out."

INSIGHTS

I'd launched my motto several months earlier, during the Brand Campaign Assessment Tiger Team meeting where we appraised the results of the new advertising campaign for our company, Boing;).

Boing;) was the largest and best-known company in the world ever to include an emoticon in its name. A rite of passage for every Boinger was learning to write Boing;) with the emoticon; penalties for not doing so were unspecified but assumed to be severe. There was a persistent but continually debunked rumor that an SVP of Engineering who wrote a company-wide email with "Boing" in the subject line was terminated for trumped-up reasons (stalking an intern) when the real reason was not using the emoticon. After you've been a Boinger for a while, it becomes natural, and seeing the letters alone feels like vandalism.

I'd been seeking just the right moment for launching my motto, and I sensed it coming. When Maryanne, our SVP of Consumer Marketing, turned to me in her I'm-one-of-those-people-who-*Gets-It* manner and asked, "So if the campaign isn't working, what's the problem? Is it the busty blonde, or the monkey with the mohawk?"

I rubbed the recently healed scar on my neck and gestured toward the PowerPoint slide projected on the conference room wall, a slide featuring a color-coded bar chart I personally crafted to illuminate the most salient insights from our recent market research about the new campaign.

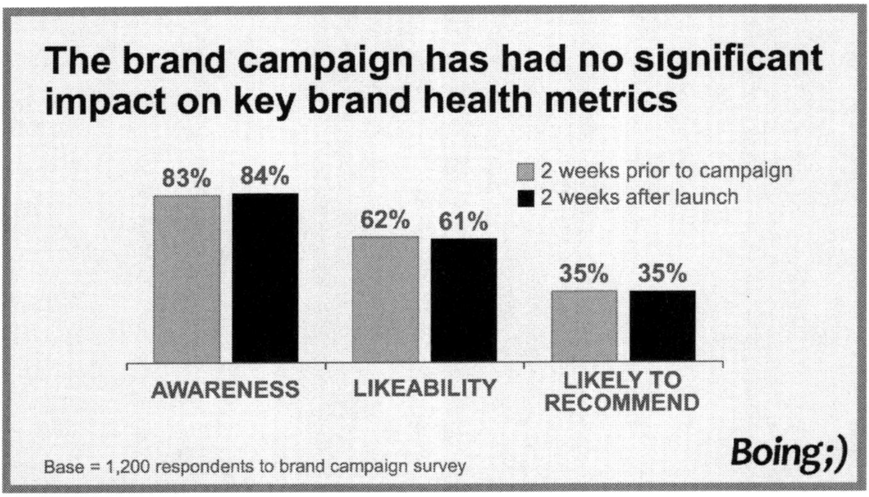

I explained, "It could be the blond. Or her bust. Or the monkey. Or his mohawk. It's likely a combination of these. The one thing the data shows for certain is the campaign isn't connecting with consumers. It hasn't significantly increased awareness of our brand. It hasn't increased our brand's likeability. It hasn't increased the likelihood to recommend our brand to friends and family. These metrics have been flat, before, during, and since the launch of the new campaign. Therefore, I conclude the campaign has had no meaningful impact, positive or negative, on our brand."

Each member of the tiger team nodded in unison, with one or more facial features wide open—eyes, mouth, nostrils. I'm pretty sure they were awed by the authority of the data.

And that's the moment, as I had the attention of the dozen people sitting around the conference room table, when I turned my head slowly, not unlike a continuous-motion sprinkler spraying life-sustaining water to the far edges of a well-tended yard, looking each person directly in the eyes before saying, "Being objective makes me effective."

Boom! Or, rather: BOMME!

Each person reacted in a different and personal way. Maryanne smiled lopsidedly and nodded in such a manner that she also seemed to be shaking her head. Her inadvertent chuckle told me her mixed nonverbal cues indicated she more than approved of my personal motto—she was impressed by it. Even, dare I say, *aroused* by it. Previously Maryanne had made some borderline unprofessional comments to me. For example, overappreciating the fit of my khakis in the elevator, or describing the muscle tone of my calves as "rigid" at the company gym. Not quite worth flagging with HR, but enough to indicate that if I was interested in spending some quality one-on-one time with her offline, outside of the workplace, she would not be completely disinterested.

Wilson was Senior Director of Marketing Insights and my manager. I'd given him a heads-up that I had a new motto and soon would be sharing it outside our team. So I was surprised when his initial reaction was to grimace at me, as if I'd just committed a social blunder—such as asking a custodian in the microkitchen about his weekend immediately after a VP had just talked about her weekend in the Wine Country, which I'd done recently—to Wilson's obvious displeasure. But I wasn't surprised to see his reaction evolve into a performance of pride as the others expressed their approval.

"Objective is your middle name, Glenn," said Huang, who was Director of Sales Enablement. Wilson's grimace turned neutral.

"That's for sure," agreed Sanjay, who was VP of Product Development. Wilson sat taller in his chair.

"Love it!" gushed Alyosha, who was Senior Director of Public Relations.

Wilson cleared his throat theatrically. "I always say, Glenn's our secret weapon." Then he expanded his chest, showcasing his tailored button-down shirt. But that's Wilson. Once he's heard everyone else's opinion, he'll form his and express it in a show-offy way. He made a point of asserting his rank over me by saying, "These are some serious implications, Glenn. Let's be sure to drill down on them during our next one-on-one."

Drill down = seek further information from a set of data that has some serious implications. *Serious implications* = the damage to the company is so great that people might get fired, and effort will need to be expended to ensure we're not among those people.

I replied, "I look forward to double-clicking on that with you, Wilson." *Double-clicking* = drilling down.

Jocelyn was a Marketing Insights Analyst and my only direct report, and she shadowed me in important meetings like this one. While the others enthusiastically endorsed my motto, Jocelyn's reaction was noticeably muted. She wore the same weary expression she usually wore, as if she was bearing a great weight. I hadn't informed her in our one-on-ones that I developed a personal motto and soon would be launching it. Perhaps she believed that I, as her manager, should have mentioned something this momentous to her beforehand. Perhaps she didn't hear me. So I leaned in toward her in the next seat and said it once more, quietly, "Being objective makes me effective."

Jocelyn nodded, and she wrote my motto on her notepad in ALL CAPS. She spent the rest of the meeting staring at me over the rims of her glasses and eating a tiny box of tiny organic raisins, one tiny raisin at a time, retracing the letters of my motto over and over until they were thick black; it was weird at the time but meaningful in hindsight.

If you haven't developed and launched your own professional motto, I recommend it. It's like an epitaph for the living. At the risk of sounding subjective, giving myself a motto that asserts and celebrates my objectivity makes me feel my thinking is even more objective than it was before my motto. It emphasizes who and what I am in the moment, in the active present tense. And it also sets aspirational goals for me to continually work toward—omnipresent objectivity, eternal effectiveness.

It was Maryanne's meeting. She was responsible for the brand campaign. "Well, these results are certainly not as delightful as we had hoped for, but we value your objectivity, Glenn."

I empathized with her disappointment. "Subjective bad news is like getting a scolding from a moody, drunken parent—random, violent, definitely unconstructive. Objective bad news is like being given a poor grade by a strict, yet fair, teacher—you know where you stand, and you know what specific steps you need to—"

Wilson interrupted. "I think we understand the challenges."

"Yeah," snorted Sanjay. "We're not getting credit for our personalization even though we're at least two years ahead of our competitors. Clearly, our users aren't seeing it in the products my team builds. Marketing only works if we get the product right."

Alyosha took some of the blame. "We could improve our messaging to the industry. For sure. The resonance scores for our press releases were kinda embarrassing, to tell the truth."

Huang chimed in. "Sales hasn't been the best internal partner for getting the message out. We'll open the kimono to our advertisers so they can see under the hood of our personalization engine. Then they'll give us great ads that are just as compelling as our great content, and we'll have a win-win." *Opening the kimono* = showing your cards = being transparent = sharing everything you know with someone you don't trust completely, such as a business partner from another company, or a co-worker from another department whose title and job description are maddeningly similar to your own.

Maryanne beamed with pride. We all did. We were witnessing one of my favorite aspects of our company's culture—nobody stands alone. We're all in it together. Blame sharing is a team sport. Maryanne started to speak, "This certainly has been an enriching—"

Wilson interrupted her. "I just want to say—sorry, Maryanne—that we'll definitely drill down and get back to you with additional insights from the data. We can always drill down deeper." Clearly, he wanted to share in the blame, too. He could give a master class on *CYA* = covering your ass. He also was a huge fan of *ROFL* = rolling on the floor, laughing. And I suspect that in the privacy of his office he occasionally ROFLCYA.

Maryanne nodded magnanimously at Wilson. "As I was saying, things didn't turn out as we had hoped. Even so, this has been an enriching meeting. In retrospect the monkey was probably a mistake."

Alyosha cooed, "But he was really cute!" The rest of us murmured our agreement. Inadvertently, I reached my hand up to my neck and felt the scar the monkey had left.

Maryanne continued. "I should've pushed back more when Darryl suggested it. My bad. Clearly we have some work to do going forward. We've identified many opportunities here. If we can just get users to view one more page each time they visit, we can grow revenue significantly." Vigorous head nodding swept around the table, stopping at Jocelyn, who was extracting a final, tiny raisin from her tiny box of raisins.

Maryanne indicated the meeting was over with her signature sign-off. "Delightful!"

Needless to say, the meeting ended on a high note, despite the disappointing findings from the research. My objectivity comforted the other members of the tiger team with the knowledge that even bad news when presented objectively identifies challenges and leads to opportunities.

In business, there are two types of people: Those who Get It and those who Don't Get It. I've always considered myself a person who Gets It. But after that meeting, there was no doubt. Among the members of the Brand Campaign Assessment Tiger Team, and, as the legend of my motto spread across the company, among all co-workers known and unknown, I became universally regarded as one of the people who Gets It.

Glenn Cregg, Senior Manager of Marketing Insights – *Being objective makes me effective.*

"That guy Gets It," I heard more than one person (two) say after passing me in the hallway over the next few weeks.

It's good to be one of the people who Gets It. Try covering forty PowerPoint slides in an hour with a room full of people who don't Get It. Impossible! Not to mention, a waste of time. But in a room full of people who Get It, we can churn through the slides in forty-five minutes and spend the last fifteen drilling down deep into the data to uncover serious implications.

Jocelyn and I left the tiger team meeting and wordlessly walked together to our building. We shared a trait common among people who specialize in *quantitative* research analyzing data—comfort with silence. Unlike most people, especially *qualitative* researchers, quantitative researchers understand that silence is as informative and data rich as a bubbly conversation.

Qualitative researchers, on the other hand, seem to regard silence as an enemy that must be attacked constantly. They can be excellent listeners, but only when other people are talking. And when the talking ends, they fill the silence with their own talk. This isn't surprising given that their work consists of conducting focus groups, one-on-one usability testing, and in-home ethnographies where a researcher engages with people in their own natural settings to understand how they use products in their daily lives.

Qualitative research tends to be more subjective than objective because you have to make judgment calls about things like whether the statement, "I don't use Boingsearch for looking up my exes," means the focus group participant actually doesn't use Boingsearch for that, despite the fact that the focus group invitation said, "We're looking for people who use the internet to keep track of past friends and lovers," or whether the respondent is too embarrassed to talk about a sensitive subject in front of a focus group of strangers.

Wilson's specialty was qualitative research, which might explain why his opinions varied with his caffeine level and his physical proximity to anyone with VP or Chief in his or her title. I had a secret nickname for Wilson—the Magic 8 Ball, after the child's toy that gives you a random, vague answer to any question you ask it. If you didn't like the answer he gave you, you could try again later, when there was a good chance he would give you a better answer.

But Jocelyn and I were part of what you might call Team Objective. Our work consisted of gathering and analyzing data, not anecdotes. We were both fluent in the one true universal language: math. So as we spent ten minutes walking back to our building, we communicated clearly to each other through the silence: The meeting was productive. My motto was well received. Maryanne doesn't get data deeply, but she's an inspiring leader. Wilson will always be Wilson.

Jocelyn confirmed all of this by looking at me skeptically, over the rims of her glasses. Despite her occasional glumness, I'd become fond of the rapport between us.

CUBES

Jocelyn and I ate lunch together every Thursday in Bytes, which was more than a cafeteria. It was a large, open-air space, two stories high, with a maximum capacity of two thousand people. It was where we chose from a variety of types of foods and cuisines available for free to all employees and their guests. It was where we attended all-hands meetings, held Q&As with celebrities, and cheered for co-workers at talent shows. It was our cathedral. Our opera house. Our multipurpose room.

Jocelyn preferred an inner table, farthest from the windows, although she wouldn't say why. While I was comfortable with it, I also was curious, so sometimes I asked her questions to try to tease out why she preferred an inner table. "Do you think those two-story windows would shatter in an earthquake?" "It's kind of bright out there, don't you agree?" "I feel like the entire campus is watching me when I sit by the windows…" with a long, expectant pause soliciting her agreement or disagreement. At the most, Jocelyn would look at me skeptically, over the rims of her glasses, acknowledging only that I spoke and she heard me. I had no preference, so we sat as far from the windows as we were able. The wobbly table closest to the tray return area was usually open, and we sat there to discuss our team's work. For, you see, those weekly Thursday lunches were where and when we conducted our one-on-one (1:1), manager-to-employee meetings.

Jocelyn reported to me. She wasn't matrixed, meaning she reported solely and directly to me. She was my team. She and I were our team. Out of the fourteen thousand employees in the company, we made up the entire Consumer Marketing Insights team, a great responsibility for two people.

Jocelyn had been reporting to me for nearly three years. I was her hiring manager, a technical term for a sort of discoverer. I pulled her résumé from the stream of résumés forwarded to my inbox by Harold from Talent Acquisition. I brought her in for a series of soul-searching, expectations-challenging, and thought-provoking interviews with Wilson, Maryanne, me, and several other people with whom she would work. We investigated whether Jocelyn was a good fit for my team and whether my team was a good fit for her. While Wilson and Maryanne both slightly preferred a different candidate, one who presented herself more confidently and less color-coordinatedly, I advocated for Jocelyn and her color coordination, and I convinced them to allow me to hire her.

Jocelyn was more than a decade younger than me, but much further along socially, politically, and personally than I was at her age. Perhaps than I am now. I learned much about Jocelyn from our lunches, which began each week discussing our team and the work we were doing, but inevitably drifted to intangible topics.

Such as guilt. Jocelyn felt guilty about everything. With every action, she generated waste. Some of it—the carbon dioxide exuding from her humid breath—fed the trees and plants (good) but also contributed to the greenhouse effect and global climate change (bad). She became animated when talking about plastic. "Every day I bring home a plastic package of frozen edamame from Trader Joe's, I extend the term of my influence on the Earth!" Plastic would be her legacy.

Jocelyn felt guilty about feeling guilty. It wasn't a religious or cultural thing. Some groups of people—Catholics, Jews, Persians, English majors—are widely known, stereotyped even, for feeling guilty about things that other groups of people manage not to feel guilty about. They *overindex* in feeling and expressing guilt. But Jocelyn was none of these, and as best I could tell, Jocelyn's guilt wasn't rooted in religious or cultural beliefs. It was a natural outcome of her inquisitive nature and her conclusion during middle school that deities don't exist, except as inspirational fictional characters, leading her to conclude all morality was a human invention.

As she told me in one of our early 1:1s, excitedly, "I realized at that young age that moral codes and behavioral norms can be only changed by the right people making the right decisions, in the right place, at the right time. And that put me in control of my own destiny. A frightening, horrifying, and yet liberating and exhilarating thing! I was determined to define a worthy destiny and lifetime goal for myself. And not a vague, self-satisfying goal, like bringing about world peace or mentoring starving children or curing disease or making a difference in my community or being a role model. A goal that lays the foundation for world peace, curing cancer, etc. A wondrous goal that serves as a platform for other goals. Something scalable, where my own little benevolent actions, as well as the actions of like-minded people, are amplified and distributed by the very nature and essence and purity of the goal itself. And the terrible fact that I haven't done it yet, after more than a decade of pondering and planning, makes me feel guilty with every breath I take that isn't making progress toward the goal that I haven't even identified!"

She followed her monologue with a combination of sigh, shrug, and whimper. And then she went on to update me about her latest project. "I completed the news consumption analysis. The most surprising finding is that moms overindex in consuming breaking news in the morning compared to other audiences; however, less surprising is that the largest share of that breaking news is about celebrities. I'll send you the results."

I became aware of Jocelyn as more than a talented and thoughtful young analyst; she was intellectual, philosophical, poetic—rare attributes in our industry.

While I shared Jocelyn's aspiration to set worthy personal goals, I didn't share her anxiety about work, largely because I've always been able to identify goals worthy of pursuing and to identify means—such as my motto—for remaining focused. But we're not talking about me. We're talking about Jocelyn, who despite her existential anxiety was a crackerjack marketing insights analyst. Every project she conducted came in on time and on budget, and the product or marketing team that commissioned it felt well served.

Two days after I introduced my motto, Jocelyn and I held our regular Thursday 1:1 in Bytes. We sat at the wobbly table with our lunches and discussed our team and its growing influence within the company. I'd chosen the day's Indian entrée, palak paneer. Jocelyn had chosen a small arugula salad, with dressing on the side in a ceramic cup; she hardly touched it during our conversation. She also had on her tray a tangelo and a package of almonds that, presumably, she'd take with her for consuming later in the day; she was almost always snacking on something.

Jocelyn had been conducting the pre- and post-launch analysis of the dramatic redesign of Boingmail, a product that for many years had been used on a daily basis by tens of millions of consumers worldwide. "I sent the preliminary survey results to Wilson, and he called me into his office."

"Ah—I saw you go in there."

"He really didn't like my analysis. He gave me some harsh feedback about the verbatims I included. I didn't censor them at all, so there were a lot of f-bombs and other profanity."

"Let me guess. 'You all suck *expletive* you *expletiving expletives.* Give me back my old *expletive* email or I'll *expletive* you!'"

"Yeah."

"I believe it's important for the product team to hear the objective truth about how consumers are responding to the redesign."

"Me, too. But Wilson wants me to remove those slides completely. He says such vile comments could only be coming from unhinged people who would respond negatively and aggressively to any changes and therefore they aren't a key segment that should be driving product or marketing decisions. That just depresses me." She took her fork and pushed a cherry tomato around her salad, circling the arugula.

I was adamant about telling the product team the objective truth. We wouldn't leave out the bad news! "For next steps, why don't you rework those slides by selecting some different quotations that convey the same sense of concern about the redesign, without profanity. And I'll talk to Wilson about the importance of sharing bad news with the product team."

"Okay. I'll send you a new draft by the end of the day." And that was it. We had a good mentor-mentee relationship. She went off to a meeting with the Data Integrity Tiger Team, a recurring meeting I used to attend but had recently handed off to Jocelyn as a stretch assignment to broaden her internal network. And I went off to my weekly 1:1 with Wilson, where I declared firmly that we wouldn't spin our results just because some of them were negative, and where the Magic 8 Ball, not surprisingly, acquiesced.

Jocelyn and I worked in Building Zed, third floor, in adjacent high-walled cubicles, or cubes. I was privileged to have a cube by the window, with a view of the parking lot through two large eucalyptus trees. Window cubes were mostly reserved for director-level employees. Hardly any senior managers like me had window cubes, and in fact, I was the only one I was aware of. Jocelyn's cube was one cube in from mine, toward the central hallway. Because I was so often in meetings and saw the relevant co-workers elsewhere, people rarely came to my cube. And people rarely visited Jocelyn in her cube. As a result, Jocelyn and I were typically the only people to visit our section of our aisle. Theoretically, the janitorial staff cleaned our cubes each night, but several times I laid conspicuous crumbs on my cube floor in order to determine whether they ever vacuumed, and each time I aborted the experiment days later by discarding the filthy crumbs myself.

So if I'd been on vacation or working from home or away on a business trip, it might have been days before anyone noticed Jocelyn on the floor of her cube, splayed like a broken bird. In retrospect, I consider it a bit of a compliment that Jocelyn lost consciousness in her cube, because I was the only person likely to find her. It was a kind of challenge to me, a way of asking me, albeit very indirectly, "Do you care about me?" If it had happened at her apartment, where she lived alone, perhaps nobody would have found her in time to help her.

I stopped at the opening to her cube and saw her there on the floor. I didn't initially realize anything was wrong, and I made a comment I regret, something like, "Lost a contact, Jocelyn?" Which would've been ridiculous, because she wore glasses. It was one of those insensitive comments that visit me during sleepless nights, when my mind wanders darkly.

On her desk was a pile of pale pink pills. They were round pills, maybe a dozen, with thick edges, allowing some to stand upright. I looked for a prescription bottle but didn't find one. Their arrangement was disconcertingly architectural, as if they'd been laid out carefully to appear to be randomly arranged. An artistic arrangement of unmarked pills, next to a glass half-full (!) of water.

I called out for help, but I don't remember any response. It was still the early part of the afternoon, so nearby co-workers might have been at lunch. As I cried out again, my voice cracking—I wasn't even sure I was making sound—I damned our high-walled cubes. They were meant to provide us with a sense of privacy, allowing us to focus on our work. But by putting up those thin visual barriers, we became oblivious to life-and-death struggles occurring just a few paces away.

As I fumbled with my iPhone trying to call Security, my mind went to a time I was conducting routine home maintenance. I found the skeleton of a squirrel beneath my condominium, in the crawl space between the soil and the floor of the dining room. It was curled up as if it had fallen asleep and never awakened. I'd been living my life completely unaware that an arm's length from the table where I ate my meals and read my newspapers and solved my Sudoku puzzles, a living being had crawled to die.

That wasn't going to happen with Jocelyn. I was there.

I knelt beside her and aligned my face with hers to discover she still breathed. This was the right thing for me to do in the circumstance, yet I felt I was being inappropriately intimate with her. I checked her wrist for a shimmering pulse, and I removed her glasses.

As I waited for Security to arrive, I held her hand; it was wrongly cold. I felt overwhelmed by emotion. I've talked about the importance of being objective, and I've denigrated subjectivity in the workplace. But I'm not an emotionless robot. I recognize the value of subjectivity in certain circumstances. I like to think if Jocelyn had been awake, the most subjective, emotive part of me would've been there, comforting her, encouraging her to be strong, to live. But in the actual circumstance, with Jocelyn unconscious and help not yet arriving and me watching her every shallow breath and castigating myself for never taking a CPR class, subjectivity felt like the wrong mode to be in. "Stay objective, save Jocelyn," I told myself as I felt a salty sludge of tears and mucus breech the levee of my upper lip.

Soon, paramedics were there, administering treatment, putting her on a gurney, confirming she was alive with acceptable vital signs. When they rolled her away, her eyes were still closed and her face was slack and motionless, but her fingers fluttered. Those flutters might have been automatic and unintentional. I took them as Jocelyn's acknowledgement of my presence—like one of those gestures some cultures use to mean hello or goodbye or sometimes both at the same time.

USERS

Jocelyn wasn't the only one struggling to stay alive. Boing;) was struggling, too. Revenue and profit had declined over a dozen consecutive quarters. Boing;) was once what we call a *top-of-mind* internet company. When asked in a survey to list which internet services they use, a majority of consumers would mention Boing;), unprompted. But even though it still had hundreds of millions of monthly users around the world, it had become what we call *aided*—most consumers wouldn't mention Boing;) unless prompted explicitly with the question, "Do you use Boing;)?" In other words, Boing;) had become like the friendly kid everybody knows a little but nobody knows well enough to notice is missing when the school bus returns from a field trip.

Boing;) was founded in 1995 by two computer engineering graduate students at UC Berkeley: Paco ("the smart one") and Stan ("the lucky one"). They were best friends in college and in the early days of Boing;), when their shares in the company made each of them billionaires on paper. You would think billions of dollars on paper would bring friends even closer. But along the way, something went wrong between them.

One legend was that Paco and Stan began disliking each other during the IPO Road Show, the series of meetings they held with investors before taking the company public and selling stock.

Stan wanted to position the new company as a portal, which he punningly called a "port hole," a type of internet company offering a range of products and services and functioning as a gateway, or portal, into the rest of the internet. Microsoft had created its own portal, MSN. Yahoo! was emerging as a portal. And of course, AOL was the portal that many people in the United States first went through to go online, use email, share information, and visit all types of websites for news, entertainment, recipes, baseball statistics, hat felting techniques, knee-obsessed erotica, and so on.

Paco wanted to position Boing;) as a digital technology company. By focusing on technology, he believed Boing;) could attract the best engineers to develop the best new products. He also believed a tech positioning would distinguish Boing;) from traditional media companies such as Disney, News Corporation, Viacom, and *The New York Times.*

There's a video on the internet of a young Paco describing this in detail during an interview, while Stan sat behind him awkwardly on a high stool. Both of them were wearing jeans and Boing;) T-shirts and sporting longish mid-90s haircuts. "Everybody knows tech companies are growth companies. They don't have to pay dividends because their stock values grow exuberantly. Meanwhile, media companies are value companies. Their stocks hold value while increasing in price slowly over time. Media companies, which can be very profitable, tend to pay dividends each year in order to keep anxious shareholders happy."

At this point in the video, the interviewer, a young journalist named Marian Sallowaskky, who would go on to co-found the influential tech industry blog, *TechNomNom*, asked, "So how does your portal positioning fit into this tech versus media divide?"

Paco became agitated. Stan squirmed on the high stool behind him. "We haven't settled on a portal position. We're a tech company. Most of the workers at a tech company are engineers who make things. Most of the workers at a media company are sales people who don't make things. A portal position would be the digital equivalent of a media position, which would be a disaster for us."

Behind Paco, Stan could be heard, if you turned the volume way up on the video, saying, "Disast her? I hardly know her."

Over the past two decades, this video has been referenced whenever a debate arises over the difference between tech companies and media companies, or whenever someone asks if Boing;) is obsolete and doomed to fail. It also has been referenced as examples of both toxic tech bro culture and terrible punning.

Despite Paco's explanation in the video, Stan's portal positioning won out with investors, and when Boing;)'s stock price debuted at 20 dollars per share in 1995 and then rose to 340 dollars per share at the height of the dot-com bubble in 1999, Stan looked like a genius. That's when Paco and Stan each bought professional sports teams.

Another legend was that they were always highly competitive frenemies: in the dorm, in Ultimate Frisbee games, in pursuing girlfriends, and in life. By the time I joined Boing;), they had long ago moved to separate corners of the country and rarely visited the main campus in the Valley, even though they still, technically, worked for the company in advisory roles. Paco lived in Portland, where he prowled the sidelines of the city's soccer franchise. Stan lived in Miami, where he could be glimpsed through the tinted windows of the owner's booth at hockey games.

By the time I joined the company, Paco and Stan's only on-campus presence was in animated form, as the cartoon narrators of a training video all Boingers were required to watch, called *Don't Touch That! Avoiding Harassment in the Workplace at Boing;)*. They also surrounded us, in a sense, through the lavendery shade of Boing;) Blue that Paco and Stan invented when they mixed cans of cheap paint to spruce up the first Boing;) office in a Mountain View strip mall. Nearly everything at Boing;) was blue, including the little blue deodorant cakes in the blue urinals.

Another way they continued to influence the lives of Boingers was through investments the company made in Boing;)'s early days. In the summer of 1999, Paco and Stan took a month-long trip to Moscow to look for opportunities to invest some of the billions of dollars in cash Boing;) had accumulated. They met with several tech entrepreneurs, including a small and extremely energetic Pyotr "Pete" Alexeyevich Protezy, who'd started a digital technology company called Tsarevich. It was being called "The AOL plus the eBay plus the Match.com of Russia." Paco and Stan convinced the Boing;) Board of Directors to invest one billion dollars of Boing;) stock for 40 percent ownership of Tsarevich. Pete Protezy quickly sold the stock for cash, which he used to invest Tsarevich money in Russian energy companies. Today he's one of the richest men in the world, and he owns professional soccer teams throughout Europe, Asia, and Latin America.

While I was working for Boing;), our core company wasn't performing amazingly. The same could be said for the core part of Tsarevich, which had to shut down its portal and online dating businesses for lack of profitability, so now it was just known as the eBay of Russia. However, Tsarevich's investment in those Russian energy companies made the stock price grow steadily over time. This made Boing;)'s stock price grow steadily over time, making all of us Boingers grateful for Paco and Stan's 1999 trip to Russia.

But perhaps the most significant way they put their stamp on Boing;) was by establishing code names for projects. If you're over a certain age, you remember the original Boingmail and its retro Courier font and *boing* sound each time you received a new email. According to company legend,

Stan gave that first email product the code name Project Ruby, after a childhood pet, and Paco gave it a different code name, Project Icon, because he thought electronic mail (email) was a new form of iconography, and the product team morphed the words together into Ruby + Icon = Project Rubicon.

Rubicon once came up during one of my regular 1:1s with Wilson. The way he pronounced it, Ruby Con, made me think he didn't know its original reference.

I said, "The Rubicon is a river in Northern Italy that Julius Caesar and his army crossed on their way to stage a coup in Rome."

"I know what the Rubicon is, Glenn."

I continued. "Upon this crossing, Caesar famously said the Latin equivalent of 'the die is cast,' meaning a battle was unavoidable, they'd gone too far to turn back."

"I know this. Seriously. I nearly minored in ancient history."

I'm not sure why I felt the need to persist, but Wilson sometimes had this effect on me. "Crossing the Rubicon has come to mean passing a point of no return."

"My patience for this discussion has crossed the Rubicon, Glenn."

Despite our kerfuffle over the word, like all Boingers we intuitively realized that Rubicon was a lofty name to assign to what eventually would become the world's most-used email service, but at the time of its naming, it was still just a series of flow charts and use cases on the whiteboard in a conference room.

Hardly anyone who actually created Rubicon was still with the company. But ever since, every Boing;) product had been given an inspirational code name like Rubicon, Eagle Eye, Exodus, Big Bang, Cure For Cancer, World Peace, Nirvana, Maximum Awesome, or Dare to Dream. Other companies in the Valley gave their projects banal, ironic, or trivializing code names. Google's code name for Gmail was Caribou; Apple's code name for the iPhone was Purple. Twitter's code name for its in-stream advertising product was Chewbacca; Facebook's code name for its news feed was DEADBEEF. Ridiculous!

By the time I joined the company, Boing;) was in decline. The era when most internet users around the world went online to check their email and were greeted with a friendly *boing* seemed as distant as horse buggies and gas lighting. Sadly, despite giving their initiatives childish code names, Google, Facebook, and other hot companies had been eating Boing;)'s lunch, and Boing;)'s revenue had been declining rapidly. This had multiple negative impacts on Boing;). It made it impossible for Boing;) to make acquisitions of promising new startups because a competitor could always pay more. It made advertisers less willing to advertise with a company seen as declining. And it made the stock grants of Boing;) employees less attractive than the stock grants of their friends working for other Valley companies. All this resulted in many Boingers becoming Googlers, Facebookers, etc.

This might sound somewhat subjective, but I believe words have magical powers, and when we use them, we deploy some of their magic. This is an objective truth acquired subjectively, over many millennia, through the collected wisdom of generations of people who Get It. Naming a project DEADBEEF means you don't take it all that seriously, and neither should consumers. Naming a project World Peace means you aspire to greatness. Never mind that Project World Peace, Boing;)'s digital scrapbook, was used at its peak by only four thousand daily users, or that the business model forecasted fourteen million daily females 25–54, or that most of the users were males in the 18–54 demographic, who arrived at the website inadvertently because they were searching for an obscure type of pornography known as scrapbooking. If the project hadn't been called World Peace, I'm certain even fewer people would have used it. The grand name allowed it to achieve its maximum potential.

Boing;) was working hard to realize its potential. The brand campaign featuring the mohawked monkey and the busty blonde was one piece of Project Resurrection, a company-wide plan with six essential goals designed to return the company to growth.

PROJECT RESURRECTION
Returning Boing;) to Glory

- Revitalize the Boing;) brand with consumers and advertisers
- Modernize infrastructure
- Reduce costs
- Grow revenue
- Build team spirit
- Create a goals-driven culture based on the Three M's: meaningful, manageable, and measurable

Boing;)

Resurrection was the company's top priority. Boingers were given a small poster featuring an image of our CEO, Darryl, staring and pointing sternly like Uncle Sam in the famous "I Want You" poster, with the caption, "Resurrection, yo!"

I put my poster on the wall of my cube, at eye level, just a slight head turn away from my computer screen, making me think several times each day about Resurrection.

Inspired by the Boing;) naming custom, I decided to give code names to my personal initiatives. In the aftermath of Jocelyn's incident, I took a CPR class at the local Red Cross every Wednesday for several weeks. I called it Project Be Prepared. I named my new fitness regimen Project Four Pack, because I had to be honest with myself—I'd never achieve six-pack abs; four-pack abs was a more realistic stretch goal. And I named my effort to help Jocelyn develop her career in a life-affirming direction Project Clarion Call; I didn't seek this challenge, but I accepted it, for I appeared to have been called to it. I couldn't suspect the myriad ways Clarion Call would challenge me, but I believed the work was worthy, so I began it in earnest.

ROCKSTAR

Jocelyn spent one night in the hospital. She Boingmessaged (BM'd) me the next day while I was at my desk.

joss2themax: hi there. i'm alive and feeling much better
joss2themax: thx for your help
glennnnn5: np. glad you're feeling better!!
joss2themax: im back at home
glennnnn5: are you in the hospital?
glennnnn5: sorry. hit enter before I got your response
joss2themax: np. they released me this morning
glennnnn5: i see
joss2themax: i have a HUGE favor to ask u
glennnnn5: k
joss2themax: wait. sorry. brb
glennnnn5: k

While I sat at my desk waiting for Jocelyn to continue the conversation, Wilson BM'd me with a cryptic message.

wilsonmba2000: pls come to my office
wilsonmba2000: immediately
glennnnn5: k

That was awkward. Jocelyn, apparently, was about to say something important. But Wilson wanted me to visit him in his office. He might have something brief to tell me; I might run to his office and run right back to my desk without Jocelyn knowing I'd stepped away. Or I might have to spend the next hour with him. I couldn't BM Jocelyn while meeting with Wilson, *could I?* I decided to chance it. Either she'd send a message that didn't require an immediate response—I could glance at it—it would annoy Wilson but not anger him, hopefully. Or she wouldn't get back to the conversation while I was with Wilson. I opened Boingmessage on my iPhone and set the phone to vibrate when a message came in. And I walked briskly to Wilson's "office," also known as the Integrity conference room.

Other Valley companies gave their conference rooms silly names, like Milk Duds, Chutes & Ladders, and Sesame Street, as if evoking childhood sweetened the sour taste of the serious, adult work that occurred in them.

Boing;) took a more inspiring approach, naming conference rooms for attributes we all aspire to embody, such as Integrity, Clarity, and Admiration. Whenever I sat down in Teamwork, Truth, or Charisma and looked across the table at co-workers, I felt a sense of purpose.

Integrity had a view of the marsh on the edge of the San Francisco Bay. Wilson had booked Integrity every day for the previous two years, and he always kept it booked six months in advance. Nominally, the room was our marketing insights war room. On the walls were charts and tables of outdated research results; on the whiteboard was a list of projects completed long ago. Wilson was a senior director, but he believed he should be a VP, and VPs got their own offices, so he granted himself his own office via the room scheduling system.

He gestured for me to sit across the table from him. I sat with my iPhone under my leg, so I would feel it vibrate if Jocelyn BM'd me.

I thought he was calling me in to follow up on one of our team goals for the quarter: *Build team spirit by supporting teammates*, which really meant *Endorse Wilson's skills on LinkedIn.* Each time I'd seen him over the previous few weeks, he asked if I'd *built team spirit yet*, reminding me I was still *in the red* for that goal. As I searched my mind for a new excuse for why I hadn't endorsed his skills yet, he surprised me by talking about an entirely different topic.

"Are you familiar with the Rockstar Award?"

What a ridiculous question! Every Boinger was familiar with the Rockstar Award.

He gestured toward a trophy displayed prominently on the rail of the whiteboard—his Rockstar Award. "It's the greatest acknowledgement a

Boinger can receive from the company. It's our Nobel Prize." He picked up his Rockstar Award and looked at it with a sly smile. He rubbed it possessively, as if wiping off fingerprints.

Wilson received his Rockstar Award years earlier for leading the focus group research preceding the rebranding of a popular photo service Boing;) had acquired. The focus group research determined that rebranding the service from *Pixxl* to *Boingphotos* would be received positively by consumers. So we did it—with disastrous results. Over the next six months, half of Pixxl users abandoned the service for a new startup service—Flickr, which Yahoo! subsequently acquired. Eventually we re-rebranded it as *Boingpixxl*, but the damage had been done. Fortunately for Wilson, that occurred well after he received his award.

He went on. "Winners of the Rockstar Award form a council of elders who protect and defend Boing;)'s culture and legacy. Our number includes many Boingers who have gone on to hold high positions at companies throughout Silicon Valley, including past and present CEOs of Boing;), Pets.com, Lockerz, and Autonomy."

I kept diverting my attention to my iPhone; it continued not vibrating. Why was he lecturing me about this? Probably he was equating himself with CEOs of major corporations in an effort to entice me to endorse his skills. He was implying he was as talented as those CEOs and might even become one himself simply because they received the same award. When you approach the world subjectively, you believe such outcomes are not just possible, but probable. I knew for a fact he wasn't equating himself with at least two former Rockstar Award winners who'd been indicted for insider trading. Then he surprised me.

"You've been selected to receive the Quarterly Rockstar Award."

I always thought people used the word *speechless* frivolously. Surely no human with a functioning vocal system is actually rendered speechless by any type of news. Surely the death of a loved one could be greeted with, at minimum, the single heart-wrenching syllable of "Nooooo!" Or a brain-bursting bit of happiness could be followed by a "wow," or an "*oh my God*." But upon hearing Wilson's statement, I had an uncontrollable biological response. The muscles in my neck, throat, and tongue tightened to the point where I was truly incapable of speaking. However, I was not incapable of grunting a guttural growl. Also, I wasn't breathing. In my non-breathing, growling, non-speaking state, I reflected upon how I occasionally imagined myself receiving the Rockstar Award. I'd delivered several pieces of what I considered Rockstar-worthy work. My brand-tracking study was the first of its kind for the company. My sports category landscape study was described by the Boingsports team as a game changer. And my idea to put a second refrigerated display case in the microkitchen of Building Zed resulted in the supplies of free Red Bull, Mountain Dew, and Diet Coke lasting well into the afternoon each day. Some people imagine their reaction to winning the lottery. Each quarter, I imagined my reaction to winning the Rockstar Award.

In my imagination, I received the quarterly email announcing winners. I scrolled down to find my name in bold letters. And as soon as I saw my name, my inbox began filling with notes of congratulations from co-workers, known and unknown, each of whom I replied to with humility and gratitude.

This time, distracted by the situation with Jocelyn, I forgot it was Rockstar Award announcement season. And this time I won. It never occurred to me that my manager would be the first to inform me. Life is like that. No matter how much you prepare and plan, few things ever turn out the way you expect.

Wilson chuckled at my reaction to the news. I couldn't speak. I couldn't breathe. I imagined myself receiving the spoils of the award, a spot bonus of a thousand dollars, which would come to roughly $617.03 after taxes and an obligatory Boing;) Employee Foundation donation were extracted, and a private Coffee with Darryl, the CEO, to discuss any topic I chose. I never had a specific topic in mind. This had always been a blind spot in my daydreaming. But as I didn't breathe and didn't speak, words formed in my head, spoken to the Darryl in my head—and the me in my head who wasn't speechless said, confidently, "Streaming music service." Then the real me fainted.

When I awoke, just moments later according to Wilson, I felt a pain where my head had hit the Integrity conference table, and I felt a vibration against my leg. All of my abilities came back to me in a rush, including my ability to speak.

"Awesome!"

He paused for a moment, perhaps wondering if I was alert enough to understand what he was about to say, but he went ahead and said it. "I'll be honest with you, Glenn. Although I think you do credible work, I didn't recommend you for this award. You have fans in high places."

I laugh-scoffed. I was a Rockstar, and there was nothing he could do about it! It gave me immunity. Tenure. Immortality! I brazenly took out my iPhone and looked at it. Jocelyn had returned to our BM conversation:

> *joss2themax*: i'm back.

I brazenly told Wilson, "I need to respond to this."

glennnnn5: hi. give me 2 mins?
joss2themax: k

I stood and nodded at Wilson. "Thanks." And I turned my back on him and his startled expression as I stumble-strutted back to my cubicle. This Rockstar Award was my opportunity to move the needle. To make a difference. To break ground. To disrupt. To pivot. To escalate. To innovate. To hockey stick! To level up!

I attempted to regain that perfect moment of clarity I experienced before fainting. I focused, I *objectified.* I determined the one thing I wanted to impress upon Darryl during my Coffee with him; the one bullet point I wanted to offer was this.

- Boing;)'s resurrection will happen if we create a streaming music service.

I didn't yet have the supporting bullet points, but I knew this was the key recommendation. I would substantiate it later with details about engaging digital natives, activating influencers, and treating an anchor product as a loss leader for building awareness of higher-margin content and experiences. Details to work out.

But first—Jocelyn. As I hurried to my cubicle, I passed Wanda from B2B Marketing, who asked, "How did you get that bruise on your forehead?"

I gave her the same answer I would later give more than one Boinger (two). "I keep bumping it on all the low-hanging fruit."

I was exhilarated, of course, by the news of my award. But as I returned to my cube—passing and looking into Jocelyn's cube, where I'd found her lying on the floor just one day earlier—my great news seemed somewhat irrelevant. It put me in a morbid mood, not at all how I imagined I'd feel after winning the Rockstar Award. I sat at my desk and typed.

glennnnn5: sorry to make you wait
joss2themax: np. i made u wait first
glennnnn5: hey, just want you to know you don't need to rush back to work
joss2themax: i'm glad to hear u say that, cuz i was going to ask for some time off
glennnnn5: sure, we can do that
joss2themax: i already looked into it

joss2themax: according to the health plan
joss2themax: a boinger can take mental health leave for up to 6 months
joss2themax: with a note from a doc
glennnnn5: o
joss2themax: stating that the patient
glennnnn5: k
joss2themax: needs time to get healthy
glennnnn5: certainly. anything I can do
joss2themax: is that a question or a statement
joss2themax: ?
glennnnn5: sorry
glennnnn5: both. i will do anything i can do. is there anything i can do?
glennnnn5: six months is a long time
joss2themax: im just requesting 6 weeks
joss2themax: sending u the form with doctor's assessment

(*joss2themax is sending you a file…click OK to download.*)
(*glennnnn5 downloaded the file.*)

glennnnn5: got it
glennnnn5: so i guess i'll see you in 6 weeks
joss2themax: thx. let me know if u need anything
glennnnn5: want me to bring you anything from your cube?
joss2themax: don't think so, but will let you know
glennnnn5: alrighty then.
joss2themax: water my plants for me?
glennnnn5: will do!
joss2themax: great, thx. and thx for calling the ambulance. youre a lifesaver!
glennnnn5: least I could do
joss2themax: ;)
(*joss2themax has signed off.*)

The medical release form was all in order. I submitted it to HR, copying Wilson. Jocelyn's date of return was set for six weeks later. There was one strange thing about the form; it was dated three days before I found Jocelyn lying on the floor of her cube.

DOGFOOD

Darryl rose to the level of CEO after starting with the company at the beginning. Several CEOs held the position before Darryl assumed it, and each was fired for one disgrace or another; Boing;) was known for its CEOs flaming out spectacularly over corporate indiscretions.

- The CEO who had an affair with his administrative assistant and then promoted him to SVP of Human Resources, a jump of seven levels.
- The CEO who lied about serving in the military and receiving nine Purple Hearts and yet still received a $113 million golden parachute as part of his severance.
- The CEO who was recorded on video at the after party of a Black Eyed Peas concert—live-streamed exclusively by Boing;)—shouting a profanity-laced tirade about the moral, intellectual, and sexual inadequacies of CEOs at a dozen other major Valley companies.
- The CEO who created a parody video (that got leaked and posted to YouTube) for the Annual Sales Conference, featuring guns, simulated drug use, and a lap dance from a stripper—called *How to Delete Your Jammy Spammy Boingmail Account.*

- The CEO who spent $2.3 million to host the launch party for the redesigned Boingsearch at her home in Atherton, on her daughter's sixteenth birthday, with the festivities focusing not on the new product but on her daughter's new BMW, a performance by the Bolshoi Ballet in her daughter's honor, and a piñata filled with truffles, caviar, and bacon—all expensed to the company.

It seemed as if every Boing;) CEO possessed a fatal flaw that eventually led to his or her downfall. One candidate for Darryl's fatal flaw was his bizarre slanguage of youthisms from the past few decades. For example, he typically started each all-hands meeting strutting across the stage in Bytes, holding in one hand a microphone against his mouth like a hip-hop artist, and holding in the other hand his crotch, saying, "Yo, yo, yo! What up Boingers?" It might not have been so strange if it wasn't coming from a middle-aged nerdy white guy, who grew up in Sacramento building computers from scratch with other nerdy white guys. Old videos show a youthful and gawky Darryl hanging out with Paco and Stan and the other early Boingers, speaking without such affects. Somehow, over the years, they crept into his speech.

Darryl was employee #5, a college classmate of Paco and Stan. They all played together on the UC Berkeley Computer Engineering Ultimate Frisbee team that beat Stanford's Computer Science Ultimate Frisbee team in a match in 1994 that included dozens of future tech industry luminaries, as documented in the near-best-selling iBook *The Ultimate Season* by Marian Sallowaskky. Darryl worked as a software engineer writing the code that ran the original Boing;) website.

According to Boing;) legend, Darryl created Dogfood, the internal tool filled with information about all the company's different departments and employees. It was built on the same website-building-and-managing platform Boing;) offered to consumers. This was an inspired choice of names for an internal portal, because *dogfood* = a product a company uses internally before offering it to consumers. By eating your own dogfood, you know what it's like to be one of your customers.

On Dogfood you could create a twiki about any topic, from the steps to take to connect a printer to your computer, to how to file software bugs, to suggested snack hacks (my favorite was combining a York peppermint patty with a banana—tasty and nutritious). Dogfood was *open source* = anyone could add to it and change it. When you created or edited a twiki, your username was logged and available for all to see.

But there was one twiki that was anonymous and read-only—no one other than the document owner could make changes to it. Therefore, it was widely believed that Darryl, the creator of Dogfood, owned the page, titled *There Is Such a Thing As a Stupid Question*, known colloquially as TISATAASQ, or *tizzatask*. It listed hundreds of questions, with the most recent at the top. One of the greatest fears of any Boinger was to ask a question that would end up on TISATAASQ. The first question on the list appeared to have come from childhood: "Are you going to finish your dinner?" The latest question appeared on the list roughly a month before my Rockstar Coffee with Darryl. It had spawned a flurry of BM messages and emails throughout the company, as did every new TISATAASQ entry: "What is Boing;)?"

Marian Sallowaskky had asked this question at the annual *TechNomNom* Pivot Conference, where Darryl was a keynote speaker. He gave a five-minute answer that Ms. Sallowaskky subsequently lampooned in a blog post titled "What is Boing;)? In 5,000 Words or Less." The article was simply a verbatim transcript of Darryl's convoluted answer, where he called Boing;) a bitchin' technology company, a rockin' media company, a consumer goods company, a home, a cruise ship, a wicked cool spaceship, a portal, a search engine, seriously dope shizzle, a life engine, a hope engine, a dynamo, a turbine, the sock in the broken pair that you didn't lose, and a whack farsighted seagull.

The next time he was asked the question, his answer was more succinct, but still somewhat rambling, spawning a new round of lampooning in the tech industry press.

But the third time's the charm. After a round of golf, reporters caught the Vice President of the United States asking Darryl, a bit too loudly, as if wanting to be overheard, "What is Boing;)?" Darryl replied simply, clearly, passionately, "Boing;) is the best damn digital company on the planet, bro!" The question showed up on TISATAASQ the next morning.

This new description of Boing;) seemed to resonate with the tech press, who began repeating it unironically, without the "bro," in articles about the company. Only one minor glitch occurred when Darryl spoke at a conference and called Boing;) "the best *damned* digital company." Predictably, Marian Sallowaskky wrote a blog post accusing Darryl of a Freudian slip by calling Boing;) damned, as if he admitted the company was "fated to spend eternity roasting in the fires of hell." Marian Sallowaskky made a name for herself by bashing Boing;), and all of us Boingers deeply resented her for it.

I didn't want to say anything during my Coffee with Darryl that might end up on TISATAASQ. So I decided I'd begin with one simple question—"How are you today?"—and ask no more. I checked to see whether "How are you today?" was on TISATAASQ. It wasn't. All subsequent words from my mouth would be in the form of a statement. I'd tell him a story that would convince him to try my idea for turning the company around by creating a streaming music service.

Darryl liked to solicit elevator pitches. Most Boingers were afraid to enter an elevator with him because he might ask them to pitch him an idea for solving a pressing problem, like, "How should Boing;) deal with all the haters?" We all knew never to enter an elevator with Darryl without being prepared for anything. So the only Boingers who entered an elevator with Darryl were the ones who'd been on *Jeopardy!*

I had half an hour for my Coffee with Darryl. It was possible he'd be running late or would need to leave early—he was a busy man—so I expected to have a solid fifteen minutes to discuss important issues. I made a PowerPoint outline of how I hoped the meeting would go.

IDEAL AGENDA
Rockstar Coffee with Darryl (CEO)

- Pleasantries. "How are you today?" (Maintain eye contact!) – 1-2 mins
- Elevator pitch about streaming music service – 1-2 mins
- Deep-dive into streaming music service idea – 11-13 mins
- Flex time. More about the streaming music service. Ultimate Frisbee. Pasta. Etc. – 15 mins
- REMINDER: Don't ask question that might end up on TISATAASQ!
- NOTE: Be prepared to improvise! ("Yes, and...")

Boing;)

On another slide, I wrote, honed, and rehoned my elevator pitch about the streaming music service, getting it down to 126 words I could recite in twenty-six seconds if I hurried. I copied the file onto the thumb drive I carried in my pocket. I wouldn't need to open that file again—I committed the contents to memory—but it made my pocket feel heavier, as if it were filled with currency. It might as well have been.

STREAMS

Darryl was late. His second assistant, an elfin woman who always wore a dark pantsuit and exuded efficiency, apologized. "He's on his way back from Menlo Park, where he's been leaning in with the COO of Facebook." I was able to maintain a calm mental state with some controlled breathing: in through the nostrils, out through the mouth, with a mindful pause in between. She seated me in a big, orange Barcalounger outside his office. A company icon, this Barcalounger had been in Paco and Stan's college dorm room, and it had the wear and tear to show for it; the stuffing was bursting out of the arm rests, and a rash of stains suggested it provided cover in many paintball fights. While nobody was looking, I took a selfie.

Darryl's third assistant hovered nearby, ready to respond to the second assistant's next whim. The third assistant was well known throughout Boing;). Her name was Felicious. She was stunningly beautiful—tall, thin, with caramel-colored eyes, perfect posture, balletic body control, and luminous light-brown skin. Her clothing budget vastly outpaced her salary, according to several female co-workers. When she walked through Bytes to get lunch for Darryl, his first assistant, his second assistant, or for herself—sometimes making four different trips during lunchtime—all conversation stopped and all eyes of all genders turned to watch her. She seemed like a person from the future, when all races have mixed and the best genetic traits from all corners of the world have combined to create a super race of perfect people.

When the second assistant instructed her to prepare some tea—which struck me as funny, because everybody knows a Rockstar Award winner has *Coffee* with Darryl—Felicious conducted a grotesque, extended, multiphase, phlegm-clearing-and-swallowing maneuver within her throat, mouth, and sinuses before growling a guttural, "Got it." It was so disgusting I had to stifle a wave of nausea. I thereby experienced for the first time something many Boingers had described to me—hearing Felicious talk and clear her facial cavities made the future seem a little less enticing.

When Darryl arrived, he smiled at me with all his teeth. "What up, yo?"

I stood, and he transferred a coffee cup from his right hand to his left and shook my hand. I've heard if your hand is warm when you shake hands with another person, they'll like you more than if your hand isn't warm. And Darryl's overly warm hand instantly made him seem smaller, less intimidating, and friendly. I found myself thinking, *I would follow this man into battle. This warm-handed, smiling, smallish man.* I followed him into his office and sat on the patron's side of his desk as his first assistant placed a steaming cup of tea in front of me before closing the door behind her. With the door's click, my left eye began to twitch.

Darryl jumped right in. "Sorry I'm late, homie. I was meeting with the peeps from Facebook. They're about to announce they've reached 600 million daily users. I never thought they'd get bigger than Boing;), but here we are. I'm sure social networking is just a fad, *amirite*? They served Kobe beef prime rib and a '64 Charles Krug cab. As I prepared to chow down, a hundred employees in their lunchroom turned and toasted me—they all had the same shizzle on their plates and in their glasses. It was sick, yo! I don't think we've met. *Hola, amigo.* I'm Darryl. It's good to meet you, Glenn. Dope name. Strong. Medieval."

Medieval? I stutter-mumbled a good-to-meet-you utterance. Fortunately, Darryl continued to do the heavy lifting.

"So, you're our latest Rockstar. What can you do that's impressive, Glenn? Know any parlor tricks?"

I spent an entire Spring Break during college teaching myself to shuffle cards in midair, in preparation for a summer job at a casino that never panned out. While I'm confident it would've impressed Darryl, and even though I had a deck of cards with me, it didn't seem to be what he had in mind. Plus, I had a skill that was more germane to the situation. "Bring up any website on your browser, and I can tell you how many monthly unique visitors it typically receives."

Darryl moved his mouse to bring alive the laptop computer on his desk. "Dude, have you memorized every website's uniques?"

"No, sir. I look at the website content and design. I see where it sits on the internet, in relation to other websites. And I google it to see what links come up. I usually can predict its monthly audience within 20 percent."

"Don't you boing it?"

"I boing it, too. But since Google's search engine is used much more often than Boingsearch, I must google it to get full information about it. In my line of work, I regularly use our competitor's products in order to understand the mindset of the consumer."

He was looking at his screen and clicking. "Can't you use comScore to get uniques?"

"Of course. I use comScore as my official source of truth for competitive data. But you asked about parlor tricks."

"Right on. Tell me about this one, yo." He turned his screen to show me the home page of a website called Guysburgh.com. It featured a lewd cartoon of a man appearing to pass gas in the form of a giant, brown, fanged monster, several headlines with the word *dude* in them, and a photo of a woman leaning over the business portion of an old photocopy machine, with her shirt up around her neck. The headline suggested clicking would result in seeing a photocopy of her breasts. The navigation bar offered the following sections of the website: Gadgets, Games, Guitars, Guns, and Girls. The page also featured an advertisement for a new movie starring Robert Downey Jr. and Kirsten Dunst in a tube top. "Have you ever checked out this website?"

"In the course of my work, to understand the online landscape, I occasionally see websites that are not entirely safe for work. But I haven't seen this one."

"Guysburgh claims to be the shizzle with young bros. We're talking with them about a deeply integrated partnership, as part of Project Resurrection. They provide the content, we provide the traffic, and the whole fam feasts on the ad impressions. As you know, since you're deeply embedded in this stuff, we have a youth challenge."

I nodded. Our youth challenge was that people younger than thirty-five, known as digital natives, rarely visited Boing;) other than to check email, and they hardly ever did that. Teens in particular communicated with their friends almost exclusively via text messaging and social networks. The only reason they had email addresses was to set up accounts on Facebook and Instagram. Once they began using those social networks, they never returned to Boing;). As a result, we had limited page view inventory to deliver ads from advertisers who wanted to reach digital natives. I was thrilled to learn Darryl was concerned about our youth challenge because my idea for a streaming music service addressed it.

"This website probably gets about thirty thousand monthly unique visitors, sir."

Darryl scrutinized my face, my posture, my sport coat, and my teacup, as if trying to find evidence of mental instability. "Dude, they say they get thirty million uniques per month. Ginormous difference there. Like, three orders of magnitude."

I pointed to his laptop. "May I?" He pushed it toward me, and I brought up the website of comScore, the online ratings service considered the gold standard of online ratings services. Not that comScore's data was perfect, but they did a nominally better job of tracking online desktop behavior than other services offering scalable cross-platform audience measurement solutions.

On Darryl's laptop, I logged into comScore and clicked a few times in order to bring up a screen summarizing traffic trends for Guysburgh.com. "In the previous month, thirty-four thousand unique visitors in the US visited the website, with monthly unique visitors fluctuating wildly over the past year, from a low of eight thousand to a high of forty-seven thousand, for an average of thirty-two thousand unique visitors per month."

Darryl received it as news he could use. "That's some whack shit, yo!"

I used the screen of comScore data for an impromptu presentation. "We can determine how Guysburgh gets its traffic by looking at the top search terms people use to get to the website. As you can see, the top search terms are either variants of *nude—naked*, *topless*, *bottomless, birthday suited*—or words for female genitalia, preceded by names of celebrities such as Kim Kardashian or Kirsten Dunst."

"Who doesn't like looking at some birthday suited Kardashian? *Amirite?*" He put his hands up mockingly. "HR violation! My bad."

I weakly nodded my consent, though I was uncertain whether I was consenting to the lewd reference or the classification of his comment as an HR violation. "Obviously, this is content that a mass audience of males regularly searches for, and they're seeing search results that lead them to Guysburgh."

"Got it."

I clicked a few times to bring up data about ESPN. "Here's an example of a website with a strong brand and with a large audience visiting deliberately. As we can see, the top search terms driving traffic to the website are variants of the brand name or represent important features of the brand's content: ESPN, ESPN live, ESPN.com, ESPN TV, ESPN sideline reporter babe. Even the typo EPSN is a top search term. Since none of the top search terms for Guysburgh includes the word *Guysburgh*, we can conclude hardly anyone visits the website deliberately, and that's why their monthly audience is so small and varies so widely."

I looked over at Darryl. He was checking his iPhone. So I continued. "Nevertheless, Guysburgh seems to be doing two things well. One, their search engine optimization is resulting in their content out-ranking erotically themed content available on other websites; this accounts for nearly all of their traffic. Two, they're convincing premium advertisers they have a large, organic audience of guys visiting their website for the other content—the gadgets, games, etc."

I *did not* tell Darryl that Guysburgh's search engine optimization efforts almost certainly involved nefarious, probably immoral, and possibly illegal activities, such as creating sham companies in international tax havens and utilizing link farms and other schemes to trick search engines into thinking their content was popular and linked-to by an army of citizen guys, rather than by an army of bots on servers in someplace like Vanuatu.

I pointed to the advertisement on the front page of Guysburgh. "While it might seem smart to advertise this Robert Downey Jr. and Kirsten Dunst movie on a website where the number four search term driving traffic to the site is 'Kirsten Dunst boobs,' with a little math we can determine Guysburgh's likely impact on box office results. Let's say the movie makes thirty million dollars in theaters. That means roughly three million people will buy a ten-dollar ticket. Even if every one of Guysburgh's roughly thirty thousand unique visitors attends the movie after seeing this ad, it means Guysburgh will be responsible for driving just one-percent of—"

Darryl interrupted my back-of-the-envelope calculation, putting down his iPhone. "Got it. I hear you, bro. What you're saying is, all Guysburgh needs is more traffic."

Then a strange thing happened. My ears felt plugged, my mouth went dry, and the room seemed darker. My ability to take in signals—sound, sight, taste, smell, touch—shut down completely for an instant. It can only be explained as a moment of cognitive dissonance; what I was seeing and hearing didn't match how I believed the world worked. "Guysburgh just needs more traffic," was not what I'd spent the previous few minutes saying. I thought I was saying, *Guysburgh is basically a soft porn website, and they're completely lying to you.*

Did this mean Darryl didn't Get It? *Is it possible to rise to the level of CEO at a Fortune 500 company without Getting It? Does working hard to Get It even matter?* I felt as if some fundamental truth had just been proven wrong, as if I just learned disease is not caused by viruses and infection but by evil little demons who inflict harm on people for infractions like passing an old oak tree without turning around three times while saying, "Please let me pass safely, little demons." I did the only thing I could do; I paused, awaiting further information.

Darryl went on. "We can give them more traffic. If they start getting millions of peeps from us, then they could drive major box office or righteous sales of men's body wash or *whatevs.* We need more monetization streams and video streams. I need more streams, yo."

My senses came back to me in a rush. This was the moment I'd been waiting for! "I think there's a better way to make Boing;) relevant again to a younger audience, both males and females."

He checked his watch. "Give me your elevator pitch, cuz I gotta bounce."

I pitched him my well-rehearsed idea for a streaming music service. "Music appeals to people of all ages, especially younger people, who dramatically overindex in consuming music. There are many popular, free streaming music services, but many, like that buggy little Swedish app Spotify that just launched in the US, are unlikely to develop the robust partnerships with music labels that Boing:) has already established. None of them do what I'm proposing Boing;) do: use a streaming music service as a lure to get young people to visit our network, then get them to click on other things while they're here. They already consume all the kinds of content we offer—sports, celebrity news, political news, fashion—on other websites. When we get them here, we can get them to stay, and we can make money from it."

Darryl jotted some notes on a Post-It. "So it's a loss leader, like the Black Friday deals at Best Buy. We get them into the store with the streaming music service, and then they do other stuff that brings us the Benjamins while they're here."

I nodded and smiled. My sense of order in the universe was restored.

The door opened, and all three of Darryl's assistants entered. His first assistant placed a packet on his desk. His second assistant adjusted the window blinds to prevent the afternoon sun from shining on his face, and Felicious removed my tea cup and saucer. Darryl came around his desk, saying, "Send me a one-pager on that streaming music shizzle. Fly ideas can come from anywhere, yo."

As we shook hands, Darryl's first assistant handed me my Rockstar Award trophy, an acrylic representation of a rock sitting on a star. His second assistant stood ready to take a photo of us with her iPhone—this soon would be posted on Dogfood for all Boingers to see. I hadn't planned to do this, but as our hands were clasped and we both smiled for the camera, I stated my motto. "Being objective makes me effective."

Darryl squeezed my shoulder tightly.
Click!

DELIVERABLES

As I walked across campus to Building Zed, I felt a mixture of elation and mortification, *elortification*. It reminded me of how I felt in college when I asked a blue-eyed young woman I'd been admiring to have dinner with me, on a date, away from the dorm cafeteria, at some unspecified restaurant off-campus with silverware and cloth napkins and a menu you hold in your hand. We'd been studying Microeconomics 1A, and every Thursday evening we spent three hours together creating supply-and-demand charts. She accepted my invitation to dinner, I thought with a gleam in her eye: smiling, hip cocked with her weight on one leg, pupils dilated, lips moist, hand touching my arm. All the right signals. Somehow that dinner never occurred.

I spent the elevator ride pondering the similarities between those momentous events, the meeting with Darryl and the dinner invitation. In both cases I prepared thoroughly. In both cases I felt exhilarated afterward. In both cases I received an acceptance to participate in an unspecified future liaison. But as soon as the elevator doors opened on my floor, I was back in the present, breaking down the meeting with Darryl, where the outcome was undetermined and largely within my control.

I hurried to my cube, undocked my laptop, and walked the halls until I found an unoccupied conference room—Vigilance. I closed the door and sat at the table. I opened a PowerPoint template titled BOMME ("Being Objective Makes Me Effective"), my own personal template I used for purposes such as this one. It was the normal Boing;) template but with my motto in the corner, in a very small font size, in the same color as the background. You couldn't see it, but I knew it was there. And I created a postmortem analysis of the meeting with Darryl.

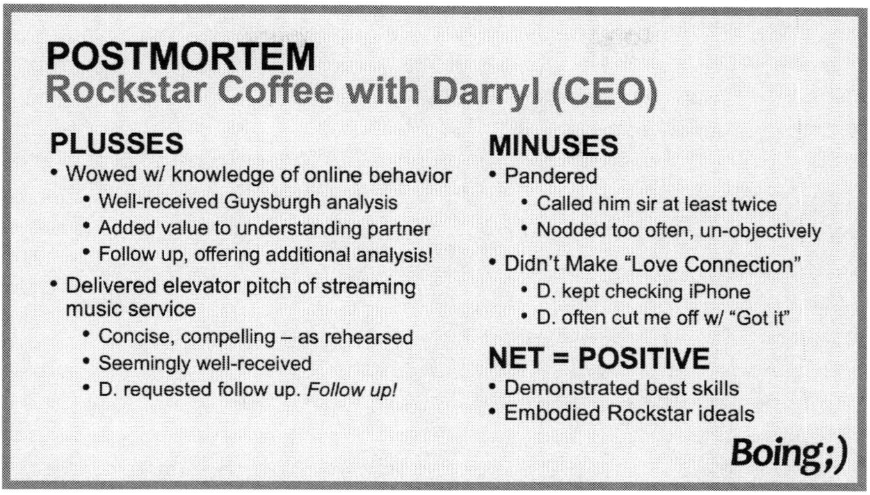

Some researchers (mostly qualitative) claim the use of PowerPoint dumbs down our interpersonal interactions. Forcing the thought process into a bulleted format simplistically suggests each issue can be boiled down to a few key elements, and we create a nation of robotic workers unable to *think outside the box* = creatively.

I believe such people overindex among those who don't Get It. I believe the following, objectively and deeply.

- The quality and depth of the information conveyed is independent of the means of conveyance (e.g., PowerPoint).
- Creating an impactful PowerPoint deck is an art form, not unlike writing a novel, directing a movie, or sculpting a realistic representation of an idealized human form from a block of marble.
- PowerPoint is merely a tool, and a PowerFul one at that.
    - o In the hands of children (or those who don't Get It), it can be a blunt instrument not suited for fine-motor-skills work.

- In the hands of a craftsperson, it's just the right handsaw for just the right mitered cut of a fine-grained wood.

Reflected in the screen of my laptop, I could see my own face, almost like a watermark on my postmortem analysis. At that moment, I couldn't be more grateful to be among those who Get It.

I began drafting a follow up email to Darryl, offering to do more analysis of websites he was considering for partnership or acquisition. In the history of the internet, Boing;) had the opportunity to buy nearly every startup that eventually became a sensation, including Google, YouTube, Facebook, MySpace, Yahoo!, and PayPal. I half congratulated, half chastised—*congrastised*—myself for being bold enough to volunteer for that responsibility now. I also reiterated my idea for the streaming music service and created a deliverable—a one-pager explaining the idea.

I don't know if other people are like me in this way—a digital document seems to me just as hold-in-your-hands satisfying as a printout of the same document. I know this might sound crazy. I'm talking about the feeling you get from having something in your possession. For me, possessing a digital representation of a thing gives me more pleasure than possessing a physical version of it. Digital stuff leaves less of a mark on the Earth than real-life stuff. It lives in electricity, in the mind, in ideas. It's fast and clean. It lives forever. Obviously, this doesn't apply to things that can't be digitized, such as a Toyota Prius, a favorite wool cardigan sweater, a piece of art, or a girlfriend.

Or a Rockstar Award, which weighs more than it looks like it should, about as much as a heavy-duty stapler or a dead opossum. Someone (me, in my jealous, pre-Rockstar days) had described the trophy as "a potato impaled on a sad star." But now that I had one, I could see it was more like a meteor and a star streaking through the solar system together on a journey of discovery and conquest.

Before I became a Rockstar, when Wilson was out of his "office," I'd go into Integrity to look at and hold his Rockstar Award. I never asked permission for admiring it; I didn't want him to have that power over me. Each time we had our 1:1 meeting, I'd glance at his Rockstar Award and amuse myself knowing my fingerprints were on it.

While I felt important and awed holding my own Rockstar Award in my hands, I got a greater sense of pride from the virtual Rockstar badge on my Dogfood profile because it was permanently affixed to my digital self. It was like a virtual tattoo on my virtual body. I didn't need to unroll my shirtsleeve to show it—it was there for all to see.

I felt the same way about my favorite files and deliverables. I kept them stored in "the cloud" redundantly—they were in my Boingmail digital locker and in another place in the digital realm that I won't divulge. I could access them at any time, from any device, from anywhere in the world.

This became useful to me during a particular hundred-day experience I alluded to at the beginning of my story, when I wasn't allowed to keep any of my physical objects, especially sharp ones. I had no fear my digital possessions might be impounded, lost, or stolen, which could happen with a Prius, a cardigan, a piece of art, or a girlfriend. They were safe forever in the cloud.

My experience with Darryl was similar—intangibly tangible, not hold-in-your-hands stuff, but just as satisfying. It was like making a deposit in the Bank of Opportunity. I saved the draft of my email to Darryl and spent the rest of the day creating Excel macros to analyze data from the latest Boingtunes Hump Day marketing campaign. I hummed to the rhythm of my mouse clicks.

EXITS

I knew I was nervous the day Jocelyn was scheduled to return to work because I was having difficulty deciding on a caffeine solution. I was in the microkitchen, trying to choose between too many options.

- Coke
- Pepsi
- Dr. Pepper
- The diet versions of all of the above
- Coffee
- Black tea
- Green tea
- Mountain Dew
- Red Bull

I usually chose coffee or a diet soda. I sometimes consumed no caffeine at all. But that day my managerial skills were being stretched. Project Clarion Call was calling me.

There are well-understood processes for welcoming a co-worker back to the office after a long vacation, after maternity or paternity leave, or after leaving the company to work elsewhere before returning a couple of years later with a higher title. But I couldn't find recommendations for managing a co-worker's return from a near-death experience. And I couldn't think of an approach casual enough to make Jocelyn feel welcome, yet formal enough to acknowledge the special circumstances of her departure and return. I certainly didn't want to put up a banner saying,

"Welcome back, Jocelyn! So glad you're alive!" But I didn't want to merely nod at her while passing her cube. The occasion called for something in between. It called for acknowledgement of the past while looking forward. It called for greater skill than I possessed. My plan was to get caffeinated and then wing it; perhaps afterward I'd have some advice to share on the internet with others facing the same situation.

While pondering my options, I saw in one of the refrigerated display cases—the one that had been added on my recommendation—a row of beverages I hadn't noticed before. Cans of Kool-Aid. Red. Apparently this was both the color and the flavor. I didn't know Kool-Aid was available in cans. This was just one more reminder that billions of people are out there doing things you don't know about until the results of their efforts appear before you. I felt the same way about boxer briefs when I first saw them. *Where did they come from? How did we live without them?*

Kool-Aid struck me as an ironic choice here, in the heart of Silicon Valley. Of course, "drinking the Kool-Aid" has become a catchphrase in corporate America, meaning "to blindly and happily follow the dictates of management, even if they might kill you." While "drinking the Kool-Aid" is often used as humor, it's hard for me to laugh at memes like this one that are rooted in tragedy, even if they resonate within the business world. In the 70s, more than nine hundred members of the Peoples Temple cult died when their leader, Jim Jones, instructed them to drink a cyanide-laced Kool-Aid-type beverage at their final all-hands meeting. Plus, while I might someday decide to drink a refreshing can of Kool-Aid, I expected to never "drink the Kool-Aid," because it's the opposite of being objective.

The Kool-Aid offered here contained no caffeine, so I selected a Diet Dr. Pepper, and I resolved to nominate the person who added Kool-Aid to our drink selections for the next Rockstar Award—for having the entrepreneurial spirit to offer an ironic beverage.

In a small way, I felt sufficiently prepared for Jocelyn's return. During her absence, I'd taken a CPR course after work on Wednesdays. At my request, my instructor, a highly competent young man named Joey, tailored my instruction toward handling a drug overdose. I described a hypothetical situation almost exactly like the one I thought I'd faced with Jocelyn. He told me CPR wouldn't help because the problem with someone who has overdosed isn't breathing- or heart-related; it's that the drugs are toxic. If such a circumstance occurred again, he recommended I make sure the windpipe is open so the person can breathe, and, if the poison is a sedative and not a corrosive acid, induce vomiting.

Joey had me practice these moves, as well as CPR, on a test dummy. And in my personal time at home I learned how to induce vomiting on myself. It was unpleasant, but it was a worthy skill to develop.

About half an hour after the caffeine turned me from an affable-yet-introverted fellow into an affable-and-nearly-extroverted fellow, Jocelyn arrived at her cube and began booting up her laptop. She looked like the same Jocelyn: alert, bemused, color-coordinated. She brought her own lunch, in a reusable cotton sack. I greeted her. "Hi, Jocelyn. Welcome back!"

"Thanks." She looked up at me from her chair, biting her lip.

"How was your commute this morning?"

"Sucky. Normal."

I watched her maybe too long, too inquisitively. Her eyes and mine turned to the desk, now clean, where pills had been spilled the last time she was there. She stood, and we walked wordlessly together to the microkitchen, where she put her lunch in the refrigerator. Before she placed it on the top shelf, she removed a package of dried edamame from her sack. She offered me some; I accepted one bean, and I chewed it dryly.

And then I did something I hadn't planned to do. I introduced her to people around the office, as if it was her first day back from a sabbatical or a very long vacation.

We peeked our heads into Integrity. "Hey, Wilson, Jocelyn has returned." He was on the phone. He gave her a wink and a thumbs-up.

We saw Maryanne in the hallway. "Maryanne, Jocelyn's back."

Maryanne stopped, smiled, took Jocelyn's hands, and looked into her eyes. "Delightful!"

We wandered the hallways saying hello to dozens of co-workers. And a wondrous thing occurred. Each co-worker greeted Jocelyn in his or her own particular way. Some acted as if nothing consequential had occurred since the last time they saw her. Some said it was great to see her healthy again. One woman, known for owning nine cats, took Jocelyn aside and spoke seriously to her, in hushed tones.

Jocelyn seemed to appreciate our co-workers' concern for her. As we walked from cube to cube, she kept looking up at me over the rims of her glasses and smiling in a searching way, as if seeking my approval, which she had, wholeheartedly. I kept smiling back at her, confidently thinking, *I know how to induce vomiting.*

Our reunion tour of the floor turned into a tour of the building, then a tour of the campus. As her tour guide, I didn't point out things she obviously already knew, such as, "Boing;) offers a beach volleyball court next to basketball and tennis courts." I pointed out things that had changed in the weeks she'd been away. "The foosball tables were moved from the entrance area of Bytes to a hidden alcove behind the fitness center. Foosball has been reclassified, as part of Project Resurrection, from a leisure activity to an exercise program." And, "We no longer receive free muffins and bagels on Fridays."

This last change was a significant loss. Legend had it the Free Friday Muffins & Bagels institution was established during the darkest days of the Dot-Com Bust. According to the legend, many Boingers had gotten into the habit of spending their Fridays *WFH* = working from home, so the campus felt like a ghost town at the end of every work week, and it was difficult to conduct meetings and *GSD* = get shit done. When Free Friday Muffins & Bagels was instituted, Boingers were enticed back to the office, WFH decreased, GSD increased, and good morale was reinstated. Presumably, we had reestablished the habit of working from work on Fridays sufficiently enough that we could now GSD without muffins or bagels.

As Jocelyn and I walked, we started to talk about other things that had come and gone in our professional lives. She surprised me by asking, "What do you think was the best exit in the history of the internet?"

The answer was obvious to me. "I think my favorite is Broadcast.com's acquisition by Yahoo! in 1999. The company barely had a viable product when Yahoo! purchased it for $6 billion in stock at the height of the Dot-Com Bubble, making the founder, Mark Cuban, a billionaire on paper. He quickly sold his stock and became a billionaire with real money. Whenever I watch the Dallas Mavericks play basketball on television and I see Mark Cuban sitting courtside beside his team, I think, 'Best exit ever.'"

Jocelyn clapped her hands elegantly, like she was applauding an opera singer. I bowed.

We naturally found ourselves in Bytes, sitting at the wobbly table near the tray return area. And thus began an unscheduled 1:1 meeting. I hadn't intended to hold such a meeting so soon after Jocelyn's return. It just happened. And it was exactly the right thing to do. Because Jocelyn had some work-related topics that were top-of-mind.

SIGNALS

In the morning, Bytes was a low-key, friendly place, not the hectic hive of activity it became during lunchtime. It had the air of a college dorm for grown-ups.

Ron from Data Systems nodded as he passed by carrying a banana and an English muffin; I nodded back.

Jocelyn waved a tiny wave across the room to a young woman I didn't know.

And Wanda from B2B Marketing stopped at our table. "Hey ya! How was your weekend?"

I motioned for Jocelyn to answer. She said, "Nice, thanks. I binge watched old episodes of *The Rockford Files*."

"I love those!" Wanda imitated the show's opening sequence, "*This is Jim Rockford. At the tone leave your name and message. I'll get back to you.*" Then she turned to me. "What about you, Mr. Objective?"

"I got caught up on my laundry."

"Doesn't get much better than that! Well, have a great day, you two!" Wanda spent the next twenty minutes bouncing from table to table before finally leaving.

In Jocelyn's absence, I'd been managing all our projects, the long-term ones and the developing ones. As I outlined the current projects, Jocelyn volunteered, "I'll do the pre-Olympics behavioral analysis."

"Great. Can you also take on the deep dive of the news junkies audience segment?" Jocelyn nodded impatiently. She squirmed as I continued speaking. "So that leaves the pre/post analysis of the fantasy hockey ad campaign, the Boingmovies customer satisfaction survey, and the celebrity fluff bucket test. We can divide those up as each of them gets closer to launching."

Then she surprised me by grabbing my arm, and, as if the words had been building up inside her, she blurted out, "I want a stretch assignment."

While there was no formal process for welcoming a co-worker back from surviving a near-death experience, there was a formal process for making a stretch assignment. My own rapid career growth left opportunities for my team—Jocelyn—in its wake, such as the Data Integrity Tiger Team membership I'd already handed off to her. "Okay. Good idea. Let me think about it and come up with a suitable stretch assignment for you."

"I have something in mind."

I paused, awaiting further information.

She continued, "During my leave, I felt relaxed and focused. Maybe it was the Zoloft my doctor prescribed. Maybe it was the lack of pressure to meet deadlines. But I still feel the same sense of clarity and purpose this very moment, now that I'm back at work." I'd never seen Jocelyn so self-assured. She seemed to realize this as she leaned toward me, "This experience has hardened me. It made me realize my #lifegoal."

When she said it, I heard the hashtag in her voice. She didn't say, "hashtag life goal." She said, "life goal," but I somehow knew she was talking about her #lifegoal in her pronunciation.

"I felt my #lifegoal start to coalesce within my mind, within my entire being. If I was religious, I would say it's a result of divine inspiration. But I'm not, so probably it was just my freaky self synthesizing my thoughts, experiences, and desires into a holistic picture."

I opened my mouth to speak; she paused to listen. I was going to say something about the moment of clarity I felt just as I was passing out in Integrity, as Wilson told me I'd received the Rockstar Award, as I realized a streaming music product would lead to Boing;)'s resurrection. But suddenly I realized I didn't want to talk about that. I wanted to hear about her #lifegoal. I was intrigued. I shut my mouth and nodded for her to go ahead.

"I realized we here at Boing;) collect zillions of pieces of information about our users, and each is a signal telling something about their needs and interests, passions and preferences. We know their demographics, the types of news they consume, the types of searches they conduct, who they communicate with, which ads they click on, the time of day they do particular things, and more. We can determine which signals are related.

For example, when a user reads an email newsletter from a consumer goods company and then does a Boingsearch for the company's product, we can assume those are related activities. When a user likes a photo posted by a friend and shares it with another friend, there's a possible future relationship between the two who aren't connected yet. By stringing together signals and their associations, we can create a *web of signals*. Users inadvertently leave behind a trail of digital breadcrumbs as they travel the digital world. We should be collecting those crumbs of information and patting them together into a sort of meatloaf of knowledge that we can then serve them to make their experiences better, to anticipate their needs in a way that's helpful, friendly, and fun, without being creepy."

Then she snort-laughed. "I can't believe I just used meatloaf in an analogy!"

"Because you're vegan?"

"No, I think it's the mouthfeel of the word *meatloaf*." She made a nasty face like she'd just eaten meatloaf. "So my #lifegoal is to extend human ability and development through digital technology. I really believe we can create something beautiful, perfect, and clean. Does that make sense?"

It made sense. It also was naïve. Every digital media and technology company leveraged data toward delivering a personalized user experience and targeted advertising. Jocelyn seemed to be talking about something a little more ethereal and impossible to test. There'd been thousands of failed startups founded on the idea of leveraging user data in the ways Jocelyn was suggesting, startups that built their own webs of signals without conducting rigorous research to understand the market and identify opportunities. Boing;) needed well-founded ideas that could be substantiated with market research, such as a streaming music service. Who could say exactly what the impact a streaming music service was likely to have on Boing;)'s fortunes, but we could conduct market research to quantify the opportunity.

She watched me closely. I stroked my chin. She tapped her foot nervously against the table, putting its wobbliness into action.

Despite my certainty that Jocelyn's idea was unoriginal and not what Boing;) needed and that her #lifegoal was a too vague for achieving greatness, I said, "That's an impressive idea. And that's a humdinger of a #lifegoal!" Not very objective of me, I know. But this didn't seem the proper moment for full objectivity. In the back of my mind, I wondered if I might regret going against my motto in this way.

She exhaled in a gust and went on. "I'd like for the web of signals to be my stretch assignment. I'd like to have permission to reach out to people across the company to discuss the idea. Maybe someone's already working on it. Maybe they ought to be. It'd be a tremendous learning opportunity for me, and it'd be a way for us to evangelize the work we've been doing."

I agreed. "Fantastic! Go for it!"

"Seriously?"

I nodded. Jocelyn jumped to her feet and did the first four steps of some sort of dance, as if she'd once performed in a musical play and still had a particular routine within her muscle memory. She looked up at the high ceiling of Bytes, and over at the two-story windows looking out on the sunny-day center of campus. She turned to me. "Do you know why I like sitting at this table?"

"I've always wondered."

"Because it's at the center of everything, Glenn. It's between the food and the refuse, the windows and the walls, the floor and the ceiling, in the center of the Boing;) campus. And Boing;)'s in the middle of the Silicon Valley, in the middle of California, in the middle of a social, cultural, intellectual, and technological revolution. And this sad, little, broken, wobbly table is like the belly button of the known universe." She repeated the four-step pattern before sitting down, with a strong "Whoo!"

Needless to say, I hadn't anticipated Jocelyn would be so joyful and engaged on her first day back from work. "Well, then, I recommend that you form a Web of Signals Tiger Team. Let me know if there's any way I can help." After all, what could be the harm in it?

RISK

In order for us to conduct, analyze, and deliver the highest quality market research insights, we needed to maintain a high level of objectivity. I was pleased to hear Jocelyn was taking Zoloft, an antidepressant medication, because I believed it would help her avoid the despair that led to her hospitalization. But I must admit I was concerned about the effect it might have on her work, and, ultimately, on Boing;). I resolved to keep an eye on the quality of her decision-making. If I thought she was straying into subjective, risk-embracing activities, I would need to intervene.

My concerns only increased as I researched the issue. A well-documented side effect of these drugs is that the people who consume them become less afraid of risks. One analysis with troubling results was conducted at DeVry University, admittedly not a highly reputable research institution. It found that widespread use of antidepressants creates a better, more cohesive community. Which sounds good on the surface but is worrisome upon further inspection.

The study looked at the Silicon Valley in early 2000s, in the aftermath of the Dot-Com Bust. At the time, 23 percent of adults living in the region were estimated to be taking antidepressant medication. According to the study, after thousands of dot-com companies failed and tens of thousands of people lost their jobs, the crime and suicide rates in Silicon Valley decreased significantly, contrary to what typically happens to a geographical region when its booming industry collapses, suggesting some key factor kept the bankrupt and disgraced dotcom employees and venture capitalists from responding to their downfalls in traditional, self-destructive ways. There was a surge in volunteerism at local schools and hospitals. Neighborhood beautification organizations were founded throughout the region. The community extension courses at Stanford were oversubscribed for the first time in a generation. The study concluded that the Valley's admirable response to the bust was a result of widespread usage of antidepressants, which made anxiety-prone people more socially engaged and less self-destructive than they normally would have been after an economic trauma.

That study was sponsored by the pharmaceutical industry; obviously, that raises a red flag. Hidden in the footnotes was a paragraph summarizing results of survey questions that weren't included in the topline findings, showing that antidepressant users who worked in the tech and finance industries—the very people who engineered the bubble—were more likely than non-users of antidepressants to believe the tech industry would continue to grow exponentially forever.

What could I conclude other than many of the major players who caused the Dot-Com Bubble (and subsequent Bust) were prone to risk-taking behavior as a result of consuming antidepressants?

I've found other examples documenting the Prozac Effect, which predates Prozac, corresponding to the introduction of the first antidepressants in the 1950s. They suggest widespread use of antidepressants contributed to increased risk-taking and reckless behavior that led to many historical disasters, including the Bay of Pigs invasion of Cuba in 1961, the deregulation of U.S. savings-and-loan banks in the 1980s and the subsequent S&L crisis, the First and Second Gulf Wars, and the election of Arnold Schwarzenegger as governor of California in 2003, along with his re-election in 2006.

On the other hand, the Prozac Effect reportedly contributed to the making of many high-quality and culturally enriching independent films by risk-taking, antidepressant-consuming directors who maxed out all their credit cards to get their movies made. It also led to the first Rickroll, which is equal parts historical disaster and cultural enrichment.

I realize this all sounds very subjective. That's my point. Bear with me. Some of the reports on the subject are truly kooky. For example, one of them concluded that all people in the U.S. have antidepressant medication in their bloodstream because when antidepressant users urinate, trace elements of the drugs wash out into the ocean, where they mix with seawater that evaporates, forming clouds that develop into rain that falls over farms, resulting in trace amounts of antidepressants making their way into the food we eat. The same study also concluded that our politicians and business leaders are aliens who're putting antidepressants into the food supply to keep us docile while they terraform Earth to match the desertscape of their home planet.

I've searched for objective, reputable analyses of the effects of antidepressants on decision making, and there's only anecdotal evidence, but it includes this critical fact: No major study has been published on this topic. That's more than a little suspicious. When you're being objective, lack of evidence is *evidence.*

GOALS

There was a pesky piece of work I'd been avoiding. I blocked out time on my calendar to finally get it done.

One of the company-wide goals for Project Resurrection was "Improve employee morale." In order to contribute to this goal, Wilson set a quarterly goal for our team. "Build team spirit by supporting teammates." I was still in the red for that goal because I hadn't endorsed Wilson's skills on LinkedIn, which was the way he wanted to be supported by teammates. To be fair, he'd endorsed my skills and Jocelyn's skills on LinkedIn, but he expected us to do the same for him. I tried several times to do it, but I kept getting caught in a spinning hypnowheel of amazement and revulsion whenever I visited his LinkedIn profile. It began with a summary of his experience.

Wilson is a seasoned, data-driven market research executive with an unparalleled track record of high-impact achievement. He is widely recognized as a dynamic speaker, strategic thinker, problem solver, solution provider, as well as a thought leader, and his advice is sought by major executives throughout the tech industry.

> Moreover, Wilson is a lifelong entrepreneur. While he was pursuing his education, he founded and sold an influential stock trading advice startup, and he co-established the world's largest pet-naming firm. More recently, he co-launched

> the fastest-growing artisanal catering startup in the Silicon Valley.
>
> On a personal note, Wilson is an avid quadrathlete, having medaled in more than two dozen quadrathlons (swimming, kayaking, running, cycling) and several super-quadrathlons. He is an internationally respected expert on Soviet-era sidecar motorcycles and has restored three of them. He also breeds and shows award-winning Weimaraners. On Sundays he enjoys watching Disney movies with his beautiful wife and children.

You might be thinking, *This sounds like a talented and fascinating guy, the kind of person I would want working at my company. The kind of person who will have a big impact.* That's the problem. If he'd been as widely recognized as he claimed to be, he probably wouldn't be just a Senior Director forcing his direct reports to endorse him on LinkedIn.

I needed help getting through this. I BM'd Jocelyn, even though she was just in the next cube.

> *glennnnn5*: hey. have you endorsed W's skills yet?
> *joss2themax*: nope. keep procrastinating
> *glennnnn5*: me, too. are you busy now? want to do it together?
> *joss2themax*: k
> *joss2themax*: checking his profile now

I waited a moment for her to catch up. Then I continued.

> *glennnnn5*: soviet era sidecar restoration. is that even a real thing?
> *joss2themax*: i know, right?
> *glennnnn5*: "Dynamic speaker and presenter"
> *joss2themax*: he isn't the worst public speaker
> *joss2themax*: he starts every preso with a joke -- i like that

glennnnn5: he started the boingmail redesign presentation with "what's worse than biting into an apple and finding a worm?
glennnn5: answer: finding half a worm
joss2themax: *groan*
glennnnn5: it would have been better if the joke was relevant to the topic
glennnnn5: what's worse than biting into an apple and finding a worm?
joss2themax: what?
glennnnn5: reading the hatemail from users who say their lives have been ruined by the new boingmail redesign

I heard Jocelyn laugh out loud in her cube.

joss2themax: lol!
joss2themax: problem solver, solution provider
glennnnn5: yes, if the solution involves him getting face time with an exec
joss2themax: i need help getting a junior engineer to instrument a page for tracking user behavior
glennnnn5: too bad for you
joss2themax: he's had a lot of jobs
glennnnn5: yep
joss2themax: none of them for longer than 2 yrs except at boing;)
joss2themax: i've always been told that's a bad sign
joss2themax: that job jumping looks bad on your resume
glennnnn5: (zipping lips, throwing away the key)
joss2themax: underwear model? whooaa
glennnnn5: (finding the key, unzipping lips) you didn't know that?
joss2themax: no
glennnnn5: there was a get to know a boinger article on dogfood about W, focusing on his career as an underwear model
joss2themax: must've been b4 my time

joss2themax: but explains why he always finds a reason to take off his shirt
glennnnn5: at the basketball court
joss2themax: at that tgif concert on the quad by the jefferson spaceship tribute band
glennnnn5: starship. at the sales conf while
joss2themax: i could've sworn it was spaceship?
glennnnn5: definitely starship. or airplane. depending on the song. it's complicated
joss2themax: this is crazy. just doing it...
joss2themax: ...endorsing now...cover me!
glennnnn5: i'm going in too -- right behind you!

Jocelyn was right. Just do it. My team-building goal was in the red, and that wasn't consistent with my personal brand. So I did what I had to do: I endorsed each of Wilson's skills, including Strategy, Management, and Leadership.

I added an additional skill to Wilson's profile: Inspiring. I saw the number of people who endorsed that skill tick from 1 to 2, as Jocelyn endorsed it, too. If nothing else, Wilson inspired me to work extra hard so I wouldn't have to report to him, a goal I'd eventually achieve!

LIKEABILITY

During the final meeting of the Brand Campaign Assessment Tiger Team, I learned who nominated me for the Rockstar Award—Maryanne.

She stood as she spoke to the team. "Thank you all for your sublime contributions. Although the brand campaign didn't have the impact we'd hoped, we had a great assessment that provided us with the insights we need to do a better job next time. The campaign failed with consumers, but it succeeded in minting a new Rockstar—Glenn Cregg—for his singular achievement in assessing the campaign."

Maryanne gestured toward me with open arms. As I nodded and thanked my clapping co-workers, I remembered a similar meeting Maryanne and I attended together, a few years earlier, assessing the results of Project Skynet.

Skynet was like Project Resurrection for an earlier era. It was designed to take all of our user and revenue data and create one holistic, all-encompassing database for optimizing traffic flow to drive monetization, brand strength, and user engagement—the way civil engineers optimize the flow of rain water into lakes, canals, and homes. Skynet was never fully implemented. Maybe that was a good thing. The name—referring to the computer system in *The Terminator* that became self-aware and adopted the stretch goal of eradicating humans—was a rare slipup in Boing;)'s legacy of creating inspiring project names.

In one of the Skynet meetings, I presented some user research to the Marketing team. It included measures for Boing;)'s brand health, likelihood to recommend, and likeability. Maryanne joked with me, "How's *my* likeability, Glenn?"

I replied, "It's always in the top quintile, Maryanne." It became a running joke between us.

Her likeability was on display again as she stoked the applause. "Being objective makes Glenn effective!" The others hooted and whistled. Wilson clapped politely and squirmed slightly, as if he was attempting to molt out of his shirt. I stood, bowed, and smiled at Maryanne. She just exuded executiveness. Partly it was the way she held herself—proudly, straightly, unperturbedly. Partly it was the way she interacted day-to-day with Boingers—always asking how we were doing, spending a moment or two longer than the typical executive to listen to our responses, before looking us in the eyes and saying, "Delightful!" Whenever the topic of Maryanne came up in less-than-polite Boinger conversation, someone usually sarcastically said, "*Deeliiiightful!*"

I sat as Maryanne lowered her arms to bring everyone back down to earth. "While we're shutting down this tiger team, its mission continues to live on within each of us as we work to make Boing;) a bedazzled member of our users' families. We still need to grow our traffic and enrichment. If we can get each user to give us just one more page view each time she visits, we can be number one again. And if we do that, advertisers will see us as a thought leader and emulsifier of their brands."

Another reason less-than-polite Boingers made fun of Maryanne was her word choice. She probably meant *beloved* rather than *bedazzled.* She often used the word *enrichment* when a normal Valley person would say *engagement.* And she regularly used *emulsifier* while talking about Boing;)'s impact on brands. Many Boingers thought she meant a different word, perhaps "amplifier" or "magnifier." But I think she meant emulsifier. It means a stabilizer, as in processed foods. To be a stabilizer of brands is a great thing, especially for likeability-challenged brands, such JC Penny when it was boycotted for selling a girls' shirt that read, "I'm too pretty to do homework so my brother has to do it for me," or Toyota when it recalled 2.2 million cars to replace faulty floor mats that jammed gas pedals and might have caused deadly accidents. In the aftermath of those controversies, both companies advertised heavily on Boing;), where their brands were stabilized, emulsified.

Maryanne gestured around the table. "It's been an honor to work with this tiger team of ribalds from every part of the company." I'm sure we all assumed she probably meant *rivals.*

In each case, I found Maryanne's nontraditional word choice to be poetic and expansive, breaking the rest of us out of our jargon-riddled and clichéd way of viewing the world. But many Boingers thought Maryanne was a dingdong.

When she finished her speech, her assistant Jefferson presented her with a bakery box. "Happy Birthday, Maryanne!" She opened it to discover a single Boing;) Blue cupcake. "It's strawberry, but I made a special request for the color."

Everyone knew Maryanne loved strawberries. Her office wall was covered with dozens of photographs and paintings of strawberries—in fields, in markets, close-up, dipped in chocolate, and being eaten by teenage Asian schoolboys. The proud look on Jefferson's face said: initiative.

Maryanne smiled her lopsided smile, except it lopped on the opposite side from usual. She spoke quietly to Jefferson, although many of us could hear her. "We should've gotten enough for everyone."

Jefferson immediately realized his mistake. In trying to show initiative to Maryanne, he completely forgot about everyone else. I don't know exactly what he was thinking, but executive assistants have a sort of tribal code of honor, starting with never making your exec look bad. His facial expression and posture practically begged Maryanne to whip him mercilessly.

Maryanne's eyes filled with empathetic wetness. She turned to the room and said loudly, "I can't believe you remembered my birthday, Jefferson! Delightful!" With that, we began singing "Happy Birthday." During the song, Maryanne spoke into Jefferson's ear. She seemed to be giving him some of the punishment he believed he deserved, because his expression transformed to one of appreciation. He counted the people in the room and began cutting the cupcake into 13 blue slivers and putting them onto small paper plates. It took a while, so we sang "Happy Birthday" a second time and then a third. In the middle of the third round, someone from Legal entered the room and told us we had to stop because the copyright owners of the "Happy Birthday" song were suing Boing;) for using it in online advertisements, and singing it at work could complicate the case.

As I received my sliver of cupcake, Maryanne came up to me. "How's my likeability, Glenn?"

I replied, "In the top quintile, Maryanne."

NODES

Jocelyn assembled the Web of Signals Tiger Team mostly with other junior-level people. The only one I knew previously was Wanda from B2B Marketing, who was a longtime Boinger and a notorious tiger team joiner; she claimed to have served on more than one hundred tiger teams. Jocelyn kept me informed of the team's progress—so far they'd met a few times for happy hour at a bar near campus.

In a technical sense, a network is a system of places connected to each other by pathways. The places are called nodes. A node is a location where something of value or importance resides. In the case of Jocelyn's tiger team, each team member was a node based in a different part of the company—she recruited team members from Marketing, Product Management, Engineering, Sales, PR, Business Intelligence, and Advanced Science.

On a network, pathways connect one node to another in such a way that each node can be accessed through other nodes. The saying, "All roads lead to Rome" sums up the essence of a network. Pick any city on the Eurasian continent. There's a road leading from that city to another city, and a road leading from the second city to a third. By following roads (pathways) through cities (nodes), you can eventually travel along a road that terminates at Rome. The pathways that Jocelyn's tiger team followed as they conducted their business included the electronic network Boingers used to communicate via email and Boingmessage and the real-life pathways Boingers followed when walking to conference rooms and driving to off-campus bars.

That old saying about roads leading to Rome could just as accurately have been, “All roads lead to Chang Mai,” or “All roads lead to every city on the Eurasian continent.” But when the saying was developed, Rome was branding itself as the most important city in the world, like how Las Vegas branded itself as the most licentious city in the world with “What happens in Vegas stays in Vegas.” Jocelyn’s tiger team took a similar approach in adopting a slogan that summarized the team’s mission and leveraged a classic internet meme—“WOS: All your nodes are belong to us.” They made T-shirts, and Jocelyn generously gave one to me. Whenever another Boinger recognized the reference, they joined a network of people who got the in- joke.

Interstitials are places and things and ideas that exist outside of a network. They’re like nodes with no pathways to other nodes, cities with no roads leading to or from them. Many things in the offline world exist interstitially. These include the dust that settles on my kitchen countertop and my thoughts and activities I don’t share with others on Facebook or Twitter. Thanks to those social networks, many things that used to exist interstitially, such as what one friend ate for lunch, or photographic documentation of another friend’s sunburned legs at a tropical beach resort, now exist in the online world, digitized, reachable from every other node on the network and ready for analysis and optimization. An interstitial that I didn’t place on the digital network was my strong suspicion that the Web of Signals would crash and burn. Nevertheless, I watched Jocelyn continue to do her primary work at a High Delivers level while throwing herself into the WOS Tiger Team with such drive and passion that she just might deserve an Exceeds at the next quarterly review.

INFLECTION

When I first joined Boing;), I received a packet of materials from HR describing the company's workplace regulations, health benefits, and vacation policy. Within this packet was a piece of literature all Boingers were pleased to discover and read. For me, it affirmed I chose the right employer, and Boing;) chose the right employee. It was referred to informally as the B&B brochure, aka the B&BB.

The B&BB said, "Welcome to Boing;)! You are among the Best & Brightest." It offered impressive statistics about the more than one hundred thousand people who'd ever worked for Boing;)—an elite group of current employees and alumni called "Boingers." Once a Boinger, always a Boinger.

- 41 percent of Boingers hold degrees in technical fields.
- 23 percent of Boingers hold MBA degrees.
- Boingers have higher average SAT scores and college GPAs than employees of Microsoft, eBay, Amazon, and Wal-Mart.
- 2,341 Boingers hold U.S. patents.
- 61 Boingers have been inducted into the Internet Hall of Fame.

- 41 Boingers have appeared on Jeopardy, more than the number from Google, Facebook, Yahoo!, and Apple, combined.
- 19 Boingers have received Webby Awards.
- 2 Boingers have received the Beyond War Award.
- 1 Boinger has received the Nobel Prize in Economics.

The B&BB went on to describe the company's many impressive accomplishments, including fastest company, at the time, to reach the Fortune 500, and first company in the Valley to become carbon-neutral. It ended with photographs of inspirational offline accomplishments by past and present Boingers, such as founding nonprofits that provide colorful T-shirts to children of color.

However, the B&BB didn't answer a couple of troubling questions that it generated among Boingers. Best and brightest of what, exactly? And perhaps more importantly: Which is better—being the worst and dimmest of the best and brightest at Boing;), or being the best and brightest of the competent and sufficient somewhere else?

Being B&B was different from Getting It. We were all B&B because Boing;) hired only the B&B, by definition. Sadly, there were many Boingers who were B&B and yet didn't Get It. Of course, the B&B overindex among those who Get It, but I've met people who Get It who aren't B&B—outside of Boing;), obviously. When I first read the B&BB, I felt a combination of inspiration and intimidation—*intimspiration.*

And that's how I felt, intimspirated, when I received an email with the enigmatic subject line, *TTTT*. It was from Darryl. I hadn't sent him my follow-up email; it was still in my draft folder, not ready to send yet. And it made no sense that he'd follow up with me. Following-up is supposed to happen from the bottom up, unless the higher-ranking person explicitly says, "I will follow up with you." And then that's usually not a good thing. Darryl hadn't done that, so this email was either very good or very bad.

My finger paused over my mouse button. I reflected on how this could be an inflection point, a specific moment that would change my trajectory, a moment that divided my life into preclick or postclick eras. I might have liked to choose the life-defining moment, but there it was, maybe. I ran my hands through my hair, straightened my collar, sat tall in my desk chair, and loosened the muscles that had tensed up in my face. I felt like Best Glenn—well-tended and blissful. It seemed a shame nobody was seeing this version of me, so I took a selfie. (Spoiler alert: I later made that selfie my profile photo on Dogfood.) Then I reflected briefly on how this email might not be a personal message of great importance; maybe it was a mass email sent to all Boingers. Then I damned my objectivity. And I clicked.

The email said that I'd been tapped to join an elite tiger team, the *Tiger Team Tiger Team* (TTTT). The one tiger team to rule them all. I hadn't known such a tiger team existed. Obviously I hadn't had a Need to Know. It explained that the Tiger Team Tiger Team decided what all the other tiger teams should be doing, and it aggregated insights across all tiger teams in order to identify opportunities and deliver results. And Darryl was inviting me to join it.

I suspected the email wasn't actually written by Darryl because it said, "Darryl would like you to join the Tiger Team Tiger Team." Also, it contained no Darryl-isms. Nevertheless, even if the actual email was written by one of his assistants, obviously Darryl himself was selecting me for this important assignment. If I had any doubt where I ranked among the B&B, it was now clear: I was among the B&B of the B&B.

The email was followed by an invitation for a recurring meeting of the TTTT, every other Thursday from two o'clock to four o'clock, in the Foresight conference room, down the hall from Darryl's office. The other attendees were high-ranking executives, including Darryl and Maryanne. I realized, *This is a stretch assignment! Darryl thinks me worthy of a stretch assignment! I am by far the lowest ranking member of the TTTT, but if Darryl thinks me worthy of being in this group, then he must think I can add value to it.*

I accepted the invitation and included a short note.

> I'm looking forward to this!
> Best,
> Glenn

In my mind, that Best in my email signature blended basic human well-wishing with everything intimspirating about working at Boing;) for B&B leaders who Get It—like Darryl.

> Best *wishes,*
> Best *regards,*
> *It's a privilege to be one of the* Best *& Brightest*
> *at the* Best *Damn Digital Company on the Planet,*
> Glenn

The meeting invite included a note, in ALL CAPS, advising me not to discuss the existence, purpose, or work product of the TTTT with other Boingers.

The meeting time conflicted with my weekly 1:1s with Wilson, so I walked over to Integrity. I rapped lightly on the frame of the open door, and Wilson looked up from his laptop. "Hey Wilson, can we change our 1:1s to a different day of the week?" I was prepared to tell a white lie, that I wanted to keep Thursday afternoons open for taking a great aunt who broke her hip to physical therapy; it was true that I had a great aunt who broke her hip, but she lived on the other side of the country.

He didn't even ask for a reason. "Not a problem, Glenn. Let's change it to Tuesday afternoons." He motioned regally with his hand, a gesture that someone else might've seen as dismissive but that I recognized as a request to close the door.

I felt very subjective preparing myself to lie to Wilson. It was a necessary part of being on the TTTT. Being named to this pinnacle of tiger teams was a trophy I couldn't display in my cube. But I cleared a space next to my Rockstar Award and "placed" an invisible TTTT trophy there in the empty space. If an eternal person spent eternity with his or her palm open in that space, it might have held at particular instances in time: bits of spinning matter coalescing into a planet, lava, seawater, a puddle of microorganisms, the trunk of a tree, a falcon's nest. But for a fraction of eternity, in that eternal person's palm would have rested the emptiness that represented one of my greatest achievements.

TACKLING

Because Darryl and I were now exchanging emails, I took the opportunity to send my follow-up to our coffee. I made it as brief as I could. I reiterated my idea for a streaming music service, suggesting we first conduct market research in order to assess the opportunity. I attached a one-pager using comScore data to illustrate how younger users overindex in consuming music online. I went ahead and volunteered to contribute to M&A-related analysis. I clicked send and thought, *I've crossed the Rubicon. The die is cast.*

Most of us probably assume the die Julius Caesar referred to was an ivory cube with a different number on each face, and that casting the die meant rolling the dice, aka letting Fate decide the next move. But as I thought about it, it occurred to me the die might be the type used to press coins, and casting the die might mean a permanent imprint had been made. A definitive decision. Which is pretty much the opposite of letting Fate decide your course. And by sending that email, I wasn't rolling the dice—I was taking a deliberate action. Would it alter the course of my life? I glanced behind me at Integrity and really hoped so.

People say, "Ideation without execution is hallucination." When you've got a great idea, it doesn't mean anything unless you can execute it, make it happen. I like this phrase. Of course, there's another meaning of execute that rarely applies in the business world.

In order to execute in business, you need to succeed with work that's foundational, boring, and unsexy—the "blocking & tackling." I've seen hundreds of PowerPoint slides of American football players in a goal-line scrum used to illustrate the importance of accomplishing the day-to-day activities required to reach a lofty goal.

I myself have used such blocking & tackling images to my own shame, because it's an ineffective and misleading metaphor. There are many other elementary skills a football team needs to master and execute in order to win, such as passing, catching, running, and kicking. Merely blocking & tackling are insufficient. Your team could be the best ever at blocking & tackling, but if it's incompetent at passing, catching, running, and kicking, it won't win. On the other hand, if you're the best in the league at the other skills but incompetent at blocking & tackling, you still could win, say, if your quarterback is the best scrambler in the league and doesn't need competent linemen blocking for him. There are many examples of tech companies that scrambled their way to success—e.g. Broadcast.com getting acquired by Yahoo! for $6 billion.

A much better blocking & tackling metaphor comes from the shipping industry. A block-and-tackle is a network of blocks (of wood) and tackle (rope) interconnected in such a way that it delivers a mechanical advantage. Before powered machinery was developed, a block-and-tackle allowed one man to do the work of an army of stevedores while loading and unloading ships. In order to achieve the goal of loading a ship before the tide went out, it was necessary that a dock worker master and execute blocking & tackling. I vowed from then on to only use images of shipyards and coin presses in PowerPoint slides about executing goals. Conventional wisdom, be damned!

I was musing on this topic while walking the hallway, when I bumped into Wanda from B2B Marketing, causing her to spill several drops from her can of red Kool-Aid.

"Whoa, Glenn!" She looked up me and smiled. "What devilish thoughts have you been thinking? You look like you just slaughtered a wild boar!"

I mumbled and apologized.

"I know what's on your mind. Thank God for Pete Protezy!"

"Um, sure. I've been checking Boingfinance regularly today."

"We all have!"

Boing;)'s stock price had risen 9 percent that day because Tsarevich reported quarterly earnings that included a huge profit on its investment in Russian energy companies. That made Tsarevich's stock price jump up dramatically. Because Boing;) owned 40 percent of Tsarevich, Boing;)'s stock price increased, too, despite the fact that Boing;) had recently reported dismal quarterly earnings for the core company.

Wanda took a swig of Kool-Aid. "Take that, News Corp! Choke on that, Marian Sallowaskky! *Amirite?*"

She was right. During the previous few years, Boing;) had been in the news many times, for reasons that didn't always reflect well on the company, including the following events that I tracked in a PowerPoint slide. I had to update the numbers regularly.

NEGATIVE NEWS ABOUT BOING;)
Since 2008 – Latest Update: 2012-02-29

- Takeover bid by News Corporation (unsolicited, unsuccessful)
- Fight for control of BOD by activist shareholder J. Reynaldo Boodle
- Boodle placed three new directors on board
- Boing;)'s search engine outsourced to Google
- Engineering and customer support jobs offshored to India
- Resignations (firings?) of 17+ senior executives
- 13 straight quarters of revenue decline
- 13 straight quarters of ad revenue shifting from Boing;) to FB & GOOG
- Tsarevich attempt to buy out Boing;)'s 40% ownership
- "What is Boing;)?" soap opera (ongoing)

Boing;)

In each of these cases, the leadership team told us Boingers very little. Perhaps there were important legal reasons for that. And yet we knew much about those issues because some Boinger continually leaked information to Marian Sallowaskky, who published it gleefully, along with her own negative spin involving *cleaning out deadwood* and *rearranging deck chairs*. Some Boingers thought the mole should be found and tarred and feathered in Bytes. Some joked that Marian Sallowaskky should receive a Rockstar Award for corporate communications.

I nodded at Wanda's Kool-Aid. "What does it taste like?"

"Fruity." She took a sip and swirled it in her mouth, making the blond fuzz above her lip shimmer in the fluorescent lighting. "With a slight bite, as if it has some Dr. Pepper in it." She extended the can toward me. "Try it."

I accepted the can and sniffed it deeply, as a sommelier inhales fragrances from a glass of fine wine. I confirmed part of Wanda's assessment. "It smells sweet, and fruity."

"You're not going to drink it, are you." It was a statement, not a question. I handed the can back to her with a shrug. "Fine. Don't drink the Kool-Aid, Mister Objective."

"I just don't—it's a little too—"

"Jeez, Glenn. I'm joking. Actually, this stuff tastes like a four-year-old's birthday party. And it needs caffeine." She patted me on the shoulder, and then we bid each other a good day and a good weekend. I passed her three more times in the hallway that afternoon, and each time we nodded crisply to each other.

BRANDING

Jocelyn knocked on the corner of my cube. Knocked perhaps isn't the right word for her giddy action. Tattooed a danceable rhythm is more like what she did. I turned from my many spreadsheets to see her smiling down at me. "I followed your lead. I created my own motto!"

I invited her to sit on the stool in the corner of my cube. She popped a chocolate-covered macadamia nut into her mouth while offering me one too. "I put it where everyone can see it."

If you haven't had a protégé follow your lead, you might not realize it's possible to feel parental pride toward a co-worker. The suspense wasn't killing me. That would be silly. But it was burning through me like a wave of fever. I accepted her nut and asked, "Where is it?"

"On Dogfood."

I pulled up Jocelyn's profile page on Dogfood. Each employee's page typically showed their mug shot photo taken on the first day of employment, the same photo on the key cards we used to gain access to buildings. This had been the case with Jocelyn's page the last time I'd seen it. She'd replaced her mug shot with a photo of a radiant woman I hardly recognized. She clearly was Jocelyn, but not the Jocelyn I was used to seeing in real life, more like the full-potential Jocelyn I always knew was there somewhere, the Jocelyn I foresaw when I hired her. Without glasses, smiling, confident, *beautiful.* I looked at the young woman in the photo, then over at the real Jocelyn, then back at the photo. They were the same person.

And that's when I saw the other changes she'd made to her Dogfood page. She'd added a nickname. She was now identified as Crazy Jocelyn.

And she'd changed her title to the new motto she spoke of. What had once read, "Marketing Insights Analyst" was changed to "Data Killer."

"What do you think?"

I struggled to put into words the overwhelming mix of emotions I'd felt in the previous thirty seconds: the pride of inspiring another person, the satisfaction of realizing that the confidence I knew had been hidden inside was beginning to emerge externally, and the extreme disappointment of seeing my employee take initiative and fail so spectacularly. Clearly, this was exactly the kind of risky behavior she might not have indulged in if she hadn't been taking antidepressants.

I cleared my throat. "One of the many charming aspects of Dogfood is that each employee can customize his or her page. This is a legacy from Boing;)'s startup days."

"Mmm hmm."

"Occasionally people have used this freedom to go beyond the boundaries of Boinger culture." Jocelyn shrank on the stool but maintained eye contact. "For example, the SVP of the Behavioral Data division once changed her Dogfood title to Queen of All Data, leading to an epic email battle with the SVP of the Advertising Data division, whose Dogfood title was Emperor of All Data. They both printed out T-shirts for the people in their orgs, leading to several tense lunchtime standoffs in Bytes, with Boingers wearing 'Long Live the Queen' T-shirts heckling Boingers wearing 'All Hail the Emperor' T-shirts as the latter group blockaded the juice bar. It was rumored the CEO of that era had to step in and broker a compromise where both execs received ten-thousand-dollar spot bonuses and replaced the nutty titles with their actual titles."

"You think my title is nutty." She popped another macadamia nut into her mouth.

"Well, I think you should remove the word *crazy* from your name. You're not crazy, and suggesting you are devalues the brand of our team. Our core attribute is *trust.* People need to trust us. They want to trust us. And nobody trusts a crazy person."

"Maybe I should change it to Trustworthy Jocelyn."

I sensed a note of sarcasm in her voice. "I'm not suggesting that."

"I thought it was funny."

"It's clever, even charming." I tried my best to laugh, but it came out as more of a burp.

"I'll change it back."

One problem solved. And then there was the motto. I thought about *data* = bits of information, which can take the form of numbers, objects, or even people. I wanted her to explain her thought process. A great manager would have done that, but I wasn't yet a great manager, despite all the training. "Data Killer is also clever. But we don't really kill data. We animate it. It arrives dry and dusty and in many pieces, and we arrange it and stitch it together and breathe life into it. So we're the opposite of data killers."

She stared (glared?) at me for a moment before disagreeing. "It doesn't feel that way to me. Data is my prey. I follow its tracks. I spy it from a distance. I stalk it, downwind, until it lingers in a place where I can take the high ground for my assault. And I don't take down the weakest stray data. I outsmart the alpha data, cornering it against the herd, and I bring it down with a swift stroke of my SQL query. And as I gut it and smear its metadata across my face and arms and take its head for a trophy, the rest of the data lies down in obedience to me and forevermore does my bidding."

Stifling a shudder, I tried to be objective. I realized Jocelyn was attempting to rebrand herself. We knew how to do that. We did it all the time, just not quite so evocatively. "Okay. Interesting. It seems to me you're not merely killing the data. You've got a purpose. Maybe you can use a word other than killer."

"How about *stalker*?" Before my face had time to form a pained grimace, she said, "No, that's not it. *Hunter*. I'm a data hunter. Wait, no, *Huntress*. I like that better. I hunt data to feed myself and my work." She looked me in the eyes and smiled. "I'm glad we had this chat!"

"Me too."

She returned to her cube, and moments later I refreshed her Dogfood page in my browser and saw the changes. She was no longer crazy; she was now a Data Huntress.

THREADS

I received an email from Joe Rupp, one of those names that's always said in full. Never just Joe. Never just Rupp. Joe Rupp, as if it was one word, Joerupp, which was, in fact, his Boing;) username: joerupp@boing-inc.com.

I looked him up on Dogfood. He was Manager of Entertainment Products Strategic Initiati. While that sounded like he was a member of a shadowy cabal, it probably just meant the job title box in Dogfood accepted a limited number of characters, and it automatically cut off part of his title. I'm reasonably certain it would've said initiatives if there'd been room in the box for three more characters.

According to his profile, Joe Rupp had been working at Boing;) for three years, after stints at Microsoft and a company called Oftly, probably a startup. He received a bachelor's degree in Asian Languages from the University of Washington. He appeared to love the outdoors and dogs—the photo on his page showed a picture of Joe Rupp, among tall trees, hugging a Labrador retriever; he looked young, fit, and full of hope, and so did Joe Rupp.

Whenever I receive an email from a product person, I focus my attention and try not to feel anxious. Product people are the ones who accomplish most of the important work at a company like Boing;). Most product people Get It, but a distressing minority of them don't. When a product person Gets It, wondrous things happen—great new products are created that transform life itself, e.g., the personal computer, the smart phone, the touchscreen tablet, Angry Birds.

However, when a product person doesn't Get It, a lot of time and money can get wasted building and launching and watching the sad demise of something that was a bad idea to begin with. There had been many terrible product initiatives at Boing;), mostly involving attempts to export the fantasy sports concept—so successful for Boingsports—to other categories.

For example, we developed a fantasy movie mogul game on Boingmovies. Users played against each other in building virtual movie empires based on the box office results of real-life movies, analogous to the way fantasy football uses the statistics of real-life football games. The reason this was such a bad idea, and I knew this from market research we conducted that the product manager refused to believe, is that, while there are legions of movie lovers out there, they're not data-obsessed in the way that legions of sports fans are. There probably aren't more than a few hundred people in the entire world who would play a fantasy movie mogul game. Fortunately, this product never got to market, not because people realized it was a bad idea but because an executive shuffle occurred, and this initiative was shut down in favor of...

A fantasy stock market game on Boingfinance. This might seem like it would be popular, because there's a lot of data about stocks, and there are lots of people who obsess over it. The problem was the people who might do this were already doing it, in the real stock market, with real money. This product launched, but all of the people involved, except for us market researchers, were stunned when hardly anyone used it. The postmortem analysis conducted by the product team concluded that it didn't fail because there was no audience for it but because the "real-time" data within the game was a couple hours behind actual stock market data. That's like saying, "We would have gotten more than moms, dads, and grandparents to attend the peewee soccer game if we'd held it in a forty-thousand-seat stadium with full concessions."

Unfortunately, enthusiasm for transporting the fantasy sports concept into other areas refused to die at Boing;), leading to...

A fantasy celebrity stalker game on Boingcelebs. It was as creepy as it sounds, and it generated several expensive lawsuits.

Steve Jobs famously said, "Apple doesn't do market research," which continues to be cited by product people throughout the Valley as justification for going with their gut instincts. Product people tend to view market insights people, like me, as bothersome gnats flitting about their eyes and ears as they endeavor to change the world. I didn't yet know whether Joe Rupp valued market research, but he wrote terse emails like a typical product person.

> To: Glenn Cregg
> From: Joe Rupp
> Subject: FW: Streaming music idea – Follow-up to Rockstar coffee
>
> Hey Glenn. Pls see thread below. Let's meet & greet. Will find time. LMK if sched not U2D.
>
> jr //u&2tr

LMK = let me know. *U2D* = up to date. *u&2tr* = up and to the right, referring to the trendline of a successful product, with usage growing over time; used as an inspirational saying among product people in the Valley; the tech industry equivalent to *Live, Laugh, Love.*

Joe Rupp's message was the latest in a dangerously long email thread with a subject line that looked familiar. I quickly scrolled all the way to the bottom. My worst fear was realized—the thread began with my email to Darryl. The full email! This meant everyone on the thread knew I was recommending we create a new streaming music service and also that I was volunteering myself to participate in M&A-related analysis. I began my breathing exercises and assumed I would experience a sleepless night of anxiety.

It was hard not to think of a famously long email thread that had become part of Boing;) lore. It happened well before my time at the company, but it's still available for reading on Marian Sallowaskky's blog. It's known throughout the tech industry as Teh (sic) Dingleberry Manifesto.

Since the founding of the company, Boingers have been encouraged to submit ideas for new products, regardless of the team they work in. Darryl expressed the sentiment this way, "Fly ideas can come from anywhere, yo." Sometimes he followed it with, "And so can bogus ideas, bro." Nevertheless, over the years many Boingers accepted the challenge.

One such idea came from a computer programmer who described it in detail in an email to his manager. The email was long, requiring much scrolling, and it overindexed in ALL CAPS compared to a typical business email.

His idea was to create an online directory that allowed people to stay connected with business colleagues, like a social network for business friends. This was before Facebook and before MySpace. His manager forwarded it to her manager, who looped in a couple of other people. All the people who were initially looped into the thread thought the idea was a good one, and they discussed its merits. However, the ALL CAPS enthusiasm of the programmer's writing style also generated lively discussion within the thread as more and more people got looped in who didn't know he had a reputation for being ALL CAPS in all aspects of his life. For example, he was the impetus for Boing;) needing to develop policies regarding a) guns on campus, and b) working while dressed in costume as a furry animal. The policies stated: a) okay as long as they are in the trunk of a car inside a gun safe, and b) okay as long as the Boinger is not meeting with, or in the sightline of, clients, executives, or founders.

As such threads move through the company, various people get looped in, then looped out, then looped back in. Eventually, Stan got looped in. Apparently, this same programmer had been stalking Stan, trying to convince him to consider the idea. So when Stan got looped in, he wrote, "That guy's a dingleberry." The thread continued, as various people discussed the idea, as well as the dingleberriness of the idea's proposer.

As you might imagine, the entire thread eventually made its way back to the programmer, who was mortified to be called a dingleberry. His response was the final one in the thread posted on Marian Sallowaskky's blog. He wrote

> To: [Long list of Boingers]
> Subject: RE: FW: RE: RE: FW: RE: FW: FW: RE: RE: RE: RE: RE: RE: RE: FW: RE: RE: RE: GROUNDBRAKING IDEA!!!
>
> THANKS FOR CONSIDREING MY IDEA GUYS.
>
> TEH DINGLEBERRY

Soon after, he left Boing;) and helped start LinkedIn. Dozens of Boingers—some who were on that email thread, and even some who called him a dingleberry—subsequently left the company to work for him. Today, his estimated personal worth is in the hundreds of millions of dollars. All that remained of his legacy at Boing;) were the policies, Teh Dingleberry Manifesto, and the phrase, "That guy's a dingleberry," which Boingers used whenever a co-worker got inappropriately enthusiastic about an idea.

Reflecting on Teh Dingleberry's experience—he'd become a multi-millionaire with many of his critics working for him—helped me relax enough to read the entire thread. I realized there wasn't anything in my initial email that a reasonable Boinger would find fault with. It's appropriate to follow up on a Coffee with Darryl. It's appropriate to request a stretch assignment. It's appropriate to propose an idea for a new product, especially if that proposal includes few ALL CAPS. I'd used it just once, while describing how younger users GREATLY overindex in streaming music compared to other categories of content, like news, sports, and lifestyles. It was unlikely anyone who read my email to Darryl would have responded with, "That guy's a dingleberry," and a quick search of the thread found zero instances of the word. Perhaps I would sleep well after all. I carefully read the entire thread to see if it contained any other surprises.

Wilson was looped in, then looped out. That was sure to create a problem for me. It was my duty to inform my manager of most things I was doing. I told myself certain activities didn't cross the threshold for needing to inform Wilson. For example, he didn't need to know I filed a ticket with facilities to replace the flickering fluorescent tube over my cube. But I'd gotten lazy about informing him of important things. Proposing a new product to the CEO was likely to be something he'd want to know about, even though I felt on firm ground for not telling him, considering that Darryl and I had an extra-orgchartial relationship thanks to my Rockstar status.

I made a note to myself to overloop Wilson into my emails to demonstrate I was a team player and not some lone-wolf, loose cannon.

All told, thirty-seven different Boingers were looped in and out of the thread that began with my email to Darryl and continued with Darryl instructing others to investigate the merits of a streaming music service. That's a lot of Boingers, suggesting I hit a nerve. None of the people looped in and out discussed the idea. They merely informed each other Darryl had made my streaming music service idea a priority. In retrospect, this should have been an important signal to me, one that suggested either everybody thought it was a great idea, or nobody thought it was a great idea but each dutifully treated it as yet another mandate from management.

I hit the reply button and crafted a short response to Joe Rupp, looking forward to meeting with him. I removed the entire thread except for Joe Rupp's message to me and the message right before that one, where Joe Rupp's manager looped in Joe Rupp. This is a best practice I learned the hard way. I cc'd Wilson. And I looped in Jocelyn. Her Web of Signals idea was interesting, but vague. I was pretty sure she was going to enjoy this opportunity to witness the execution of a well-thought-out idea.

FRIEND

We met in the Harmony conference room—Joe Rupp, Jocelyn, and me. Joe Rupp wore the standard uniform of a Boing;) product guy who intended to rise into management—blue, button-down, long-sleeved shirt with the sleeves rolled up; khakis; and a belt. Product people at Boing;) who had no such ambitions wore jeans and either T-shirts sporting ironic messages or sports team jerseys.

Jocelyn already knew Joe Rupp. He was a member of her Web of Signals Tiger Team. They'd begun calling it the WOS ("woss"). And Joe Rupp loved the WOS.

"The WOS," he said, with a messianic gleam in his eye, "has the potential to disrupt every existing form of communication, consumption, and transaction." *Disrupt* = provide consumers, via a new technology, with a new way of doing something. Automobiles disrupted horse buggies as a method of travel. Television disrupted radio as a way to be informed and entertained. Text messaging replaced phone calls as a way of communicating; interestingly, the ability of phone companies to extract roughly the same amount of money from each of us every month, year-after-year, regardless of the communication method we use, has not been disrupted.

As we discussed the streaming music service, Joe Rupp kept bringing the conversation back to the WOS and its disruptive potential. "The thing I like best about the WOS is that it gives us an opportunity to ride the mobile platform shift to the cloud while unlocking big data to develop new monetization streams, at scale."

Jocelyn explained, "These are the sorts of exciting things we've been talking about with the WOS."

Joe Rupp agreed, "The winners of Web 2.0 are proving to be whoever delivers the greatest relevance and personalization, but it's largely about moat building. The winners of Web 3.0 will be whoever snarfs the most nodes while decentralizing legacy power structures, thereby dynamiting moats altogether. The WOS solves for that, big time."

I wondered if Joe Rupp was taking antidepressant medication. I tried to bring the conversation back to reality. "When you have an idea in your head, it's difficult not to have it infuse your every thought. Recently someone said to me, 'Can you believe all the digital billboards they've put up in the Valley? So distracting. So annoying!' I hadn't noticed them, but after that, I saw them everywhere, and I found myself obsessing over catching the transition from one image to another. Once someone directs your attention to something, it moves from the background to the foreground, and you overindex in noticing it."

Joe Rupp could see the connection I was making. "The WOS isn't an obsession. It's a framework for synthesizing emerging technologies. Take your streaming music idea—"

"It's an opportunity to re-engage digital natives and connect them with a broad range of our products and services." I felt I had to interrupt because once a product person starts talking, it can be difficult to get a word in.

"I get it. And I don't need to be obsessed about a streaming music service to notice that many Boingers wear headphones at their desk as they listen to music all day. They're listening to Pandora, iHeartRadio—"

"And Soundcloud, Last.fm, and probably half a dozen others. They also all have Facebook open, which might—"

"Which might make us worry about Facebook launching a streaming music service."

"So we should get to market with a streaming music service before they do."

"They're not gonna do that."

"But they might."

"Look, Glenn, we all want to be part of the solution, right?"

The conversation paused for an instant. In my mind, and I'm sure in the minds of both Jocelyn and Joe Rupp, the entire phrase Joe Rupp had just invoked played out in full. In my case it was in the voice of an early career mentor who once worked as a local news anchorman and still had an authoritative, manly voice. "Glenn, you're either part of the problem or part of the solution."

Joe Rupp was the first of us to get back on track, which kind of pissed me off. He stepped to the whiteboard and began drawing interconnecting circles. "Let's visualize the situation."

Who wants to be part of the problem? Nobody! If a sane person wants to be part of the problem, it's only because he believes that's the best approach for achieving a different, better solution. When someone invokes this saying, he really means, "I hate your idea."

That's essentially what Joe Rupp was saying to me with his interconnecting circles. "We can use the WOS to personalize the streaming music service. You want to know what music your friends are listening to, right? And you want that to inform the music that gets recommended to you, right?" Joe Rupp had a way of panting between phrases, Labradorly.

"Totally right," said Jocelyn.

"Actually, a large number of my friends have dramatically different tastes in music, and I don't want my streaming music service to be informed by their love of Rhianna, Bruno Mars, and Yugoslavian jam bands."

Joe Rupp looked at me as if I'd said something both immoral and insane, like "We should test experimental AIDS treatments on children who study Ancient Greek in elite private schools." He explained it to me like I was five, "It absolutely needs to be social, in order to be personalized, which means every person gets the right song at the right time."

"Why?"

Joe Rupp panted a couple of times. "Why does it need to be social?" He erased the circles and drew a new picture, a set of interconnected squares. He wasn't satisfied, so he erased the squares. He drew a pyramid, then he shook his head and erased it. He drew a funnel pointing down and then erased it. He drew a foursquare box and began filling each box with phrases such as *Innovator* and *Fast follower*. Then he mumbled to himself and erased it. He exhaled in a huff. "It just does. In order to drive huge engagement, in order for it to be personalized, in order for us to optimize it toward increasing streams, it needs to be social, at scale. That's just a known fact."

"Actually, many studies, including at least two by our own Boing;) Advanced Science team, show that getting recommendations from people who are similar to me, whom I don't know, is a much more successful way to drive engagement than getting recommendations from my friends. Have you seen those studies?"

"I've seen the studies."

"And?"

"They're very academic. They don't represent the real world."

In my career I've encountered many unreasonable product people, and I've learned a technique for staying calm while talking to them, where I maintain eye contact and also slowly turn my face away and downward, giving me the appearance of being both submissive (with my face pointed away) and dominant (with the eye contact). I used this on Joe Rupp. "From my point of view, assuming you need a social component is just as academic."

Joe Rupp turned to Jocelyn with his mouth agape and his palms up in disbelief.

She opened and began eating from a bag of roasted *pepitas*. "Social is just one component."

"That's right," said Joe Rupp, using what might have been a technique or might have been his natural way of trying to influence others, where he maintained eye contact while raising his chin until he was looking at me down the bridge of his nose. "The algorithm will recommend songs based on social signals from people you know, signals from people like you who you don't know, and also business considerations, like whether the music label buys ads on our network. We're going to lay out the use cases, scope out the project, and draft a roadmap. Is that okay with you, Glenn?" He said that last sentence semi-sarcastically.

"Sure." I refused to match his in-the-gutter tone. "As long as we conduct market research at the beginning in order to understand our target audience and identify opportunities."

Time passed, as much as thirty seconds, while Joe Rupp thought about it. That's an insignificant amount of time in the context of a lifetime. But it felt like a ridiculously long time for responding to such a simple statement. For a fruit fly, thirty seconds is the equivalent of ten days of human lifespan. Ten days!

Eventually he said, "Is it really necessary?" I was beginning to wonder, *Does Joe Rupp Get It?* I wondered further when he said, "We'll get a bunch of smart people together in a room and figure this thing out."

"Why limit yourself to a handful of people in a small room? Market research is like getting all the smart people together in a limitless room. You should always conduct market research before embarking upon an important project such as this one."

That must've sounded condescending, because Joe Rupp grabbed his iPhone and checked his messages, the typical response from a product person who feels offended.

Jocelyn smoothed the situation, using a time-honored technique for wooing a product person—rather than tell him how you'd solve a problem, ask him how he'd solve it; a product person needs to think he came up with the idea for the solution. She offered some *pepitas* to Joe Rupp, who put out his hand to receive them. "The key is identifying opportunities and challenges, and there are many ways to do that, including market research. Sometimes market research shows us that the target audience should be entirely different from the one we assumed it would be. Most of the time it helps us avoid bad decisions and improve on good ones. But it's your call. What approach do you recommend for assessing the opportunity and understanding the target audience?"

Joe Rupp clearly had heard all of this propaganda about the benefits of market research, but not from Jocelyn, with whom he seemed smitten. Her geeky enthusiasm and—for lack of a more professional word—*cuteness* made him willing to put market research into the product roadmap. He leaned toward Jocelyn, looking into her eyes and chewing *pepitas*. "I suppose we should conduct some market research."

Jocelyn had done it. I looked at her to silently congratulate her, but her eyes followed Joe Rupp as he began writing, on the whiteboard, *Next Steps* = action items for each of us to work on. "Jocelyn, you'll scope out market research on the interest in a streaming music service, paying particular attention to the needs and interests of digital natives. Glenn, you'll confirm that budget is available for conducting the research. I'll make a list of use cases and draft a roadmap." He checked his iPhone. "We still have a few minutes. We need a code name."

I suggested, "How about Project Philharmonic? It refers to music, but it also invokes teamwork and common cause in creating beauty."

Joe Rupp cringed, pressing his neck against his shirt collar. He wrote "Project Melody" on the whiteboard. "How about this? I went to middle school with a hippie girl named Melody who wrote ironic phrases on photos way before the existence of Tumblr and Pinterest. This streaming music service reminds me of her. Plus her name is music related."

He seemed to think Jocelyn would be impressed by this display of sentimentality. I thought it was a boneheaded move, because, based on personal experience, talking about one female while trying to impress another almost always leads to a reduction in time spent with the target female. It was unclear how it was affecting her; she nodded nonchalantly. So Project Melody it was.

When I returned to my desk, the first thing I did was email Wilson a brief synopsis of the meeting with Joe Rupp and request permission to dedicate some of our team's budget to conducting the research. I wondered whether I should assign a project name to my new effort to overloop Wilson into things. I decided against it and instead created a recurring meeting with myself in Outlook that reminded me every day at three o'clock to "Loop." Eventually I realized I had, inadvertently, created Project Loop without going so far as to formally name it. If I'd thought it through, I would have assigned an actual project name to this initiative, a name that aspired to reach the heights of interpersonal communication, such as Project Parlance or Project Interlocution—no doubt that would've made it more successful than it turned out to be.

Right after I created the Loop meeting, I received an email notifying me Joe Rupp wanted to friend me on LinkedIn. Technically, you connect with people on LinkedIn, rather than friend them. But thanks to Facebook, the word "friend" has become the generic verb used to indicate the establishment of any persistent connection on a social network. Joe Rupp wanted to be a node on my network. Many Boingers did this—as soon as they met a co-worker, they friended them on LinkedIn. My threshold for connecting with people on LinkedIn is much lower than it is for the other social networks, so I accepted Joe Rupp's invitation.

SPONSOR

I slept poorly the night before my first TTTT meeting. I was, of course, anxious about the meeting and my ability to contribute to it. People commonly compare adult anxiety to the anticipation of a kid waiting for Santa. But as far back as I can remember, I always thought the Santa story had to be a myth—there were too many logical inconsistencies explained away illogically by parents.

A young me asked, "How does Santa get into apartments? Apartments don't have chimneys."

My mom said, "Santa enters apartments through the window."

I responded, "Reindeer can't fly."

My dad explained, "Santa's reindeer are magical."

I countered, "In order to visit a billion households around the world within twenty-four hours, Santa would need to visit at least eleven thousand houses per second—difficult to imagine even for a magical being."

My mom and dad said together, "Eat your soup."

And yet Santa clearly did exist, because presents were delivered with "Santa" written on the "From" line of the gift tag, meaning Santa had to be a scalable solution, evenly distributed throughout the world, at roughly the same distribution as children. All of which meant Santa = parents.

There was no TTTT orientation brochure. There was no How To Prepare For Your First Secretive Corporate Tiger Team Meeting video to watch on YouTube. Nevertheless, there almost always are things a person can do to prepare for a scheduled event.

I memorized the Dogfood information about all of the attendees—name, title, start date, degrees, direct reports—and I looked, anonymously, at all of their LinkedIn profiles. I boinged and googled them and tried to find any crumbs of information about them that would help me understand the arena I was about to enter. I found a lot of professional headshots as well as amateur photos of smiling people standing shoulder-to-shoulder. I found bland statements made at conferences and in press releases. I found short Twitter streams from years ago as they tried and then abandoned what was then the hot new thing.

"My first tweet, here it is!"

"Is this thing on?"

"Eggs for breakfast, again. #boring"

I did not find peace of mind.

I arrived at the Foresight conference room a few minutes early. It was my first time in that hallowed room where Boing;) executives made unsuccessful multi-billion-dollar offers to buy nearly every major startup in the history of the internet. There were other conference rooms as big at Boing;), but only Foresight had a long mahogany table with a supersized projection screen that filled an entire wall. I felt like I was on the bridge of the Starship Enterprise or in the situation room at the White House or in the mead hall of the gods in Asgard.

Darryl's third assistant, Felicious, was there, preparing the room. Watching her was like watching a goddess perform a sacramental rite, until she made that phlegmy noise. It lasted for what seemed like a full minute. I thought maybe all she needed was an over-the-counter allergy medication.

She connected her laptop to the room's projection system via a cable that snaked out of a console in the middle of the table. She plugged it in and watched the projection screen. It remained blank. She tapped keys on her laptop. No response from the projector. "Daaaaamn it!" she shouted, in a shrill, nasally voice.

"What's the matter?" I asked.

"The stupid projector isn't working. It never works! This is supposed to be a technology company!"

"Maybe the cable needs a jiggle."

"You don't think I've tried that?" She jiggled the cable, pointed at the blank screen, then snarled at me.

There are people who run away from an explosion, and there are people who run toward it. When the explosion is a snarl from an excessively attractive woman, I'm typically one of the people who runs away. However, when the explosion is a problem with digital equipment, I run toward it. I stepped up to her laptop, and Felicious took a step back to give me room.

I reconnected. I jiggled. I pressed the various laptop keys that make different projector models jump to attention. Then, after pausing a moment to assess the situation, I identified the problem. I told Felicious, "Watch the screen, please." She turned her attention to the screen as I quickly reached over and pressed the projection system's power button, turning it on. An image of her desktop appeared.

She huffed, "Thanks."

I nodded crisply as the other TTTT members began arriving. I greeted each of them with a hello and a handshake. The group seemed to be a combination of Darryl's direct reports and other influential people from across the company. I wasn't sure yet where I fit in, although one day Darryl would explain it to me, precisely.

The meeting was called to order ineffectively by Hank, Darryl's Chief of Staff. He was a large man who had a small presence, except when he was threatening physical violence, which occurred more often than you might expect. He spoke softly while the others chatted among themselves. I could barely hear him. "This meeting of the Tiger Team Tiger Team will come to order. Please welcome the newest member of the team, Glenn Cregg, who leads the market research analytics team."

Darryl was sitting next to me. He spoke loudly, "Yo, yo. Let's settle down, people." They became quiet. Darryl put his overly warm hand on my shoulder. "Be cool to Glenn, yo. I invited him to join us because I think he'll make some dope contributions to our team."

I waved to the room. "Hi, everyone. I'm happy to be here." The others greeted me with a variety of salutations.

Hank's voice took on the monotonous tone of an airline gate attendant repeating the same instructions about boarding he'd repeated thousands of times before. "You all got the pre-reads. Let me remind you of the ground rules. There are dozens of tiger teams operating across the company. We're here to accelerate the work of the most promising ones, not to advocate for our own tiger teams or those supported by our own team members. This is a strategic advisory team, not a tactical advisory team. Brainstorming rules apply. There are no bad ideas. No personal comments. No whiteboarding. Who wants to start?"

Several people began talking at once. The voice that rose above the din belonged to Sousie, the VP of Corporate Strategy. "*…will have the* *biggest im*pact." The others stopped talking, ceding the floor. "Sorry. Didn't mean to shout. I know we've talked about this before. We have frickin' godzillabytes of data but no data valuation platform." She wiped a spot of spittle from her lower lip and straightened the lapels on her blazer as she turned expectantly to Ted, SVP of Product.

He was a small, charismatic man with an enormous head made doubly enormous by his helmet of wiry black hair. If the series of events making up his life hadn't led him to become the chief product officer of a Fortune 500 digital media and technology company, he could've been a televangelist, a cult leader, or the benevolent dictator of a small, tropical country with enormous oil reserves. He asked her with a smirk, "Are you referring to the Data Integrity Tiger Team?"

She smirked back—I couldn't tell if they were flirting or fighting. "You might've heard me say that if you all hadn't been shouting your asses off. Their mission is off target. I simply don't understand how a data-driven company can get by without a frickin' *world-class* data valuation—"

"Perhaps because we have an *implicit* data valuation platform through our *world-class* display exchange." Bartleby, the SVP of Advanced Science, interrupted. He split his time between a job at Boing;) and a faculty position in the Computer Science department at Stanford. Darryl had nicknamed him Brainiac, though he didn't resemble Superman's DC Comics nemesis Brainiac, who was bald and green and tall and chiseled. Bartleby was pale and rumpled. He was, however, bald.

Sousie sighed. "Guys, we need an *explicit* data valuation platform."

Bartleby explained professorially, "What matters most is that our data valuation platform be world-class, regardless of whether it's implicit or explicit. And it is. World-class."

"I'm with Brainiac," said Jamie, EVP of Sales. Regularly voted Best-Dressed Boinger, his graying, heavily gelled and combed hair always had the same gauge stripes as his pinstripe suits, giving him a sense of having been thoroughly combed from head to foot. "Anyways, building an explicit data valuation platform is a two-hundred-million-dollar solution for a two-dollar problem. We faced this at Proctor & Gamble, and we decided we didn't need better ways to leverage the data; we needed better storytellers."

Hank mumbled quickly, as if his statements were less valuable than the others, "Stories are important. We should double-click—"

Sousie rolled right over Hank. "I'm talking about investing. And P&G's situation was different. All their problems were solved when they badassedly changed their target audience from women to moms."

Jamie said, "That was a smart business tact—"

"No, it was a bold and brilliant strategic pivot for a ginormous multinational. Women have a butt load of needs and aspirations, whims and worries. But moms are all about the kiddos. Moms just want to believe the household products they buy are not only safe and effective but make their children better human beings. Aaaaannnd, I'm the one who made that recommendation to P&G while I was at McKinsey."

Walter, the CFO, chuckled. "You're telling an inspiring story about investing in order to inspire us to invest. Well-played, Sousie."

She half bowed to Walter, who had a reputation at Boing;) for making memorable statements during quarterly earnings calls with stock market analysts that either amused them or terrified them, such as, "I know it's been a while since we've reported revenue growth, but our guidance for next quarter is that we'll see very, very, very slight growth. *Boing;)!*" And "We've had some leaks to tech bloggers about new products, and I assure you we'll find the persons involved and prosecute them to the full extent of the law. I'm glad we do business in Florida, because they still enforce the death penalty."

"Delightful!" Maryanne was there, too.

Sousie smiled with her lips at Maryanne, letting that "Delightful," hang in the air for a moment before continuing. "When I was at McKinsey, and also when I was at BCG, and even during my stint at Bain, we found that implementing a data valuation platform was the first step toward driving mondo pivots for incumbents."

Ted shook his big head. "Incumbents pivot off pre-existing strengths. This isn't one of our current strengths. So it shouldn't be the fulcrum of our pivot." Susie snorted. Ted stood and stepped toward the whiteboard on the wall. He picked up a marker from the tray. Everyone else shifted in their seats, either sitting taller or slumping deeply, as if bracing themselves for something. For the first time, Darryl put down his iPhone and gave his full attention to the meeting.

Hank bellowed in a suddenly confident and forceful tone, "Step away from the whiteboard, Ted!"

"If you'll just permit me to diagram it, I can—"

"Step away from the whiteboard!"

Darryl said, "You know the rules, dawg. No whiteboarding in TTTT."

Ted shook from toe to head, with his big hair shaking a moment longer than the rest of him. He defiantly opened the cap on the marker and moved it toward the whiteboard. Hank rose from his seat, reminding all of us just how large he was.

Hank explained matter-of-factly, "I was a state champion wrestler in high school. In Iowa. And Iowa is the Silicon Valley of high school wrestling. There is a grown man in Des Moines who lacks full function of his right shoulder as the result of one of my half-nelsons."

Ted rubbed his hair with the hand holding the marker. He inflated himself with a deep breath, and he let it all out until he looked like just a weird little man with a huge head. "Criminies, Hank. You don't have to make threats. All I wanted to do is visualize the situation."

Sousie said, "You know the frickin' rules, Ted. We make rules for a frickin' reason."

Ted put the cap on the marker and held it tightly in his fist, returning to his seat. The rest of them exhaled in relief. So did I. I didn't know what crisis had been averted; apparently it was a big one.

As Ted sat down, he spun the marker between his fingers. His defiant posture and tone returned. "All I'm saying is the data valuation platform shouldn't be the fulcrum of our pivot. Have none of you seen my TED Talk?"

This led to a flurry of talk-shouting from all members of the TTTT. As the sounds coming from their vocal cords mixed into one cacophony, I lost track of their sentences and connecting words, like "I agree with you, but—." I could parse only brand names and buzzwords.

"Silver Lake." "Leverage." "Apple." "Installs." "Microsoft." "Poison pill." "Pepsi." "Make-goods." "Google." "Relevance." "Facebook." "Social graph." "Boing;)." "Tech debt." "BHAG." "Resurrection."

It seemed to me they'd invented a new language in order to think big thoughts and develop disruptive strategies—the way Newton had to invent integral calculus in order to work out his laws of motion. It was like the language of Olympus, known only to the gods, and I felt like an errand boy, hiding behind a wall while the gods hurled their bolts and spells at each other.

"Influencers." "Venn diagram." "SWOT analysis." "Golden parachute." "Boomers." "Millennials." "Platform shift." "Home page sets." "Innovator's Dilemma." "Patent portfolio." "At scale." "Zuckerberg." "Gates." "Warren Buffet." "ROI." "God." "Steve Jobs."

Through all of it, Darryl shook his head. His face flushed, and he began tapping the table rhythmically with the middle finger of his right hand. He interrupted this one-upmanship contest by standing and outshouting the rest of them. "Yo, yo, yo, *yo*! Chizzle the frizzle out!"

They quieted, glanced at each other sheepishly, sipped from various cups and mugs, and waited for Darryl to speak. He held out his palms in disbelief, pulsing them several times as he extended his arms outward with each pulse.

"Seriously, people! My ninjas be trippin'."

Ted and Susie exchanged shrugs, as if neither understood what Darryl had just said. Later that day, I looked it up on UrbanDictionary.com—Darryl was trying to say his team wasn't functioning smoothly and effectively.

"Here's how we gonna play it. I neglected to have Glenn tell us a little bit about what he does. Yo, Glenn."

"Me? Now? Okay. Well, I lead the Consumer Marketing Insights team. There are two of us. We analyze user behavioral data and conduct market research in order to evaluate marketing campaigns."

Darryl sat back down. "Glenn's the dude with that fly motto, 'Objectivity breeds effectivity.'"

Ted asked, "You're that guy?"

I answered, "Sort of."

Sousie laughed, "I wrote that on the whiteboard in my office after I heard it from Darryl. 'Objectivity breeds effectivity.' Frickin' fantastic!"

Hank interjected, "I did that, too."

Jamie said, "Priceless!"

"Actually, my motto is 'Being objective makes me effective.'"

In the long pause that followed, Maryanne winked at me supportively. Maryanne always gave great feedback. Finally, Sousie admitted, "That's good, too."

Ted observed, "It rhymes like the other one."

Jamie countered, "It's a little longer, though."

Bartleby declared, "I prefer the first one." The rest of them agreed through nods and utterances—they thought Darryl's version was better. Obviously, I wasn't going to change my motto. But I noted their feedback.

Darryl asked, "Glennster. What's your opinion about the data valuation platform?"

I looked each person in the eyes. "I agree it's an issue that needs to be solved, although I don't feel sufficiently knowledgeable about the facts to have an opinion one way or another."

Maryanne cooed, "That's refreshing, Glenn."

Bartleby grinned. "I suppose none of us is fully informed about all possible facts."

Jamie laughed. "Except for Sousie."

"LOL!" blurted Sousie. "I just act that way sometimes. My bad."

I continued, "When I was a member of the Data Integrity Tiger Team, the topic of a data valuation platform didn't come up. I handed off my membership on the team to my direct report, as a stretch assignment."

Darryl patted me on the shoulder. "Right on, Glenn. Stretch assignments are the shizzle for Boing;) employee development."

The rest of them uttered supportive statements about the shizzality of stretch assignments.

Jamie combed through his hair with both of his hands. "What if we instruct the Data Integrity Tiger Team to model a couple of different scenarios, with revenue implications? Aggressive and conservative, of course."

Ted spun the whiteboard marker in his fingers. "Agreed. But let's also model a change-the-world scenario, just to make sure we're thinking big enough. Sometimes it's not enough to think outside the box. Sometimes we need to build a bigger box that doesn't require people to step outside of it to think."

The rest of them agreed enthusiastically.

Hank mumbled, "We'll bake that in."

There was a moment of silence. I could hear Maryanne tapping away at her iPhone. She looked up at me, just as my iPhone vibrated in my pocket. I took it out to see a BM.

> *Maryanne1776*: this group always argues. you're a good influence, glenn! ;)

I looked up at her and smiled. She winked at me.

Hank cleared his throat and said, in his confident mode, "All righty then. Next topic."

We discussed a few more tiger teams and their work products. Rather, they discussed them while I watched and listened. In each case, Darryl would solicit my opinion, and I'd admit I wasn't extremely knowledgeable about the situation, until Bartleby introduced a new subject. "I just heard about a new tiger team called the WOS. I'm getting the impression people are excited about it."

Sousie asked, "W-A-S?"

"W-O-S. Web of Signals. It's a plan to track and optimize every on-network action. Has anybody heard of it?"

The others shook their heads, no.

I piped up, "I've heard of it. In fact, I encouraged its creation."

Maryanne asked, "You sponsored the WOS Tiger Team?"

"Sponsored?"

"Typically, an executive sponsors a tiger team so its mission emboldens a larger strategy."

"I'm not an executive. I didn't realize there was a process."

Darryl chuckled. "It's cool, bro. I'll sponsor it. If my homie G-Cregg endorsed it, that's good enough for me."

"I'll get you invited to their next meeting, chief," said Hank.

"Sweet!" Darryl turned to me. "Tell us about the WOS Tiger Team, Glennster. Why did you believe in it enough to sponsor it?"

What could I say? That I didn't believe in the WOS and its potential to transform how the world uses digital media and technology? That I went along with it as part of Project Clarion Call? That I was merely trying to give Jocelyn a reason to go on living? That, at heart, maybe what I really was doing was trying to ensure my managerial record, which already included one employee's emergency hospital visit and subsequent personal leave, didn't include an actual death? That it all made me feel like a cynical, terrible person? I took a deep breath and explained.

"My direct report, Jocelyn, was away on personal leave. When she returned, she was newly energized by the idea of the Web of Signals. She's always been a productive, valuable employee, so I encouraged her to develop a tiger team to investigate the idea."

Walter demonstrated his ability to terrify stock market analysts. "And what is the idea? It sounds like it might require doubling our data center footprint. That would destroy our operating margins, crash our stock value, and drop our market cap to the level where we would be easy pickings for private equity vultures." They all looked at me wide-eyed, wondering whether the WOS had such potential to destroy the company.

"I don't think Jocelyn's idea is that dramatic. She says consumers drop a trail of digital crumbs wherever they go on the internet. We should be collecting those crumbs in order to understand their needs and interests, and patting them, along with meaty content and advertising we know will appeal to them, into a 'meatloaf' of relevant, personalized experiences that we can serve them as they visit our network."

Sousie said, "That's essentially what I advised Arthur Andersen to do with their accounting practices when I was at Deloitte. If they'd listened to me, things might have turned out differently for them."

Walter changed his tone, "It still sounds expensive. But this has the potential to unlock the value of our owned-and-operated businesses, which could quadruple our stock price and make everyone in this room helicopters-and-house-staff rich." He looked toward me and squinted. "Except for Glenn."

While the others murmured positively about helicopters and house staff, Bartleby made a proposal. "The Advanced Science team has a couple of tiger teams focused on harvesting and leveraging signals and on delivering personal relevance. It sounds to me like they should be merged into the WOS to form a White Tiger Team."

The others agreed with high fives, table slaps, and fist bumps. "Yes!" "Frickin' A!" "Yep!" "Uh huh!" "Delightful!" "Booyah!" "Sounds good." "Right on, right on, right on."

Their enthusiasm surprised me. "What's a White Tiger Team?"

Ted explained, "It's a rare, special tiger team with direct access to the best company resources. We've created a White Tiger Team only once before, to work out the search alliance with Google. This would be the second White Tiger Team. I think I hear angels singing. Do you all hear angels singing?"

The others nodded. They heard angels singing. I heard the air conditioning system start up and begin blowing air from a nearby vent, making the blinds bump rhythmically against the window. It sounded more like angels being spanked.

Hank summed up the situation. "We'll assign an admin to the team, give it queue-jumping privileges for booking conference rooms, and provide T&E budget for fact finding they might need to do at conferences."

Darryl stood up. "Word. This is exactly what we need to focus on, to make our pivot from being a brokeass portal to being the best damn digital company on the planet. Because I'll tell you—and this stays right here, between these walls—I'm getting wicked pushback whenever I tell advertisers and investors we're the best damn digital company on the planet. Some actually laugh at me. True dat. We're not proving it to them in our products and our user experiences. This WOS White Tiger Team shizzle could be the savior of the company, yo."

Maryanne turned to me with her brow furrowed. "Glenn, are you okay? You should be very proud."

I must have looked ill—eye twitching, mouth-breathing deeply and rapidly. I wondered to myself, *Am I hyperventilating?* I took a long, deep breath through my nose and held it as long as I could, long enough for all of them to furrow their brows like Maryanne had. Then I released my breath slowly through my mouth.

Sousie, then the rest of the TTTT, clapped, applauding me and what they thought was my foresighted conception of the WOS Tiger Team. I couldn't actively control my thoughts or actions. My mind and body returned to center position, as if I were automatically rebooting after a system failure. I nodded to the room and said the only thing I was capable of saying at that moment.

"Being objective makes me effective."

PARTNER

The TTTT meeting was over. I wasn't quite sure what had happened. I hadn't understood much of the material, and yet I seemed to have made a meaningful contribution. Darryl gave me a thumbs-up as he rushed with Felicious to his next meeting. Everyone else thanked me for joining the team, and each of them made a point of telling me they looked forward to continuing to work with me.

I stopped Hank and asked him about the pre-reads. He explained, "Darryl doesn't think you need the pre-reads. It's all very confidential information, above your pay grade. It's okay for you to hear about them during discussions, but you don't need to have that information in your possession."

"I don't have a Need to Know?"

"That's right."

"Okay. Thanks. Let me know if there's ever anything I should be pre-reading." I was disappointed, of course. It seemed to me that the B&B who Get It and were talented enough for stretch assignments such as the TTTT had a Need to Know. But I had more important things to do than indulge in self-pity.

As I was about to return to Building Zed, Maryanne beckoned me to join her in the Mentor conference room, just down the hall. It was small and windowless, and it contained two chairs beside a round table that nearly filled the room. Maryanne remained standing, and I did, too, so we stood closer to each other than normal.

I thought she wanted to discuss the TTTT meeting, but she had another issue on her mind. "I'm speaking at an upcoming panel on marketing to moms. I'd love to wow them with some great insights showing that Boing;) understands moms better than anyone. And of course, when it comes to getting great insights, I thought of partnering with you."

"Thank you. I'd be happy to partner with you on this." My natural impulse was to half-bow, as a way of acknowledging the compliment, but there was no room for it, so I remained stiffly upright.

"Fantastic! Really, Glenn. You do such good work uncovering enriching insights. If I told you, you had a beautiful body of work, would you hold it against me?"

It took me a moment to process her comment. I thought it was a reference to a country song. Maryanne had always been clever, so such a reference wouldn't have been outside her skill set. I also thought it was a joke. And I suspected it was a veiled invitation. Or not so veiled. I made the decision to laugh, probably coming off as forced and nervous, because Maryanne's response was to guffaw like a camel, forcedly and nervously. In doing so, she put her hand on my shoulder and leaned toward me, just close enough to touch.

I thought, *This is really happening. She's holding her body against mine.* It seemed like a hug. People hug. Co-workers hug when they share important news with each other. Hugs are cool. So I put my hand tentatively on her shoulder, resulting in Maryanne leaning into me, warmly, fully. We stood there for a moment before separating.

I should probably mention that Maryanne wasn't unattractive. Rather, she was actually attractive, not just for a woman who was older than me, although not that much older, but for a woman, period. She could regularly be found each morning pedaling briskly on an exercycle in the Boing;) gym in shorts that showcased her freckled knees. And outside of the gym, her choice in clothing was both professional and also showcased her fitness. She had breasts. Definitely breasts you were aware of; she regularly displayed, tastefully, a hint of cleavage, as a little reminder: "Breasts are here." Her eyes were bright. She had an endearingly lopsided smile. I tried not to consciously think about these aspects of female co-workers because such thinking can interfere with conducting business. This is one area where it's inappropriate to objectify. But these attributes were top-of-mind as we embraced.

Maryanne opened the conference room door and followed me out. "Thanks so much, Glenn. I really appreciate this. I'll send you details about the moms panel."

By the time I reached my desk, I'd received a flurry of BMs, a virtual pile of messages on my virtual desktop, from co-workers informing me of the latest Boing;)-themed post by Marian Sallowaskky. It was time stamped four fifteen, just fifteen minutes after the end of the TTTT meeting.

> My sources tell me the geniuses at Boing;) have created a White Tiger Team for just the second time in the company's history. The first was formed to figure out the details (more like the ransom demands!) for outsourcing their search engine to Google. What momentous work could this new White Tiger Team be doing? And what's up with the escalation of tiger team names? As you know from reading my blog religiously, tiger teams are things that fading companies create in order to try to "entrepreneurialize" their bloated, deadwoody workforce. Is this the first step in Boing;)'s miraculous turnaround or one more rearranging of the deck chairs on the RMS Boing;)? Put your thoughts in the Comments section below. And be nice, people!

There were just nine people attending that meeting: Maryanne, Bartleby, Jamie, Walter, Ted, Hank, Sousie, Darryl, and me. And eight of them weren't me. And one of those eight people had to be Marian Sallowaskky's mole. And I was the mole's team member!

PROJECT

My next hour-long 1:1 with Wilson was like nearly all of my 1:1s with Wilson, with one key difference: I was a TTTT member. It was like having a secret identity, like having my latent superpower emerge and manifest, and now I could fight crime anonymously at night and still make it to work on time in the morning. I liked keeping secrets from Wilson; there's probably a word in German for the pleasure derived from keeping a secret from a person you don't respect.

The part of the meeting that was the same was Wilson's. We almost never talked about work during our 1:1s, unless by work, we meant Wilson. I'd been tracking the information he conveyed to me in a PowerPoint slide.

M8B

EDUCATION
- Self-described prodigy
- BA Psych in 3 years; MBA in 1 year
- Graduated *summa cum laude*
  "the highest *cum laude* of them all"

MARRIAGE
- Karyn = Wife
- "Love at 1st, 2nd, and 3rd sight"
- Model, like M8B
  - Graced covers of auto magazines
  - While M8B modeled underwear
- "Glamour, impersonated"

CHILDREN
- Jaryn and Taryn = beautiful, fit kids
- At ages 3 and 6, vocabularies 3x peers
- Headshots make talent scouts weep
- Already being recruited by Ivy League

PET
- Springsteen = beautiful, fit Weimaraner
- "Not a pet, a working member of family"
- "Best in Show" at regional dog shows
- Loves to fall asleep at M8B's feet

Boing;)

On this day, the topic of conversation was Wilson's wife and her latest grand accomplishment. "As you may know from my LinkedIn Profile, Karyn started a catering business, an *artisanal* catering business."

"Catering wedding parties, bar mitzvahs, events like that?"

"Catering *extravaganzas*. Weddings, bar mitzvahs, bat mitzvahs, *quinceañeras*, anniversaries, birthdays, holiday celebrations, product launch celebrations, and more."

That's how it went with Wilson. "So she doesn't cater parties. She caters *extravaganzas*."

"Correct. *Extravaganzas* only. If you need a caterer for your party, try Craigslist. She's only been doing this for two months, and with my extensive network of business contacts, combined with her charm, beauty, and unparalleled work ethic, she's already the go-to caterer to the stars of the Silicon Valley. She catered the wedding of the lead engineer of Google Plus. She catered the bat mitzvah of the daughter of the CCO at Hewlett-Packard. She's catered dozens of *extravaganzas*."

I struggled to find something to say, half out of a need to further the conversation until it happened upon something useful, and half out of a need to further the conversation until the time of our meeting elapsed. "Does she specialize in any type of food?"

"Indo-African fusion, by way of Texas, via Barcelona. Her motto is: *Small plates, big smiles*."

"I approve of mottos."

"I know you do." He paused as he looked at me. If he'd been smoking a cigarette, he would've slowly exhaled a stream of puffy-cloud smoke, before saying, "Karyn had her motto before you had yours."

Needless to say, I was stunned. Selecting and launching a personal motto is not a competition! It's a self-improvement project that also benefits society. This was already a few months after I'd launched my motto. And he just said she'd been catering for just two months. Wilson seemed to sense I was thinking in this direction.

"She already had her motto when we met in graduate school."

We'd previously discussed Karyn's graduate work in theater. "Don't theater students expect to do anything but catering when they graduate?"

"She didn't know what it referred to when she came up with it. She just liked the sound of it. *Small plates, big smiles.* Her first thought was that it referred to pottery. So when we got married and bought our first home, we installed a potter's wheel and kiln in the backyard shed. Her pottery is exquisite, but that wasn't her true calling—there's less demand for handmade pottery than you'd think. Then she thought it might refer to plate tectonics, so she studied geology for a semester at San Jose State before learning that all tectonic plates are large, by definition. Then she thought it might refer to dental plates, which naturally create 'big smiles;' 'small plates' is a technical term for children's dentures. So she investigated joining Dentists Without Borders to help them fix cleft palates and other dental problems in third-world children. But she quickly realized, from the brochures, that she doesn't like looking into other people's mouths. The meaning became clear eventually, after she spent years wowing her husband, her children, and her many dinner guests with her cooking and food-presentation skills. *Small plates, big smiles.*"

"You must be very proud."

"There ought to be another word, because 'pride' doesn't do justice to what I feel." He sniffled, nearly tearful. "She's being considered for the pilot episode of a cable reality show, *The Caterers of Silicon Valley.*"

I found myself wondering whether I should be making more of an effort with Wilson. It's probably clear I didn't respect him or feel him worthy of being my manager. Or anybody's manager. This wasn't about me. It was about Wilson.

There's a fascinating phenomenon in business, where the skills a person needs to succeed at one level are not necessarily the skills he needs to succeed at the next level. Rumor had it Wilson was a very good market researcher. Sheila at Consumerology, a boutique market research and consulting company based in San Francisco, for whom Wilson had previously worked, once told me Wilson was a fountain of market research lore and wisdom whenever they traveled the country conducting focus groups with consumers. She also said, "He's funniest person I've ever met."

I had to ask, "Are we talking about the same Wilson?"

In video games, when you've completed a set of tasks, your character levels up to a new set of powers and skills. For example, when you go from Level 41 to Level 42, you might gain the ability to vanquish foes with the haunting beauty of your avatar's voice rather than with swords and daggers. Sadly, in the corporate world, leveling up doesn't automatically come with a new set of powers and skills. Wilson's ability to conduct focus groups and amuse co-workers hadn't made him an effective manager.

As he droned on, "Every day I reflect on how blessed I am to be married to a woman who is so talented and intelligent and resourceful and attractive—to all genders—," I realized I needed to master a new skill—managing upward. It pained me that Wilson was upward, but that didn't alleviate me from the necessity of managing toward him. That required more than looping him into email threads. It required caring, truly caring, about things that mattered to him, such as his wife's impromptu problem solving at a catering event. "—and the family's dog jumped on the steam table and began nibbling the sirloin medallions."

"Oh, my! What did Karyn do?"

"Well, she shooed the dog away. And then she garnished the medallions with sprigs of parsley."

"That's resourceful."

"Very. Karyn said the people who ate the nibbled medallions raved most about how delicious they were. She's thinking of having that dog nibble on all of her medallions!"

I smiled a real smile; I didn't have to force it. Only a misanthrope wouldn't smile at the thought of nibbled medallions. "Speaking of catering, we could cater to the needs and interests of our users by conducting some market research on an idea that's been gathering momentum, a streaming music service."

"Fine," was all he had to say about the issue. He continued his tale about Karyn as if I hadn't interrupted him and as if he hadn't just committed hundreds of thousands of Boing;)'s dollars to a research project. But that was how decisions got made.

Eventually we got to the part of the meeting where Wilson asked me about me. It was a regular feature of our 1:1s, and it meant our time was nearly up. "How're you doing, Glenn?"

I gave my typical response: "No complaints." This was usually when Wilson rose from his seat to signal the meeting was over. But he remained seated. "How's Jocelyn adjusting since she returned to work?"

He'd never once asked about Jocelyn since the period three years earlier when we were interviewing for her position and chose her out of many applicants. He didn't inquire about her while she was in the hospital or while she was on personal leave. I wondered if he truly cared about her well-being, or whether he was asking for the same reason I'd been wary of discussing Jocelyn with the TTTT—her physical and mental well-being had become a part of my career well-being.

"She seems better. She's been enthusiastic and engaged and is—"

"Got it. Fantastic!" That told me he didn't truly care about Jocelyn. But it also made me realize that, while I was looking out for myself somewhat with Project Clarion Call, I also truly cared about Jocelyn. I cared about her objectively; Wilson cared about her subjectively.

When I got back to my desk, I looped Wilson into a dozen different email threads about the streaming music service and the WOS, and I sent him a team update, copying Jocelyn, thanking Wilson for his leadership and support.

COOKIES

Project Clarion Call had a clear goal: Increase the likelihood of Jocelyn remaining alive. While I neglected to create a formal roadmap with milestones for the project, I did follow a process.

Each time Jocelyn and I met for our weekly 1:1 (Bytes, wobbly table), I presented her with a "cookie," or reward. It varied each time. Sometimes it was tangible; sometimes it was intangible. These cookies are different from the small digital files, known as cookies, that websites place on your computer to track your actions as you surf the internet. Such cookies are the private investigators that tell website publishers and advertisers how they might best anticipate your needs and get your attention. This can be compelling, providing relevant content that's likely to appeal to you, such as targeting you with ads for a medication that can heal a physical ailment you're suffering from. Or it can be creepy, delivering the same "Visit Orlando" ad to you wherever you go on the internet, merely because you clicked on a story about Justin Bieber getting ticketed by an Orlando police officer for driving 130 miles per hour.

The type of cookie I was giving Jocelyn wasn't creepy. I gave her the first one a couple weeks after she returned from personal leave. "You know that one-pager you submitted yesterday?"

Jocelyn frowned and said, "I'm sorry. I tried boiling it down—"

"You'll be receiving a five-hundred-dollar spot bonus for this latest contribution to our body of knowledge about Boingnews."

"What? Wow! But I didn't do anything special. It was just a one-pager. And I didn't even keep it to one page."

"You turned in a three-pager for a one-pager assignment. That's a 300 percent delivery!"

"The point of a one-pager is to keep things brief and simple. I expected to get a reprimand. I deserve a reprimand."

I made a mock-stern face and said, in a mock-gruff voice, "Don't do it again!"

She nodded and shrugged. "Okay. Thanks."

Another time, I'd received a Starbucks gift card for attending an on-campus talk about leadership by the CEO of Starbucks. I regifted it to Jocelyn, without even giving her a reason, saying, "You can probably make use of this."

She replied, "Sure. Thanks."

One afternoon, Wanda from B2B Marketing, whom Jocelyn had recruited for the WOS Tiger Team, stopped me in the hallway and called Jocelyn a dynamo. When I passed that feedback on to Jocelyn, she smiled and blushed. "Nice. Thanks."

I'd begun thinking of Jocelyn as having two personalities, happy and sad. Sad Jocelyn was different from depressed Jocelyn, whom I'd seen before her hospitalization but not since. My theory was that the antidepressant medication transmogrified depressed Jocelyn into sad Jocelyn. A life-preserving improvement, for sure. Nevertheless, this categorization of Jocelyns turned out to be a useful way for me to determine what kind of cookie to give her. Happy Jocelyn received intangible cookies, aka *attagirls*. Sad Jocelyn received tangible cookies—real stuff—although ironically, never an actual cookie.

At our 1:1 after my first TTTT meeting, happy Jocelyn was eager to share exciting news. "My WOS Tiger Team is being merged with a couple of Advanced Science tiger teams into something called a White Tiger Team, with Darryl as the sponsor."

I couldn't let on I knew about this; doing so would reveal the existence of the TTTT and my place on it. "*The* Darryl? CEO Darryl?"

"Yes!" Her enthusiasm energized me and made my charade easier.

"Wow! Awesome! Wonderful news!"

"He's going to attend our next meeting, tomorrow. You know, this makes me feel like my #lifegoal is on the right track."

"Do you have any work to show yet? Roadmap? Launch deck?"

"We don't have a roadmap, since it's not a formal product yet. But we have a project-scoping deck of about a dozen slides, describing the Web of Signals and how we could be leveraging it. It gets pretty out-there. Like, we think patents could result from this."

Jocelyn shifted her gaze toward the windows, with a near-far look in her eyes, as if simultaneously examining an object up close and also staring at the horizon. She grabbed my arm and asked, "Am I missing something? What am I missing? Does any of this matter? Please say it matters!"

I inadvertently pulled my arm away, then immediately regretted it. I tried to push my arm back toward her, but she clasped her hands together. "Of course it matters. All of it matters. I'd be happy to look at your deck, to see if it's Darryl-worthy."

"Darryl-worthy?" Jocelyn stuttered and moaned her way through the words, as if saying them caused her great intestinal pain. More like, "*D-dd-d-aaaarrrr-yyyllll w-w-worrrrrthyyy*?" It was sad Jocelyn who continued, "I don't know if it's Darryl-worthy. Of course, I want it to be Darryl-worthy. I've never had to make anything Darryl-worthy. What does Darryl-worthy even mean?"

I tried talking her down. "You've already done a lot of Darryl-worthy work. Your analysis of the new Boingmail was Darryl-worthy."

"That wasn't even Wilson-worthy. It's why I ended up unconscious on the floor of my cube. I could have died!"

This was the first time Jocelyn's incident had been mentioned directly by either of us. I went from feeling like the captain of a sturdy sailing ship, steering it confidently in perfect weather, to feeling like a child who's never taken swimming lessons, wrestling with a bloodthirsty barracuda thirty feet below the surface of the ocean. I did what I usually do in such situations: I paused, awaiting further information.

Jocelyn sniffled, and tears began flowing from the inside corners of her eyes, down along her nose, and off the edge of her upper lip, splashing soundlessly on the wobbly table, as if her face was designed for efficient runoff. She used a brown paper napkin to catch most of it. I handed her more napkins from the dispenser on the table.

She said, "I'm sorry."

"Don't be."

"But I am."

"Then be sorry. Very, very sorry." Tears began forming in my eyes, too.

She giggled. So did I. At that moment I could tell she, like me, spent more time than most calculating what to say before saying it. And here we were giggling uncontrollably. Rolling giggles built into guffaws and then fell back down to giggles before building again. We giggled and cried. Other Boingers noticed us, but they kept their distance. As a result, what we were doing felt private, even in such a public setting.

I went for more napkins. When I returned, Jocelyn had controlled her giggling and crying. So had I. We dried our faces. And we returned to work-related topics.

"I would love for you to review our deck, to see if it's Darryl-worthy."

"I'm sure it is. And if it isn't, I'm sure it won't take much work to get it there. Remember, I've met personally with Darryl, and I survived."

Jocelyn looked at me skeptically, over the rims of her glasses. It felt like a good sign. Not quite happy. But no longer sad.

"Also remember, Darryl must think the WOS is a good idea, because he volunteered to be the sponsor of your White Tiger Team."

"Did he? How do you know?"

"Darryl is the CEO. He can sponsor any tiger team he likes, right?"

Jocelyn nodded. I felt relieved. I thought I'd inadvertently revealed my secret identity. But Jocelyn wasn't in an inquisitive mood.

We never again acknowledged our giggle/cry-fest. But I color-coded that 1:1 meeting orange in my Outlook calendar, just so I had a reference point I could return to should the need arise, because it felt like a milestone in Project Clarion Call. I could have coded it in two colors, because it also marked an actual roadmap milestone for Project Melody. It was the day Jocelyn said, at the end of our 1:1 meeting, "The research for the streaming music service is *in field*," meaning the market research was actively being conducted with consumers.

I later learned from Jocelyn that Darryl attended their first White Tiger Team meeting, as did several Advanced Science guys who'd been on the tiger teams that got folded in with the WOS Tiger Team. The prelaunch deck she and I reworked to make Darryl-worthy was appreciated by Darryl, who asked smart questions and provided constructive feedback, including calling the WOS "fly dope shizzle." I gave happy Jocelyn an *attagirl.*

I learned from observation that Jocelyn's involvement in the White Tiger Team was allowing her to extend her internal network. In addition to Joe Rupp, three young Advanced Science guys began hanging out at her cube—a tall one with wispy facial hair; a loud and stout one; and a short one who wore stereotypical nerd clothing ironically—lab coat, pocket protector, horn-rimmed glasses. They laughed a bit too hard at her jokes and gesticulated full body in ways that might've looked embarrassing to a typical objective observer but were slightly charming to an objective observer with subjective experience dealing with an emotionally fragile co-worker who appreciated the attention.

SURVEY

I continued to loop Wilson into almost everything. I also sent just him and me follow-up emails where I asked direct questions, such as, "This good with you?" and, "Am I missing anything?"

In every case, Wilson didn't reply. It began to disturb me.

I received emails from him that weren't replies to my emails. A recent one was an email he forwarded to Jocelyn and me, informing us about a new goal for Project Resurrection—reducing time spent by Boingers in meetings by 25 percent, which was achieved when most teams transformed their daily stand-ups and weekly check-ins into breakfast and lunch meetings, because meeting while eating didn't count as a meeting.

I did a quick search of my inbox to confirm that, indeed, none of the Loop emails I'd sent to Wilson resulted in a response from him. I forwarded one to myself, and it entered my inbox within seconds, confirming, at least, that something was working.

In another time and place, I might've walked into Integrity and asked Wilson directly, "Are you receiving my emails?" But this was the Silicon Valley in the early twenty-first century, where there's an unstated rule that you don't talk in the analog, offline, IRL, face-to-face world with a person when you could use a digital intermediary, such as email, IM, text message, or Twitter. Obviously, this wasn't true all the time, but it was true for cases like this that didn't occur during scheduled meetings. This was a Valley cultural practice that might seem strange to outsiders in the same way that non-natives find it strange that Thai people don't ever point the soles of their feet at other people or that Boston drivers regularly run red lights. It wouldn't, however, have been weird for me to BM a co-worker, "Have u been getting my emails?"

I didn't BM that question to Wilson because I didn't want him to know I was paying special attention to whether or not he was receiving my messages. I assumed a key tenet of managing upward was appearing not to be managing upward while doing it. (I later learned it's acceptable, even expected, to notify the upward target that you're managing toward him or her. Sigh.)

I needed to get to the bottom of this. I crafted an email I thought would attract Wilson's attention and get his reply and confirm whether he was receiving my emails.

> To: Wilson
> Subject: Need your help prioritizing request from Maryanne!
> Priority: HIGH
>
> Hi Wilson. Maryanne just pinged me with an urgent request for a re-cut of the brand campaign research results by demo. Working on the Boingmail segmentation you requested. Both seem urgent. Which is higher priority?
>
> Best,
> Glenn
> (Sent from my iPhone, pls excuz tipoz)

The message wasn't sent from my iPhone; I sent it from my laptop at my desk. I added that touch to give it a greater sense of urgency. Truth be told, Maryanne had made this request, but not urgently, and I'd already completed the work, but I hadn't sent it to her yet.

I received a reply from Wilson moments later.

To: Glenn
Subject: Re: Need your help prioritizing request from Maryanne!
Priority: HIGH

Maryanne's request more urgent. Thx.
W.
(Sent from my iPhone)

I had my answer. Wilson had been receiving my emails. I didn't know for sure he'd been reading them, but probably he had. So I had to assume he received, and read, an email from Jocelyn that I'd looped him in on. That email included topline results from the Project Melody survey.

A market research survey is a wondrous, peculiar thing, a combination of art and science. Imagine a Michelangelo statue that's beautiful and breathtaking and also provides feedback about which demographic group spent the most time viewing it, along with the emotions it evoked in viewers (joy, sadness, anger, envy, etc.), and you'll understand the power of a well-crafted market research survey.

Market research can be expensive. The larger the sample size, the more expensive the project. *Sample size* = the number of people who answer every question of a survey. At the same time, the larger the sample size, the more statistically significant the results will be. *Statistically significant* = meaningful and providing an opportunity to drill down and uncover serious implications. So each project sets a sample size that optimizes the project's budget with the amount of knowledge the company seeks to gain.

Let's say there are four people in a home—mother, father, daughter, son—and all are asked, "Do you like cheddar cheese?" The son doesn't like cheddar cheese. The rest do. That's three likes and one dislike. Seventy-five percent of the sample likes cheddar cheese. Can we extrapolate these results to the entire United States? No—a very small sample of four respondents within the same home isn't representative of the entire population; it isn't statistically significant. There are many types of biases that might skew a very small sample's results, either too much—they might eat cheddar cheese as part of a daily religious practice, or too little—they might refuse a particular cheese because their ancestors hailed from Devon, England, where for millennia the local Ticklemore cheese has been overshadowed by cheese from the nearby village of Cheddar.

In order to accurately understand how many Americans like cheddar cheese, we would need a representative sample from across the country, distributed proportionally—we'd survey more people in California, the most populous state, than in Wyoming, the least populous state. We'd need a large enough sample, which turns out in this case to be four hundred, to receive statistically significant results—64 percent of Americans say they like cheddar cheese. For what it's worth, that family of four overindexes in liking cheddar cheese, a differentiating attribute worthy of affixing to a family crest.

DECKS

The sample size for the Project Melody survey was two thousand. As soon as that many people answered the survey, it came out of the field and went into data processing. Within a couple of weeks, we had results.

The vendor for the project was, not surprisingly, Consumerology. Their quantitative division consisted of one person, a guy named Xiang, who received a master's degree in statistics from a university in China. That university might've been China's equivalent to MIT, or it might've been China's equivalent to the College of San Mateo. I'd never heard of it. Either way, Xiang was a very smart young man who deeply understood the data and could take you on a tour of the weeds—where *weeds* = detailed minutiae that are often essential but sometimes irrelevant. He was less skilled at seeing the big picture. My preferred vendor for this project would have been MillerMüller, a boutique market research and consulting company based in Redondo Beach that specialized in quantitative research and the big picture. But one of the compromises I had to make in order to get this research done was to go with Wilson's previous employer, Consumerology.

Xiang sent a PowerPoint deck with topline results to Jocelyn, who forwarded them to me, and I forwarded them to Wilson. Usually we took these decks created by vendors and presented them as-is to key stakeholders within the company. But sometimes we made significant changes in order to bring the research to life and make it more *actionable* = leading to action and tangible benefits. For example, this was an actionable insight from one of our market research projects.

- Females 25–49 with children in the home want fewer stories about Kim Kardashian and more stories about inspiring women who overcome challenges.

When we put that insight into action, we received an 11 percent increase in page views from that demo. Truth be told, the inspiring stories of women overcoming challenges were mainly about Kim Kardashian, who overcame many challenges, such as her controversial home sex video, her struggles with body image issues, her reality-show marriage to NBA player Kris Humphries, and her divorce 72 days later.

Actionable also has a technical meaning within the legal community = grounds for suing someone in a court of law. Therefore, we had to be careful about evangelizing actionable insights to the legal department, because they thought we were talking about suing competitors, i.e., for patent infringement.

Decks from Xiang often required significant reworking in order to illustrate the big picture. As soon as Jocelyn forwarded the results to me, she knocked on my cube and peeked her head in. "I'll rework Xiang's deck. Unless you want to."

"I can do it."

She exhaled in relief. "That would be great. I'm in the weeds with the WOS." Her initial impression was the same as mine. "I expected the results to be better."

I strongly believed the streaming music service was the key to Boing;)'s resurrection and the product that would lead Boing;) into the Great New Days that would be even better than the Good Old Days when celebrities and politicians regularly said "Boing;)" and when all Boingers could afford homes in Palo Alto. Jocelyn, however, strongly believed the WOS held the key to the door leading to those Great New Days. So I wasn't sure I completely trusted her to be objective about the Project Melody results. But that isn't the reason I wanted to rework the deck myself. The reason was—I thought I'd found something that needed to be fixed—a *data anomaly* = an artifact within a data set that skews results inaccurately.

At the risk of sounding subjective, data isn't always accurate or true. A certain level of quality has to be achieved within a data set for it to be useful for analysis, analogous to how water from a muddy mountain stream needs to be filtered before it's drinkable.

Let's say we want to know how many individual people saw one of the most popular photos ever published on Boing;)—of Taylor Swift at the beach wearing a tankini. We know how many views the photo received: 14.9 million. People who don't Get It will say, "14.9 million people saw the photo." Not true. Many people viewed it multiple times. In fact, when we applied proper mathematical principles to the data, we discovered that 9.3 million unique users viewed the photo, with teen males, teen females, and middle-aged males overindexing in viewing the photo multiple times. Once your data is clean, you can be truly objective with it.

Xiang's analysis concluded that the millions of people using or potentially using a streaming music service were already perfectly happy with the options currently available, and there was no room in the market for a new service, even if it was dramatically better than the existing ones. It all came down to one data point showing most people thought YouTube was an excellent streaming music service. If many fewer people had responded that way, we could've concluded a Boing;) streaming music service would have a good chance of success. But I thought I'd found an anomaly in the results for Question 17. Here's that question with the percentage of respondents who chose each answer.

Q17. If YouTube disappeared today, how would it affect your music listening habits?

a. It wouldn't change my music listening habits at all. (22%)
b. It would change my music listening habits somewhat, but I can find all the music I'm interested in somewhere else. (8%)
c. It would make it difficult for me to find and listen to the music I like. (18%)
d. It would be a travesty. Life would hardly be worth living. (52%)

Note the percentages add up to 100. 22 + 8 +18 + 52 = 100 percent. This means all people who answered this question are accounted for.

But we only asked Question 17 of the people who, in a previous question, said they considered YouTube to be a streaming music service, and only one-third of the sample said that. As a result, only one-third of respondents were asked Question 17. So the 52 percent of respondents to Question 17 who thought YouTube was essential ("It would be a travesty... [if YouTube disappeared]"), represented only 17 percent of the total sample. (52 percent of 1/3 = 17 percent). Therefore, Xiang's conclusion that YouTube was an essential streaming music service based on Question 17 was a little bit like asking only the children attending a wedding reception what flavor ice cream should be served with the wedding cake and then declaring that "cotton candy" was the preferred flavor of the entire guest list.

Faced with a conundrum about how much importance to place on a question only asked of one-third of the sample, I asked myself, "What would a Rockstar do?" I was so deeply in the objective zone I'd forgotten I was, myself, a Rockstar! I went far down the thought path of imagining what an imaginary Rockstar would do before I realized I already knew what Rockstar Glenn would do.

First, let's look at the results from that other question, the one that determined who would answer Question 17. This was Question 16.

Q16. Do you consider YouTube to be a streaming music service?

a. Yes, definitely. I use it all the time to play songs on demand. (27% of respondents chose this answer)
b. Sort of. It's more like a video site that also offers music. (6%)
c. Not sure. (40%)
d. Probably not. I don't think of it much when I want to listen to music. (17%)
e. Definitely not. It's for dogs on skateboards and rants from demented teenagers, not a place for music. (10%)

This question was asked of all two thousand people who took the survey. Only those who answered A or B to this question were asked Question 17. I realized what we needed to do was have all two thousand people answer Question 17.

While we couldn't go back and contact everyone again, we could use the available results to, essentially, achieve the same thing, by combining results from Question 16 C, D, and E with results from Question 17. These new results would be called Question 17x. I created a slide to visualize it.

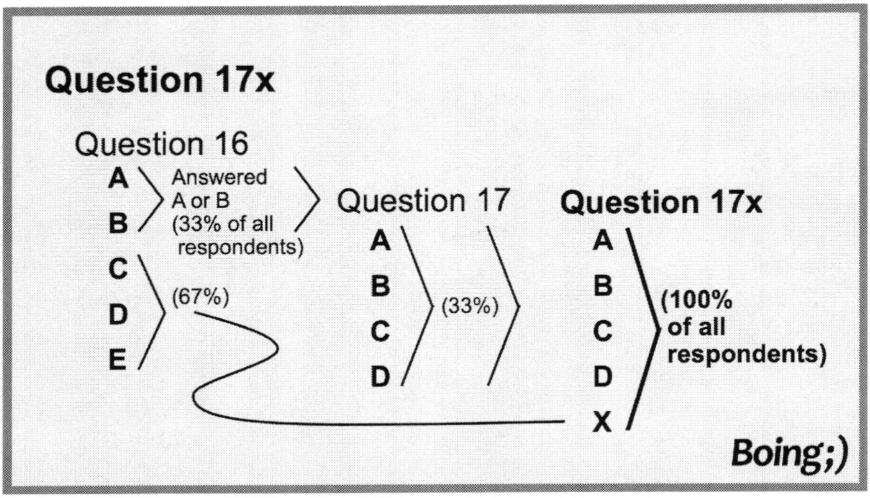

When I combined responses from Questions 16 and 17 in this way, I got these percentages for Question 17x.

Q17x. If YouTube disappeared today, how would it affect your music listening habits?

a. It wouldn't change my music listening habits at all. (7%)

b. It would change my music listening habits somewhat, but I can find all the music I'm interested in somewhere else. (3%)

c. It would make it difficult for me to find and listen to the music I like. (6%)

d. It would be a travesty. Life would hardly be worth living. (17%)

x. I don't consider YouTube to be a streaming music service. (answered C, D, or E to Question 16) (67%)

It all came down to that one question. If a majority of respondents felt the loss of YouTube would be a music listening travesty, then it meant most of them were perfectly happy with the streaming music options already available to them, and it wasn't worth the investment and risk to build our own streaming music service. That's what Xiang's analysis concluded.

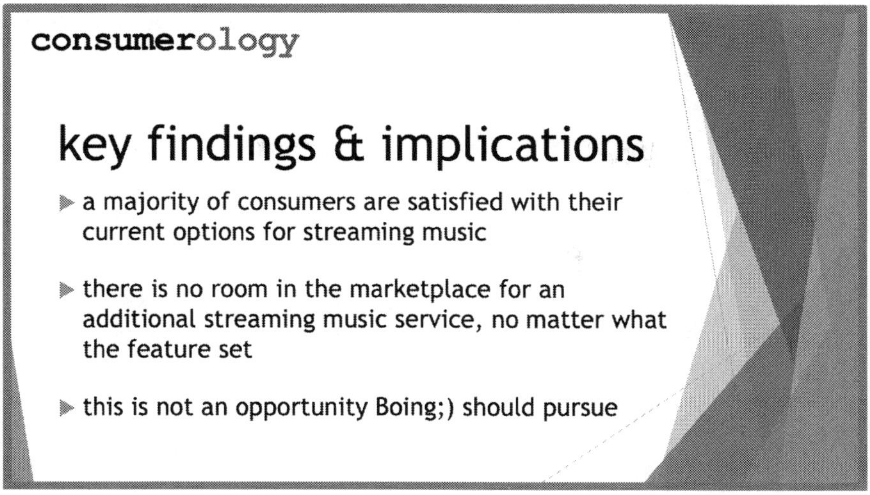

By fixing the data anomaly to form Question 17x, I changed the percentage of respondents who felt this way from a majority (52%) to a small minority (17%), and that suggested we had an opportunity.

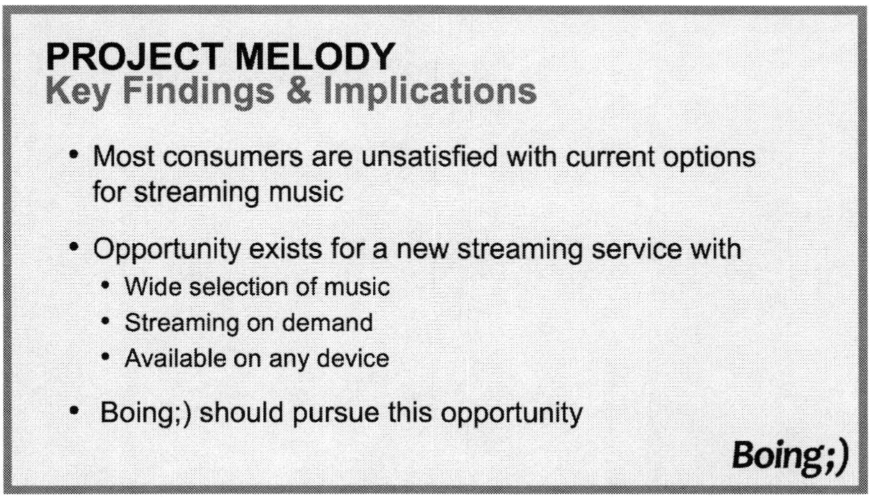

This turned the key findings and implications around completely.

This should not affect your trust in market research. The greatest value of research comes from the interpretation of results. When an analyst such as Xiang doesn't see or understand the big picture, the interpretation can be literally the opposite of what it should be.

There was one additional important thing I needed to do—schedule a meeting to present these results.

Imagine a co-worker saying, "If I just had more money, I could really accomplish my lifegoals." Would you then ask that co-worker to give you money that you'd never repay? Of course not!

Now substitute "money" for "time," and you can understand the basic challenge of scheduling a meeting. Time is the most precious commodity any of us has to share. Asking people for their time, that you won't replenish, is necessary in order to hold a meeting. This is why scheduling a meeting requires confidence and grace. I know of more than one Boinger (thirteen) who cracked under the pressure of scheduling meetings and left the company to do "consulting." But it's easy if you're confident the time you're requesting will be well spent. I saved the reworked deck to my hard drive, my thumb drive, and my digital locker. And I scheduled a meeting to review research results for Project Melody.

DEMO

Before giving an important presentation, I fuss over my slides, working and reworking them so that each flows seamlessly into the next. I choose distinctive and differentiated colors for each chart. I carefully pick each image. I craft each bullet point as if it's poetry, conveying the most meaning with the fewest words. I make sure every footnote is anchored in exactly the same spot. It's important to pay attention to the details.

I was giving the Project Melody research deck the polishing it deserved while sitting in a common area on the first floor of Building Zed, when dozens of people filed past me into a nearby conference room, Generosity. It had windows for walls, so I could see the group sit in rows facing away from me, waiting for someone to lead their meeting. They were all wearing T-shirts, sports jerseys, or hoodies. That meant it was probably a Product team meeting.

They were surprisingly quiet for such a large group. I forgot about them as I flipped through my slides like cards in a deck, searching for anything that might be out of alignment. Eventually, our chief product officer, Ted, arrived, walking briskly, his hair swaying like foliage on a windy day. He saw me out of the corner of his eye and turned to me blankly, without skipping a step. Then he recognized me from the TTTT with raised eyebrows and a slight smile. I nodded as he entered Generosity and took his place at the front of the room.

I was nearly done finalizing my deck—futzing over the RGB values in my charts—so I found myself trying to catch Ted's remarks through the open door. He spoke for a moment and then sat down to yield the floor to a tiny woman in a Boing;) Blue wheelchair and a bearded, bear-sized man. Together they represented the size range of the adult human body. I reoriented my chair and discreetly cupped my hand to my ear so that I could hear them.

The tiny woman said, "A lot of you might've seen our demo. We won Hack Day eighteen months ago, and we've been building and refining ever since. We set a goal of building a lightweight social app that prizes authenticity over perfection."

The huge man raised his iPhone. It was connected to the projection screen behind him so that everyone could see what he was doing. "We're calling it ChatPic, a visual messaging app where you take a picture with your phone and then send it through the app to a friend." He took a selfie and overlaid a word so that it looked like it was coming from his mouth, "Hey!" And then he clicked the send button.

The tiny woman's phone beeped. She smiled with a thumbs-up. She took a selfie and spent a few moments moving her finger across her phone. He received her reply, which appeared on the screen—cartoonish glasses and a smiley face overlaid on her selfie. The crowd applauded, as a little window in the corner counted down from seven. When the counter reached zero, the image disappeared with a silent, animated *poof*. Several people muttered, "Whoa," under their breath—it was clear that *poof* made a big impression.

The giant guy grinned at Ted. "Probably the most important feature of ChatPic is that the images are ephemeral. They disappear seven seconds after you open them. Because they aren't permanent, the focus is on the asynchronous emotional moment you created with a friend." The crowd murmured over the implications of such a feature.

Ted stepped to the front. "Thanks guys. Great demo. We'll keep noodling and find a way to incorporate those features into Boingmessage. The challenge is that it goes against the primary use case of Boingmessage, which is permanent messaging. Nice work, though. Who's next?"

A guy in a Pittsburgh Pirates jersey with hair to his shoulders jumped up. He held his phone high. "If you've got an iPhone, you can try out the demo for yourself. Open Safari and go to loopsy.internal.boing.com. Make sure to give it permission to use your phone's camera." Many people, including me, followed his instructions; several others grumbled. "If you've got an Android, sorry. Get an iPhone. Seriously."

Those with iPhones began playing with the demo, filming videos of those with Android phones as they frowned and tried to see what was happening. It was an app called Loopsy, and it let you take a short video, which instantly began looping. I took a video selfie of myself rolling my eyes, and then I watched it play over and over on my phone. "There's tons of use cases for this. Sending funny loopsies to your friends. Cheering for your sports team. Reporting news."

Someone asked, "Can you share these on social networks?"

"Yep. That's the plan."

It was fun, and impressive. I tried right then to share my loopsy on Facebook, but the social sharing function wasn't enabled yet.

Ted got up and said, "Nice stuff. We're thinking about incorporating this into Boingmail so that people can email loopsies to their friends and family." The long-haired guy sat down with a shrug.

One after another, people or groups demoed their ideas. Each of them elicited the same response in me—*I want that now!*—and based on the reactions in the room, others felt the same way. Sadly, none of them were ever launched as Boing;) products. Over the next few years, I'd experience déjà vu as I watched other companies succeed with the same basic ideas I saw presented at that meeting, in products such as Snapchat, Vine, Instagram, Waze, Tinder, Chromecast, Fitbit, Twitch.tv, LINE, Periscope, and WhatsApp.

In each case Ted thanked the presenter(s) and then explained to the group how they were thinking about incorporating the idea into an existing product. The mood of the room became progressively worse with each presentation, until the end, when Ted stepped to the whiteboard and began filling it, from the upper left to the lower right, with text and diagrams, speaking authoritatively the entire time. He looked like that PBS painter with the huge halo of hair, but instead of painting a scenic landscape on a canvas with a trowel, Ted painted the big picture of the entire digital media and technology industry on the whiteboard with black, red, green, and blue markers.

He began by drawing a lattice of atoms with little arrows flowing through, signifying electrical current. "Silicon is uniquely effective as a semiconductor because it has four valence electrons in its outermost shell, which gives it the ability to gain or lose electrons equally at the same time." I remember this because I wrote it down. However, the rest of my notes were a jumble of words and indecipherable drawings written in a fit of ecstasy.

He talked about how news distribution evolved from expensive printing and physical delivery of newspapers to nearly cost-free delivery of digital content over the internet. He explained Moore's Law, the innovator's dilemma, first movers, and fast followers. He diagramed the venture capital industry, unicorns, and dragons. On that whiteboard he laid out the entire universe of possibilities, and he pinpointed Boing;)'s unique place in that universe, right there in the Generosity conference room, on a Thursday afternoon, with the setting sun shining through the blinds. Through it all he somehow managed to make Boing;)'s product strategy, which had always seemed a mystery to everyone but Ted, look like a bold and brilliant plan for certain global domination.

I don't remember many other details, but I was enthralled. Apparently, so were the people whose demos had been demolished. They all exited Generosity as if leaving a revival—smiling, laughing, high fiving, and walking briskly with renewed sense of purpose back to their cubes.

Ted was the last to emerge. He looked exhausted, depleted. "Hey, Glenn. Did you catch any of that?"

"I sure did!"

He acknowledged my enthusiasm with a weary nod. "See you later."

As I watched him trudge off, my excitement drained away. I began forgetting what he'd said and remembering only the amazing demos. What was missing from all of it was market research that quantified the opportunities. But I had in my lap, on my laptop, a highly polished deck that did exactly that about Project Melody.

EVANGELIZE

We met in the Foresight conference room to review the Project Melody research results. This was the same conference room where TTTT meetings were held. There had been two TTTT meetings between the first one, where Darryl approved the White Tiger Team, and this Project Melody meeting. Each had been similar to the first—the other participants argued and insulted each other until Darryl said something like, "Glennster time, yo," and I expressed my opinion, leading to a smoother, more constructive conversation. It felt good to have some of the most important and powerful people in the company listen to me. I'd begun to feel at home in the Foresight conference room.

Usually, Foresight was reserved for Darryl's exclusive use. But every conference room that was big enough to accommodate all the people who needed to attend this meeting was booked, and Felicious let me use Foresight because Darryl was scheduled to be in New York that day.

Felicious and I had developed a playful relationship. Once, when I was helping her with the projection system, she asked, "Does anyone call you Glenn-Glenn?"

"Nobody."

"Can I call you Glenn-Glenn?"

"I don't see why not."

She snort-sniffled quickly. "But I'm only going to call you Glenn-Glenn if nobody else does. I want to be the only one who calls you Glenn-Glenn. Will you promise that if anyone else calls you Glenn-Glenn, you'll tell them they can't call you that?"

I've learned, from real-life observation of the well-documented nerd-and-beauty phenomenon, that if an amazingly attractive person of the gender to which you subscribe asks if she or he can be the only one to do X to you in public, even where X = something embarrassing, you agree. While X rarely leads to a romantic entanglement with the amazingly attractive person, it often leads to persons who are significantly more attractive than you finding you more eligible than they previously found you.

"I agree."

Felicious smiled.

Attendees of the Project Melody research results meeting included Maryanne, Wilson, Jocelyn, and Joe Rupp. Also attending were Joe Rupp's manager, Paige, and Boingers from Engineering, Corporate Communications, Business Development, Business Management, Editorial, and Sales. Altogether, twenty Boingers attended the meeting, fifteen in person in the Foresight conference room, and five remotely on the phone.

Since the day I launched my motto—*Being objective makes me effective*—the attendance rate of my meetings had increased significantly—a benefit I didn't foresee. All of the invitees of this particular meeting attended, along with three uninvited interns, giving the meeting an unprecedented, for me, attendance rate of 117 percent. Clearly, there was a lot of interest in this project.

As I clicked through my PowerPoint slides, I had my audience's full attention. They laughed when I meant for them to laugh. They gasped when I intended for them to gasp. They applauded when I didn't expect them to, more than once (thrice). I received more than one "Delightful" (seven) from Maryanne. The presentation was going well until I got to the slide with a bar chart showing the results from Question 17x.

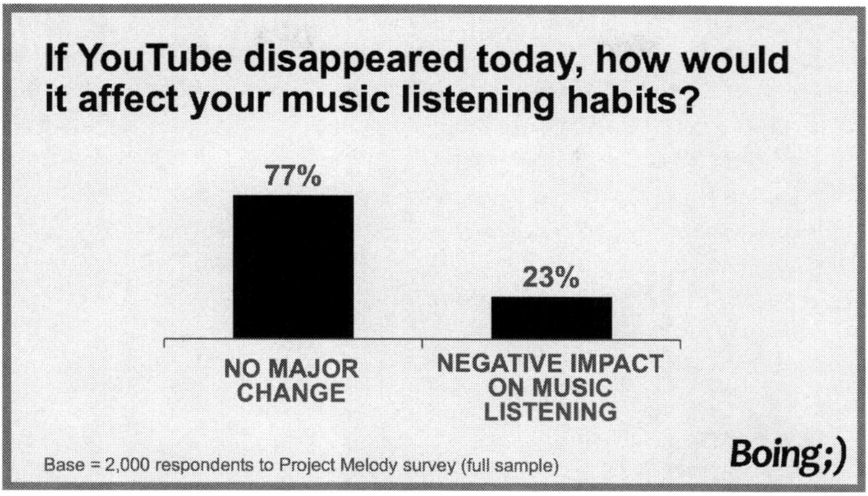

In order to craft this chart, I combined the results from Question 17x to form two buckets—"No major change," and "Negative impact on music listening."

Jocelyn immediately realized I had dramatically reworked Xiang's deck. She raised her hand high, like an eager student warning her teacher that she's about to ask a question without being called upon. "How did you get these results?"

At that moment, the door opened, and Darryl entered.

"Hi, Darryl. I'm sorry. I thought you were out of—"

He gave me a thumbs up. "I'm not here, bro. Don't catch me up. Keep rockin' it." He took the only open seat, next to Jocelyn, and they exchanged an elaborate greeting, beginning with their hands clasped arm-wrestling-style and ending with a fist bump, with a patty-cake clapping duet thing in the middle.

Also, during that extended handshake, Wilson stopped tapping on his iPhone and hid it in his pocket. He put on a blissful smile and turned what he'd previously described to me as "the good side" of his face in Darryl's direction, which meant he could only see the projection screen by glancing sideways awkwardly.

Darryl's attendance certainly raised the stakes. Of course, he could attend any meeting he wanted to attend. He was the CEO. On the plus side, Darryl's presence increased the attendance rate to 124 percent, which had to be a Boing;) record.

There was a rumor that Darryl had given an actual Get Into Any Meeting card, made of titanium, with his signature etched onto it, to a talented employee named Sid Daturin. According to Sid's Dogfood profile, he reported to Felicious, and his title was Change Agent. His profile picture was of a palm tree. His name didn't show up in searches on Boing;), Google, Yahoo!, Bing, or LinkedIn. But some Boingers experienced Sid walking into their meetings, flashing his titanium card. They said he rarely spoke, but when he did, his words were illuminating.

Jocelyn asked her question again. "How did you get these results? I don't remember the question being worded this way." I'd created a backup slide for just this circumstance. I jumped to the appendix to show it.

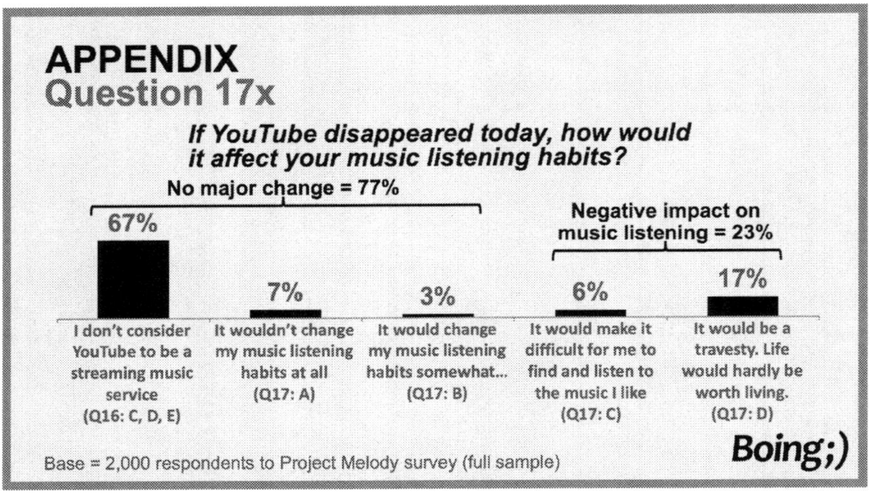

"Great question, Jocelyn. As you can see, I rebased Question 17 to the entire sample by combining partial results from Question 16 in order to fully and completely understand the competitive threat posed by YouTube as a streaming music service. Clearly, for a strong majority of respondents, YouTube isn't an essential source for streaming music."

Jocelyn looked at me skeptically, over the rims of her glasses.

I continued, "I felt that the original set of questions didn't adequately probe consumer perceptions of YouTube as a streaming music service. We try to anticipate every possible angle when we write surveys, but sometimes we miss something. Fortunately in this case, I felt that the information we needed was in the data set, if we combined results from two of the questions."

Turning back to Jocelyn, just as she was folding her arms and opening her mouth to respond, I said, "We can talk about this offline."

Jocelyn closed her mouth and smiled tightly. She kept quiet for the rest of the meeting, but she did so in a protesty way; she opened and consumed a package of pretzels loudly.

Fielding tough questions from the audience is all part of giving a presentation. The Magic 8 Ball took a turn. Wilson treated each presentation by his team as a dissertation defense. Darryl's attendance skewed the tone of Wilson's questions a bit—each question seemed designed both to trip me up and to impress Darryl—but I embraced the challenge.

"Why have a sample of two thousand respondents? Why not one thousand? It would be cheaper."

"Two thousand respondents gives us deeper statistical significance for each demo. We especially wanted to have deep results for digital natives."

"Why isn't Grooveshark listed as one of the streaming music competitors? I use Grooveshark all the time."

"The Consumerology team—you know them well—recommended we take it out because in their opinion, Grooveshark hasn't made it on the radar of most consumers yet. So you're ahead of the curve, Wilson."

"In one word or less, describe the difference between the music streaming habits of digital natives and the habits of baby boomers."

I made a deep sound in my mouth and throat. "Booooom-cha-boooooom-cha."

"Dubstep?"

I nodded. Wilson raised his eyebrows and reluctantly smiled a closed-mouthed smile.

With each question, Wilson turned and nodded slightly to Darryl, who sometimes nodded back and sometimes was busy trading doodles with Jocelyn on her notebook. With each answer, I nodded slightly to Wilson and then to Darryl.

"Do digital natives stream music on their PCs, tablets, or phones?"

"Yes."

"Yes, what?"

"Yes, they stream on all of those."

"Which do they stream on the most?"

"Their phones, when they're connected to Wi-Fi."

"Why didn't you say that the first time?"

"Because that isn't what you asked."

"*It is* what I asked."

"You asked what devices they use to stream music, and you used *or*, which in a list of more than two items is typically *inclusive*, meaning, 'Do they stream music on any one of these?' The answer to that is, 'Yes.'"

"All right. Good answer."

Darryl looked up from Jocelyn's notebook, with more of the page's surface area black with ink than white. "*Inclusive or.* That takes me back to my hacker days. Right on!" He returned to doodling.

"If we create a streaming music service, will it offer bluegrass?"

"If you want bluegrass, Wilson, then I'm sure we can offer bluegrass." I turned to Reva in Business Development, and she nodded.

"I'm not a big bluegrass fan. Just asking." Wilson sat back in his seat, indicating that he had no further questions.

I clicked to the Key Findings & Implications slide where I made the big recommendation.

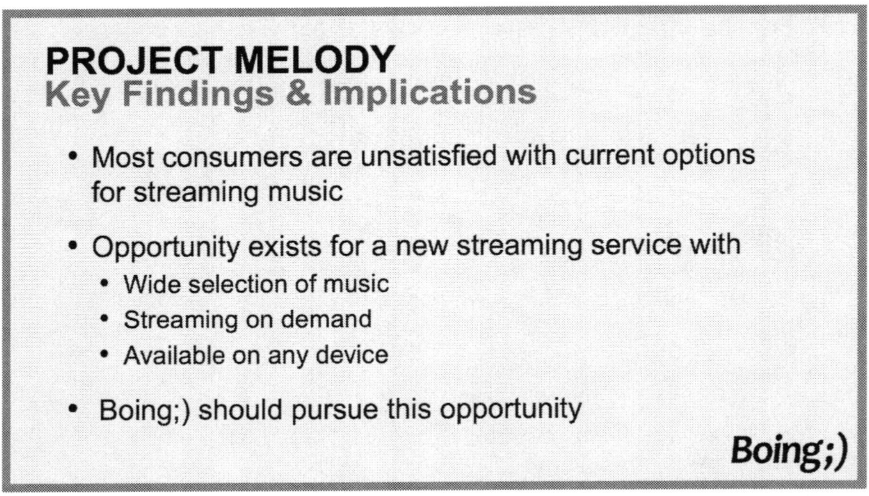

"So based on all the research I have presented, the opportunity is clear—"

Darryl interrupted me. "Yo, Glenn. *Un momento, por favor.*"

I extended my arm to Darryl, giving him the floor. He stood and said, "This research is the shizzle. I think we all know what needs to be done next. I consider this a big part of Project Resurrection. Let's get this done and give those bitches at Apple, Facebook, Google, and Amazon a smackdown. *Amirite*?"

Several of us muttered versions of, "Yes."

He cupped his ear with his hand, "I can't hear you. *Amirite*?"

We all said, more loudly, in unison, "Yes!"

He pointed, Uncle Sam style, at each of us as he chanted like a cheerleader. "Resurrection, yo! Resurrection, yo! Resurrection, yo!" Then he raised two fingers in a V on both hands. "Peace!" And he left the room.

One of the interns tapped me on the arm. "Great job evangelizing." *Evangelize* = spread the word about a technological opportunity. I half-bowed in appreciation, even though I wasn't sure if she was talking about Darryl or me.

Of course, "evangelize" has a religious connotation. When you evangelize your idea across a company like Boing;), many people treat you as if you're attempting to convert them to a cultish religion. For example, the enthusiasm Jocelyn, Joe Rupp, and the Advanced Science guys had for the WOS was so fervent it was nearly religious. When they talked about the WOS, their eyes filled with a divine fire. It was as if they believed they belonged to a select group of people favored by a powerful deity. They used technical jargon designed to separate the devout from the heathens, words like "signals," "relevance," "authentication," and "personalization." They spelled personalization, "p13n." They also used a lot of words that have special importance in religious contexts, like "inspire," "meaning," "conversion," and "faith." And sometimes they combined both types of words, as in this sentence from an email evangelizing the WOS.

> To: [Long list of Boingers]
> From: Joe Rupp
> Subject: Web of Signals (WOS)
>
> ...The Web of Signals (WOS) will leverage discreet artifacts of implicit user behavior and explicit feedback in order to optimize relevance, maximize conversion, and create deeply meaningful p13n experiences within savior products, which will incentivize authentication and accelerate monetization, at scale, restoring faith in Boing;) as an essential daily destination delighting and inspiring billions of global consumers and a no-brainer must-buy for thousands of the world's top brand advertisers...
>
> jr //u&2tr

Project Melody wasn't as dependent on magical thinking. We had research results that clearly defined the opportunity. The next steps were obvious to everyone in attendance. Paige, Joe Rupp's manager, turned to him. "I want you to be PM on this, Joe Rupp."

Joe Rupp and Jocelyn exchanged worried glances that I interpreted to mean he'd been hoping to be product manager of the WOS, which hadn't been greenlighted yet. But the company had priorities, and Project Melody was now one of them.

After an awkward pause, I presented my ending slide—an image of rows and rows of people at desks looking at screens while wearing headphones. Unfortunately, on nearly all of those screens was Facebook; nevertheless, it allowed others to visualize the opportunity for a successful streaming music service.

I ended the meeting with what had become my signature sign-off. "Thank you for your time, your attention, and your generosity." In retrospect, maybe I should have stuck with my motto; a signature sign-off was a little show-offy.

DRIVEN

There's a period of time after you give a successful presentation—it might last two minutes, it might last two weeks—when the world seems sharper. Senses are heightened. Edges are more defined. It's more than a post-performance high. Giving a presentation is like doing a fire walk that creates a defining moment, dividing your life into stages before and after the experience. The effects can be slight. For example, each of the people who attended your presentation might pass you in the hallway with a sly smile, as if you shared a secret. Or they can be large, for example, an email might be sent by an executive informing a wide audience that, based on new research conducted by Glenn Cregg, Boing;) would be developing a streaming music service.

I was in my cube feeling proud about that very email I'd just received from Ted, evangelizing the greenlighting of Project Melody, when the Advanced Science guys came down our aisle in Building Zed. I assumed they were there to see Jocelyn, as they were nearly every day. But they walked past Jocelyn's cube to mine.

The tall one with wispy facial hair took the lead. "I have to admit, Glenn, I thought the streaming music service was a stupid idea, but the data is irrefutable."

The ironically nerdy one was wearing a Boing;) Blue lab coat with a stethoscope around his neck. "I agree. The necessity of this project isn't intuitive, but the results show it's something we should do."

The loud and stout one said loudly, "It's something we must do!"

As they discussed the merits of Project Melody, using their signature, awkward, full-body gestures and overly loud laughing, my mind drifted, pondering the fact that they weren't like most people. Advanced Science guys were data driven.

If you live near an interstate highway, you might notice that a couple of children on your block have asthma. You might ask yourself, "Do they have asthma because they've been breathing particulates generated by all the cars and trucks driving the nearby highway?" Even though you can't see the particulates, you know, or believe, they're in the air. You might query a friend who lives in a neighborhood far from the highway, who might say, "No kids on my block have asthma." That might corroborate your fears, but not enough to move away, because you don't have asthma. Or, your far-from-the-highway friend might say, "All the kids on my block have asthma," which might lead you to think, "It's all a matter of chance," redirecting your thoughts toward understanding why your neighborhood has so many feral cats.

If an Advanced Science guy were to consider buying a house on your block, he'd conduct research in order to understand whether living next to a highway has statistically significant effects, good or bad, on people's health. When the data shows that the closer you live to a major highway, the more likely you are to develop asthma, he'd conclude that regularly breathing in the particulates expelled by cars and trucks increases the likelihood of developing asthma. But he wouldn't stop there. He'd quantify the risk and put it in human terms, especially if he were starting a family, with statements such as, "For every thousand children living near a highway, seven of them will develop asthma, three more than develop asthma in places with better air quality."

While he might get a great deal on an historic, early 1900s Victorian mansion, built with Philippine mahogany and Italian marble, just one block from the highway, even the most historic-homes-obsessed Advanced Science guy would consider that house to be as uninhabitable as one in the middle of a nuclear waste dump. He knows his child's likelihood of getting asthma from living next to a highway is small, but he also knows the likelihood of getting asthma is much lower if he lives in an ugly little post-war cookie-cutter ranch house, on the slope of a little view-less hill, far from the highway. That's where you'll find neighborhoods full of Advanced Science guys and their families.

So it's no surprise that when the data showed Boing;) should develop a streaming music service, the Advanced Science guys were among the first Boingers to get excited about it. They trusted data more than they trusted, well, anything else.

The tall one said, "This data tells us Project Melody is likely to be transformative."

The lab coat one went next. "Disruptive."

And then the loud one, "*Eminently scalable*!"

"Inspiring."

"Awesome."

"*Rational meets emotional*!"

"Web 3.0."

"Social graph 4.0."

"*One giant leap for the singularity*!"

Jocelyn poked her head out of her cubicle, looking like she wanted to say something. The lab-coated one greeted her. "Hey, Jocelyn." Then he looked at his watch and frowned. "Uh oh, guys. We're late for the QBR!" They all wave-nodded at me and filed quickly past Jocelyn. As soon as they reached the central aisle, they were jogging.

Jocelyn looked over at me, cube-to-cube. I could tell from her posture and the frowny way she said, "Got a minute?" that she didn't share the Advanced Science guys' enthusiasm for the research results.

"Of course."

We squatted in Courage, a room with a rectangular table for eight. Jocelyn sat on one side of the table, and I sat across from her. She'd brought her laptop, and she opened a spreadsheet. "I checked the results from Xiang, and they were very different from the results you presented."

"I found an anomaly in Xiang's analysis. Look at Questions 16 and 17, where we asked about YouTube."

Jocelyn found the relevant data in the spreadsheet.

Our back-and-forth felt like a championship-level table tennis match. *Jocelyn 0, Glenn 0.*

I served first, "As you can see, the raw data shows most respondents to Question 17 think YouTube is an essential source of streaming music. But look at the base—that question was only asked of one-third of the sample. We're trying to determine the mass audience interest in the service, beyond YouTube loyalists. So I combined the results from 17 with results from 16, but just for the respondents who didn't answer 17. That gave me a composition of the full sample, which I called Question 17x. It showed a strong majority of respondents to be swayable."

Jocelyn was impressed; her eyebrows made the same upward, curvy motion that many people's eyebrows made inadvertently whenever they said the word, "Boing;)." One point for me.

Glenn 1, Jocelyn 0.

While I was explaining the above, Jocelyn made the same calculations I'd made. Then she cross-tabulated results from Question 17x with results from another question that asked how much music people stream in a typical week. "YouTube loyalists are the heaviest streamers. Here's how 17x looks cross-tabbed with streaming volume." She turned her laptop so we both could see the screen. She was right.

Glenn 1, Jocelyn 1.

If I'd cross-tabulated those results, it would've suggested my interpretation of Question 17x was…"incomplete" wasn't the right word. Jocelyn found a more accurate word, "deceptive." Another point for Jocelyn.

Glenn 1, Jocelyn 2.

We weren't looking at the pretty slides I'd presented; we were looking at raw data in spreadsheets. Marketing insights analysts like us read spreadsheets fluently. When we see tables of numbers, we visualize the charts and trends in our minds, not unlike how Nero from *The Matrix* understands raw data pouring down the screen.

I had one more ace up my sleeve. One more bullet in my deck. One more stream in my player. "Look at Question 3, where we asked about favorite services. I think most of the respondents who answered 'None of the above' would have answered 'YouTube,' if we'd offered it as a choice." Unexpected insight—point for me.

Glenn 2, Jocelyn 2.

Jocelyn scrutinized me. "I thought YouTube *was* a choice for that question. I added it to an early draft of the questionnaire."

I scrutinized her back. Her eyes were steady as she peered at me over the rims of her glasses. I saw her pupils dilate, as if she could control them at will to take in more raw data. So with her greater dilation-driven powers of perception, she might have noticed the slight tensing of muscles in my jaw line or the faint rush of blood to my cheeks that suggested I was the one who removed YouTube as an option for Question 3. And she might have sensed I was being disingenuous when I said, "It's possible Xiang removed it."

Glenn 2, Jocelyn 3.

Jocelyn moved to the Question 3 portion of the spreadsheet. While it showed Pandora was the favorite of more respondents than any other service—14 percent named it as their favorite streaming music service—it also showed that the most popular response, with 44 percent, was "None of the above." She cross-tabulated those results with results from Question 16. I'd done that, too, so I anticipated how she would interpret it. "It's pretty obvious that almost all of those 'None of the above' respondents are YouTube loyalists, which means YouTube is the most popular source for streaming music." I knew that—no point.

Score remained *Glenn 2, Jocelyn 3.*

I said, "YouTube might be the most popular, but not for a majority of respondents."

Glenn 3, Jocelyn 3.

"YouTube loyalists are the very people we need to win over. They drive most music consumption."

Glenn 3, Jocelyn 4.

"The data suggests we can create a category-leading product with or without winning over YouTube loyalists."

Glenn 4, Jocelyn 4.

"At some point we have to admit the story we want to tell isn't supported by the data."

Glenn 4, Jocelyn 5.

"At some point we have to make judgment calls."

Glenn 5, Jocelyn 5.

Jocelyn closed her laptop; she placed both of her hands, palms down, on top of it. She watched me as she took a deep breath and then exhaled in a huff through flaring nostrils. "These don't feel like the judgment calls of an objective analyst. They aren't data driven."

"They *are* data driven. Xiang's deck contained a data anomaly. It needed to be reworked. His decks always need to be reworked. So I reworked it."

"That seems really subjective. What happened to your motto?"

For a long time, I regretted the part of the conversation I'm about to relate. But I don't regret it now, as I'm telling it, because later events changed my perception of it, from regrettable to warranted. Not unlike how Xiang's key findings and implications changed when I reworked results from Question 17. I said what I was thinking, unfiltered. "You've never liked the idea of a streaming music service, because it pulls attention from the Web of Signals."

I thought I saw a glimpse of sad Jocelyn. "You're right that I think Project Melody is an unnecessary diversion, and maybe I didn't work as hard on the questionnaire as I could have—"

"A-ha! I knew it!"

But mad Jocelyn took control. "Don't interrupt me!"

"You just admitted you've been sabotaging Project Melody!"

She spoke with a tense pause between words, as if her speech rate was limited to one word per second. "You aren't letting me finish my statement. I expect you to let me finish my statement."

She didn't shout those words, but the effect on me was the same. This was a new type of interaction with Jocelyn. "I'm sorry I interrupted you."

She spoke in a lower volume. Not whispery. Forcefully, angrily, confidently, but quietly. I had to lean in to hear her. "You manipulated the research results. That's just wrong, Glenn."

I matched her volume level. "*Manipulated* isn't the right word." Why were we talking so quietly?

"What is the right word?"

"Fixed. That's the right word. I reworked the deck. I fixed the anomaly, Jocelyn."

"You *fixed* it?" I saw it on her lips more than I heard it in her voice. Jocelyn chuckled, quietly, disturbingly. She continued softly, in that staccato cadence, "*Fixed* is the perfect word. It means *repaired.* But also means *improperly influenced the outcome*, like fixing a boxing match, which is how I see it."

I mumbled, "*Fixed* also means *castrated*."

Jocelyn laughed loudly in a burst, "Ha!" It broke the quietness spell. And for an instant, I thought things would be all right between us, and this was just a normal disagreement between co-workers. But then she said, "Project Melody wouldn't have been greenlighted if you hadn't fixed the results."

"I suppose you think the WOS should be greenlighted instead of Project Melody."

She paused and smiled a self-satisfied smile. "The WOS has been greenlighted. Oops. I guess I forgot to mention it. We're already developing a prototype. The good news about Project Melody is that the WOS can power the recommendation engine."

Jocelyn adopted a bizarre pose. She crossed her arms, dropped her jaw, mouth breather-like, and opened her eyes wide as if she were horrified. Then I realized she was mirroring me. I didn't know whether she was doing it consciously, suggesting she'd received leadership training, or whether she was doing it unconsciously, as one of her natural empathy skills. Either way, seeing her like that made me realize I was stunned. The WOS had been greenlighted. That meant Jocelyn and Joe Rupp and who knows who else were planning to make Project Melody a WOS test case!

I remained in mouth-breather mode. "Are you and your team of WOS groupies trying to undermine my idea? Project Melody would resurrect the company if people just let it! The WOS is another in a long line of enticing, vague, improvable solutions to problems real people don't have that would take hundreds of millions of dollars of investment in platforms and infrastructure just to test. And Project Melody shouldn't be that test!"

"I see. Then why did you encourage me to work on it?"

"Because I thought it would keep you alive."

Jocelyn looked at me skeptically, over the rims of her glasses. "I've thought of you as my mentor, but we're past that now."

She stood and walked out, closing the door behind her quietly, without even a click. I wondered if that was one of the beneficial effects of the antidepressant medication—no ragey door slamming. I would have felt better if she'd slammed it.

I was convinced I was right, that I'd objectively assessed the research results and organized them in the proper way. But that moment, when the door closed without a sound, was when I first wondered whether I'd made a mistake. Jocelyn's anomalous behavior meant something, although I didn't yet know what. Had my *-jectivity* strayed from *ob-* to *sub-*? Had my Rockstar Award gone to my head, turning me from a high-value GSD employee into just another self-important CYA dingleberry who doesn't Get It? Had I drunk the Kool-Aid?

I looked out the window at Boingers playing hacky sack and began considering possible implications if Jocelyn were to share her concerns about my analysis with Joe Rupp or Wilson or Darryl. Or Marian Sallowaskky.

SEASONED

I was sitting in my cube when my iPhone rang. The call was coming from a blocked number. This was uncommon, but not unprecedented. I swiped the answer-call button, raised it to my ear, and said, "Hello."

"This is Marian Sallowaskky." I paused, awaiting further information. "I write a blog about digital technology and media companies."

"I know who you are, Ms. Sallowaskky." I spoke quietly so that nobody in an adjoining cube could hear me.

"Please, call me Marian."

I kept calm. "How can I help you, Ms. Sallowaskky?"

"Okay, if that's the way you want to play it. I guess I'll have to treat you like a hostile witness." She seemed to be flirting with me. So this was how she consistently received the company's most secret information!

"Hold on a moment."

She replied as if she'd won the first round of what was sure to be an epic match. "Of course."

I walked down the hallway as casually as I could, avoiding eye contact with a succession of co-workers—including Wanda from B2B Marketing, Wilson, and Alyosha from PR—by pretending to be checking emails on my phone. I found the nearest open conference room, the little, windowless Valor. I closed the door and sat down. "Why are you calling me?"

"I've been hearing about Project Melody, and your name keeps coming up. My sources tell me it has the potential to return Boing;) to its glory days."

"Who's been saying that?" As far as I knew, I was the only person who'd been saying that.

"You know how this goes. I can't tell you who my sources are. I'd like you to tell me more about Project Melody."

I thought about hanging up. That was the proper, safe thing to do. And yet, if she was going to write about Project Melody, who better than me to influence how she did it? Should I give her the truth? Or should I give her misinformation? The truth could be traced back to me. But misinformation couldn't. "Project Melody is a new location-based check-in app that lets you share photos from your mobile device with people near you, whether or not you know them."

"Come on, Glenn. You're Mr. Objective. You can do better than that." I could hear her typing in the background.

"What did you call me?"

"You're the guy with the motto: *Being objective makes me*, meaning you, *effective*. It's *deeeelightful*! I've been wanting to chat with you ever since I heard it. So be objective and tell me something I don't know about Boing;)'s plans for a new streaming music service."

I paused. While I take pride in being comfortable with long silences, she was even better at it. I broke first. "You seem to know a lot about me. Do you know where I live?"

"Glenn, please. I'm not stalking you. I'm trying to interview you, off the record. I don't know where you live, and I'm not going to show up at your home. I haven't checked you out on Facebook, Twitter, or Tumblr, although I did take a looksee at your LinkedIn page. Nice profile photo, by the way. But you shouldn't call yourself 'seasoned.' Makes you sound like you're ready to be barbecued. Suffice to say, I know how to use the Google like a demon. So if I wanted to find out nearly anything about you, I could."

I terminated the call. Since I hadn't brought my laptop, I instinctively reached for a marker next to the small whiteboard on the wall, in order to diagram the situation. But this wasn't something I wanted to make public in any way. I could write it out and then erase it, but sometimes you can faintly see what people wrote, even after erasure. And there was a rumor that all Boing;) whiteboards were digital, where everything written on them was stored in a database somewhere. So I put down the marker. I would have to map this out in a PowerPoint slide that only existed in the cloud storage of my own mind.

Marian Sallowaskky knows who I am

- She could've gotten my cell phone number from any Boinger—it's listed on Dogfood
- She knows about Project Melody
- One of the TTTT members is her mole
- Her mole has been talking about me
- She knows about my motto
- She's trying to make me a mole

At that moment, my phone chirped a single note, like a succinct song bird, signaling I had a new text message. It was from her.

> great chatting with you glenn. let me know if you change your mind—would love to pick your big brain. xxoo m.

I didn't have a company-owned mobile phone. That benny was saved for directors and above. So my iPhone was personal. Otherwise I would've deleted all traces of that woman from my phone, and I would've worried that the company had a record of her contacting me. But I felt safe—only a court order could force my wireless carrier to provide data proving Marian Sallowaskky and I had communicated.

STEALTH

My next 1:1 with Jocelyn was more of a 1. I arrived at the wobbly table and waited. And waited. Jocelyn didn't show up. So I was unable to give her some news in person.

I'd received an email from the SVP of Human Resources informing me Jocelyn had won the Rockstar Award for that quarter. The email instructed me to let her know she was chosen for her "enterprising contributions to a promising new stealth initiative."

I was going to tell her at our 1:1. But since she didn't show up, I sent her a pithy email while I sat at the wobbly table, twenty minutes after our 1:1 was scheduled to begin.

> To: Jocelyn
> Subject: 1:1
>
> Sorry you didn't show up to our 1:1. So I was unable to tell you in person that you've been selected to receive the quarterly Rockstar Award, reportedly for your "enterprising contributions to a promising new stealth initiative."
>
> Best,
> Glenn
> (Sent from my iPhone)

As I continued sitting there, I realized she was committing a type of mutiny. I could've indulged in self-pity or anger. However, such thoughts only led to sleepless anxiety-filled nights. Instead, I focused my mind on pondering and solving a difficult question. Why do managers sometimes not notice achievements by their team members that others see? I didn't nominate Jocelyn for the Rockstar Award, and it hadn't occurred to me to do so. I certainly thought she was Rockstar capable, but in my mind she hadn't yet done anything Rockstar worthy. Evidently someone else felt differently. Similarly, Wilson had told me he didn't think my work was Rockstar worthy, and he didn't nominate me for the award when I received it. And although Wilson received the award, I didn't see anything Rockstar worthy in his accomplishments. Is it possible the default state of human beings is not seeing Rockstar potential in others? Or could this be a defect particular to people like Wilson and me, who scrutinize information for a living?

As I pondered my ability to see or not see Rockstar worthiness in others, I nearly concluded it comes down to a simple truth. *It's difficult to step out of the weeds in order to see the big picture.* I didn't get around to fully concluding this because my thought chain was interrupted by a more urgent thought. *I hope Jocelyn is safe.* I assumed she was skipping our 1:1 on purpose, in protest of my analysis of the Project Melody results. But what if she was lying on the floor of her cube again? Probably the Advanced Science guys would have found her by then. But that thought interrupted my thinking.

I walked back to Building Zed with some urgency—not running, but walking faster than my normal speed. When I got to our aisle, I found Jocelyn sitting at her desk, conscious, alert, working, crunching a carrot. No spilled bottle of pills. No ambulance.

I stood at the threshold of her cube and waited for her to acknowledge me. I cleared my throat. "Hey. Do you need something from me, Glenn?"

"You didn't show up for our 1:1."

She frowned. "Sorry. I forgot. "Can we reschedule?" She seemed neither apologetic nor defiant. She seemed busy.

"Did you get my email?"

"I don't know. I shut off my email so I could focus on this new WOS deck."

"Before you open that email from me, can I do something on your computer?"

She took her hand off her mouse. "Sure."

She scooted her chair back in order to give me room. I stepped behind her desk and put my hand on her mouse. I opened her inbox and deleted the message from me. I then went into her deleted items folder and deleted it again. When the email program questioned my judgment with a message window—"Are you sure that you want to permanently delete the selected item(s)?"—I confirmed. Jocelyn watched me do this but didn't comment. I was beginning to realize I'd been granted a *do over* = an opportunity to do something right the second time when I'd done it wrong the first time.

I asked, "Will you join me for a moment in a conference room?"

We walked down the hall to Valor. I sat in the same chair I used while talking to Marian Sallowaskky. She sat across from me, looking curious. I forced a fake smile that relaxed into a real smile on my face. She shrugged as if to say, "What?"

I sat straighter and cleared my throat dramatically. "Congratulations are in order. You've been selected to receive the quarterly Rockstar Award for your excellent work on the Web of Signals."

Jocelyn looked at me skeptically, over the rims of her glasses.

LAUNCH

This wasn't the Old Boing;), where it took years to bring a new product to market. Darryl had been talking for months about "GSD with urgency, yo!" And that call to action reinvigorated Boingers. So Project Melody moved along rapidly, with all the various teams working in parallel in order to deliver the product just three months after the greenlight.

The product was named Boingstream, and it was the new central feature of the Boingtunes website. Launch was scheduled for a Wednesday because Marketing wanted to leverage the long-standing Boingtunes feature, Hump Day New Tunes. *Hump Day* = the day in the middle of the five-day workweek, Wednesday, also known among working-age digital natives as the "middle finger" of the work week.

I was surprised to learn that a financial services company had stepped forward to sponsor the launch of Boingstream. When you visited the Boingstream website or downloaded the Boingstream app, the sponsoring company's logo was displayed prominently. When you streamed songs, an audio advertisement described how the company's financial advisors were "Wall Street-smart." When you played a music video, a preroll ad for the company played before the video, and a postroll ad played after the video. The company paid nearly five million dollars to sponsor Boingstream's launch because someone in Sales convinced them Boingstream would allow them to reach and engage young consumers just entering the lifestage when they needed help managing their finances.

This was very good news; Boingstream was generating revenue from day one, which had been moved up a day at the last minute to try to squelch other Boing;) news that was dominating Silicon Valley—Ted had left the company. Marian Sallowaskky reported it on her blog.

> I feel on a first-name basis with Ted, even though we've never met in person, mainly because of that hair—that's some intimacy-creating hair, my friend! But my friend Ted won't return my emails, calls, tweets, or IMs. He won't visit my farm on FarmVille! (Why won't you accept my Friendship Fertilizer, Ted?)
>
> Thankfully, some of the usual *highly placed sources with knowledge of the situation* do visit my farm. So I can tell you that Boing;)'s chief product officer left—drumroll, please—without sending a G&GL.
>
> I know! Unbelievable!
>
> Those of you who read my blog religiously know it's customary for a digital technology executive to leave a company with a Goodbye & Good Luck email that quickly gets leaked to journalists like me. Oh, sure, G&GLs are typically bloated combinations of self-congratulation and don't-burn-that-bridge fluffery. But a G&GL indicates that order exists in the universe. Even boneheads who get caught banging their interns send out G&GLs. When a major executive like Ted leaves a company like Boing;) without one, there are only a couple of possibilities. 1) Either he was immediately terminated for some major infraction, or 2) he could no longer take the internal politics and deckchair rearranging and quit abruptly. I can't leave you hanging like this, without clues to the mystery.
>
> Several of my sources tell me that Ted recently tweeted:

> *Another day at Boing. #punctuationnightmare;)*
>
> That tweet doesn't exist anymore. (Let me know if any of you hooligans screencapped it—will pay CA$H!) But it would explain the leaving without a G&GL. At Boing;), not punctuating properly is a fireable offense!

So the Boingstream launch was moved to Tuesday in the hope of changing the conversation from the departure of the company's top product executive to the launch of a cool, new product.

We had a spectacular launch party in the afternoon. A stage was set up in the middle of campus, outside Bytes. Thousands of Boingers showed up to see the band we hired for the occasion, Wheeezer, a Weezer tribute band. We had booked the actual Weezer for Wednesday, and we still ended up paying them, but on Tuesday they weren't back yet from a show in Copenhagen, and it was determined that it was more important to move the launch up a day than to have a performance from the actual Weezer. Fortunately, the San Francisco-based Wheeezer was available.

Darryl began the event as he began all others, strutting the stage. "Yo, yo, yo! What up Boingers?" He stuffed his microphone in his pants as he used both hands to clap rhythmically above his head until the Boingers in the crowd were clapping along with him. Then he pulled the mic from his pants to say, "Right on, Boingers! Respect."

Darryl passed the mic to Randy, the VP of Boingtunes, who pantomimed wiping it off with his untucked shirt tail. Randy let much of the crowd's energy dissipate as he spoke for several minutes, beginning with, "It's an honor and a privilege to be standing before you today, more than a dozen years after I started my career in the music business as marketing associate for Napster," and ending with, "Boingstream represents the latest great rest stop on the highway toward the future of digital entertainment. Thank you!"

Darryl leaned over Randy's shoulder like a backup singer and said something that filled me with pride. "Boingstream is the latest reason why Boing;) is the best damn digital company on the planet, yo!"

I usually think less of a person, briefly, who uses the phrase "reason why," because it seems redundant to me. The reason is why. Why is the reason. It should simply be the reason, or it should simply be why. But I was able to forgive Darryl in this instance—the reason was he so clearly Got It.

Then Darryl pointed at me. I was standing near the stage, hoping to be close when Wheeezer started playing. "Yo, yo, yo. I'd like you all to meet Glenn Cregg. Get on up here, bro."

Needless to say, I hadn't expected that. I stepped onto the stage, and Darryl wrapped his overly warm arm around me and told the crowd, "I always say, fly ideas can come from anywhere, yo. Glenn here had a fly idea for a streaming music service, and he conducted the research showing the tremendous opportunity it offers for making Boing;) the shizzle with young peeps. If it weren't for the Glennster, we wouldn't be here today announcing the launch of this bitchin' new product."

Darryl had one more surprise for me. "As recognition of your contribution, dawg, I'm giving you a special Rockstar Award."

I was speechless, but I remained upright and conscious.

Felicious stepped up to the stage and handed a Rockstar Award trophy to Darryl, who pushed it into my midsection when I neglected to take it from him. "Glenn is the first-ever two-time winner of the Rockstar Award. Let this be an inspiration to all of y'all—keep the fly ideas coming!"

There was an unwritten rule that a Boinger could only win the Rockstar Award once. Apparently, that rule had been un-unwritten. As the assembled Boingers clapped and cheered, Darryl announced, "And now, it's my pleasure to welcome to the Boing;) campus, the best damn Weezer tribute band on the planet, Wheeezer!" We stepped off the stage and stood right in front as the band began to play Weezer's hit song, "Buddy Holly."

Wheeezer played a thirty-minute set of music, including my favorite song of Weezer's, "Troublemaker," as an encore. Everyone at the Launch Party received a Boing;) Blue Boingstream T-shirt and a commemorative set of Boingstream earbuds. Cupcakes were served. All in all, including the party expenses, Boingstream cost thirty million dollars to develop, launch, and advertise.

After the Launch Party, I took a long, ambling walk back to Building Zed. And what a walk it was! The sun was shining. The temperature was just a degree or two below sweat inducing, with a very slightly chilling breeze that felt like nature's kisses on my face and neck. The sky was pale blue, like the eyes of that girl who never had dinner with me. Several songbirds were frolicking in the air, or fighting, or both, singing as they frolic-fought. A skywriting airplane was puffing out a proposal; during my walk its message grew from, "Mary," to "Mary will you marr." Workers were planting blooming tulips in flower beds along a walkway—they paused to wave at me, in my Boingstream T-shirt over my button-down shirt, with the signatures of Wheeezer still drying on my chest. One Boinger after another, as I passed them, looked up from their phones and nodded and smiled and said "Hello" and "Great job!" A ladybug lit on my Rockstar Award and turned its inscrutable face toward me, as if to congratulate me, and then it flew off in its herky-jerky, ladybuggy way.

As I passed the gigantic Boing;) sign on the corner of campus, about to cross the street to Building Zed, the Google Street View car drove by. It was a Toyota Prius outfitted with a 360-degree camera on a pole sticking out through the top, taking photos for Google Maps. The next time I looked at that intersection in Google Maps, it showed a picture of me, my face blurred, beside the Boing;) sign, in my Boingstream T-shirt, holding my second Rockstar Award, about to cross the street, commemorating my magical journey back to my cube. It was the best moment of my life.

The lyrics of "Troublemaker" were still ringing in my ears when I got to my desk—the song seemed to have been written about me and my carefree, can-do attitude. I placed my new Rockstar Award with my old one, leaving space between them for my imaginary TTTT Award. And I sat at my desk to review the very first results showing how consumers were responding to Boingstream. As I pressed my mouse to see the data, my finger trembled.

RESULTS

The Boingstream service had opened for users at six in the morning, Eastern Time. We began gathering data and conducting a survey as soon as people started using it. Some of the key behavioral metrics we tracked included total users, total streams, and streams per user. We asked a few different questions, but two were the most important.

- How satisfied are you with Boingstream, on a scale of 1 (Not at all satisfied) to 10 (Extremely satisfied)?
- How likely are you to recommend Boingstream to friends or family members, on a scale of 1 (Definitely will not recommend) to 10 (Definitely will recommend)?

A team in Bangalore was collecting real-time data. Real-time meant the data was delayed a few hours; many a Boinger had noted the irony of this. So by mid-afternoon, Silicon Valley time, I had several hours of data. The results were mixed.

The behavioral data was very positive. It showed nearly two million users had already tried Boingstream, with a healthy streams-per-user count of 7.4. Considering that tens of millions of people used the Boing:) home page every day, and considering that we plastered it with marketing messages to "Try Boingstream—free music on-demand," it's not surprising that this occurred. We were very good at getting millions of people to try our new products once.

The survey data was troubling. It showed an average satisfaction score of 3.5 out of 10, and an average likelihood-to-recommend score of 2.4. For both of these questions, we also asked, "Why did you choose this rating?" These were some typical responses, all from the 18–34 demo we were targeting.

- "No. Just no."
- "stupid recommendations. seriously, dubstep?!? what is this, middle school?!?"
- "Bad timing, dudes. I'm glad Spotify is finally here in the US. It's sick!"
- "Would be better if this was simply a link to YouTube."
- "Why would I use this when I have Pandora, iTunes, Amazon, and a dozen other, better services that understand my musical tastes and do a better job of helping me discover new music?"
- "Pls stop making new stuff and just fix my boingmail pls"
- "boingstream sux. theres zillions of songs you don't have that are on youtube. youtube rox. bitches!!!"

Over the next few hours I watched the data trickle in, with the numbers gently changing every few moments, delayed by a few hours, as if I were sitting by a real-life stream watching rubber duckies that had launched a few miles upstream eventually pass my vantage point. The streaming audience peaked around six thousand users per minute in the middle of the morning and was steadily falling off, to about one thousand users per minute after the launch party. If positive word of mouth had been spreading, we'd see users per minute increase throughout launch day. If no word of mouth was spreading, we'd see users per minute roughly hold steady. Since users per minute were declining rapidly, the word of mouth likely was negative. I found examples of it on Facebook and Twitter, calling Boingstream, "lame," "buggy," "slow," "stinky," and "about ten years too late."

I'd seen such unpromising results before. And in every case, the same pattern occurred, as inevitably as the sun rises and sets each day.

- Millions of users tried the new product.
- Nearly all of them rejected it.
- We made slight tweaks to the product that were barely noticed by users.
- We increased our marketing efforts but were unable to entice a mass audience to try it again.
- Usage of the product continued to decline.
- Eventually, later than we should have, we shut it down.

In the course of my work, I sometimes felt like Cassandra, the princess of Troy in Greek mythology, with whom Apollo fell in love. He granted her the power of prophecy, but when she didn't return his love, Apollo cursed her so that nobody would believe her. So everybody ignored her when she said, "A team of elite Greek soldiers is going to hide in a large wooden horse and leave it outside the gates of the city, while the rest of the Greek fleet pretends to sail away in defeat. Our guys will bring the wooden horse into Troy as a trophy, and in the middle of the night, the Greeks will emerge from the horse and open the gates of the city while their navy sails back and murders us in our sleep."

Of course, her prophecy came true with disastrous results.

I didn't feel like Cassandra because I thought I could truly *see the future.* I felt like her because my co-workers never believed my dire predictions of future results based on data trends. The data told me, irrefutably, that Boingstream would fail. Considering the money invested, the failure would be spectacular. It was only a matter of time. If the initial ratings had been two points higher, we might've had an opportunity to tweak our way toward making a popular product. But that wasn't going to happen. I knew this as surely as the Titanic's engineer knew that, with just a small portion of the ship flooded, the entire thing would go down within hours, even though the ship showed no signs of sinking when he first analyzed the data.

Many times before, I'd made efforts to evangelize fellow Boingers with data-driven prophecies. For example, I'd sent an email about Boing;)'s digital scrapbook saying, "Project World Peace is not gaining sufficient traction with the target audience and risks tarnishing Boing;)'s reputation with consumer-goods advertisers interested in reaching moms ages 25–54. We should shut down the product immediately."

Nobody heeded my warning. In fact, we kept World Peace running and tried several different Scrapbook Night events sponsored by major advertisers, all of whom were greatly disappointed by the number of women who participated. The Scrapbook Night event on a chilly winter night in Madison, Wisconsin, was attended by three moms and seventeen homeless men. As a result of World Peace's failure, Boing;) was required to deliver millions of dollars of make-good advertisements.

By the end of the day, I knew from watching the real-time data trickle in on my screen that Boingstream would fail. I knew something else. I knew my chart based on Question 17x had been used extensively to convince Boingers and the sponsor that Boingstream would be popular among digital natives.

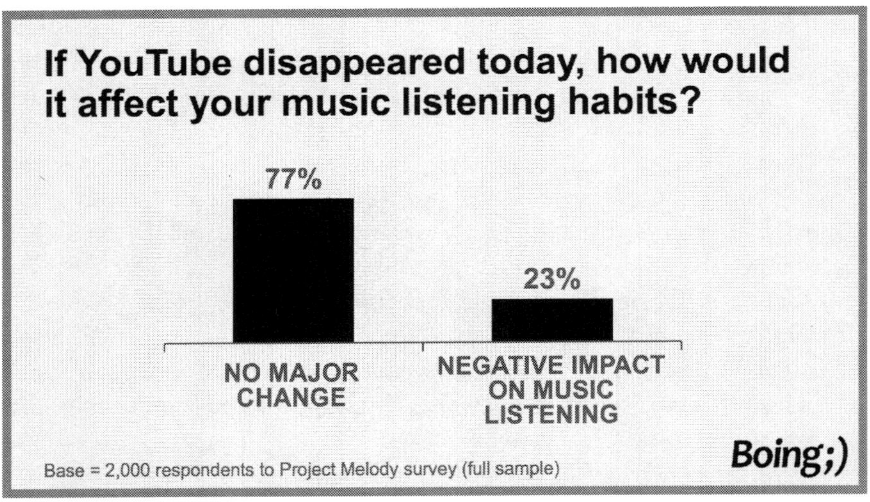

It would've been appropriate for me to feel worried or embarrassed or frightened. I felt none of these. I still felt the sense of fullness—sunshiny, blue sky-y, Rockstar-y, ladybuggy pride and joy—that I felt during and after the launch party just a few hours earlier, but with an apocalyptic twist. I knew the world was going to end. I knew Boingstream would go down in flames, that it might be Boing;)'s last gasp, that stockholders would rebel and call for Darryl's resignation, that thousands of Boingers would be laid off, that the tech press would cite the date and time of the Boingstream launch—perhaps right during Wheeezer's "Troublemaker" encore—as the official date and time of Boing;)'s demise. And I knew nobody would believe me when I told them.

But it was my job to tell them. I crafted a short email to the Boingstream Tiger Team. I provided initial results from the data. I explained I'd never seen a product rebound from such poor initial results and that even product improvements and additional marketing were unlikely to make a significant difference. And I wrote, "I'm sorry I got all of you to believe that Boingstream would fix Boing;)'s problems." I reread that apologetic line several times before deleting it. And I sent the rest of the message.

I got up from my chair and began walking, aimlessly. My memory of this walk is fragmented, a collage of images. I remember seeing the refrigerated display case in the microkitchen with one lonely can of Kool-Aid remaining. I remember the Tetris-like pattern in the floor tile next to one of the toilets in the men's room. I think I saw a crow, alone and cawing beside an open window, in the Courage conference room. I'm sure I ended up outside, where I'm pretty sure I watched the skywritten marriage proposal spread and twist illegibly in the wind. And though I have a clear vision of it in my mind, it's hard to believe I really saw the Google Street View car doing donuts in the Boing;) parking lot.

I found myself in Maryanne's office, in Building Alpha, standing before her desk, surrounded by photos, drawings, and paintings of strawberries and people enjoying strawberries.

She looked up at me, with sad eyes, as if she knew what I knew, and believed me, which couldn't have been the case. She wasn't on the Boingstream Tiger Team, so she wouldn't have read my email. She was a sensitive, perceptive person, so she might have noted the despair in my face. But no—she had her own troubles. "Oh, Glenn! My presentation at the Marketing to Moms panel was a disaster!"

OFFLINE

I had provided Maryanne with a few slides describing how Boing;) delights moms with our various products. One of the slides described the search terms that moms overindex in using compared to other demos. Some of them weren't surprising, but others suggested a secret mom world I hadn't been aware of before I conducted the analysis.

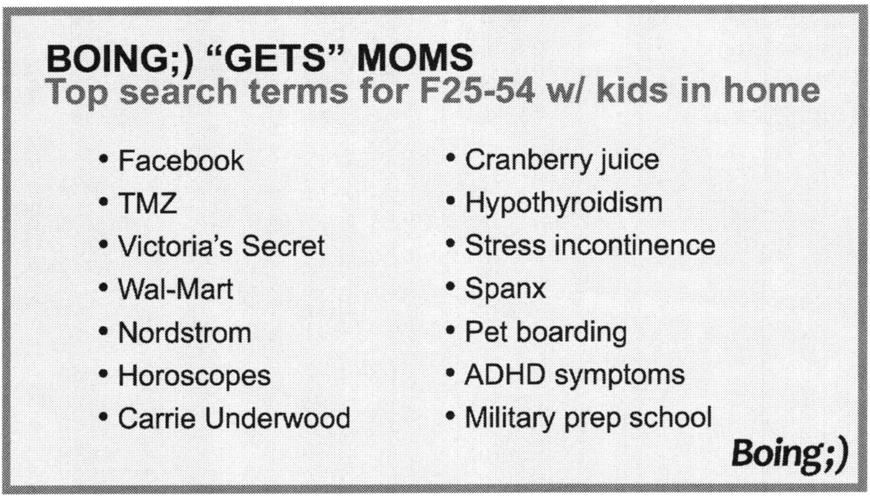

Maryanne had been especially delighted about these search terms. She was certain they would be received warmly by her audience, as proof that Boing;), and by extension, Maryanne, Gets It about moms.

As a way of explaining how badly her panel went, Maryanne showed me the latest blog post by Marian Sallowaskky.

> The Marketing to Moms panel at the annual Digital Media Cavalcade seemed like an easy break between buffet lines. It turned out to be as fun as a Restoration Comedy. (For those of you who weren't English majors, think, *30 Rock*. Or Katy Perry. Or the first Dot-Com Bubble. Over-the-top hilarity!)
>
> The panel was moderated by my former pupil, who has become an accomplished teaser-outer of ridiculous statements by executives (*proud sniffle*). Enjoy!

THE MUM EQUATION

Dramatis Personae

MISS FOGGYBOTTOM, Senior Vice President of Marketeering at The Best Damned Digital Company on the Planet

PHINEAS WILDEHAMMER, SVP of Marketeering at another, larger, less-damned digital media company, and scrivener of books and treatises about mums

DR. GRISELDA WATCHMEE, Professor and purveyor of truths and pronouncements about the mum demographick

MRS. FORCIBLE, Chief Marketeering Officer at Ye Olde Esteemed Consumer Products Manufacturer

LACY UNDERGARMENTS, moderator, scrivener on the topic of the Technologickal Arts

FOPS and PHANATICS of Digital Computation

Scene: A gilded Las Vegas ballroom.

Discover Foggybottom, Wildehammer, Watchmee, and Forcible seated, empaneled as a jury, on a stage. The occasion is a discussion about Marketeering to Mums.

Enter Lacy Undergarments, to the applause of Fops and Phanatics.

LACY: Let's begin with a question. How many of us are mums? A show of hands, please.

Hands raised by Lacy, Watchmee, Forcible, and many of the Fops and Phanatics.

LACY: Thank you, mums, you may put your hands down. Mr. Wildehammer, you are a man.

WILDEHAMMER: Thank you for noticing.

LACY: Why on Earth is a man on a panel about delighting mums with digital media and technology?

WILDEHAMMER: As you know, Lacy, I've written many tomes about the purchasing behaviors of mums. Like most of us, I have a mum. And I live with a mum, my wife, whom I have been led to believe I have, from time to time, delighted.

Titters from the Fops and Phanatics.

LACY: Fair enough, Mr. Wildehammer. Dr. Watchmee, you are a mum.

WATCHMEE: And a professor. So I have deployed the skill of lecturing my children to sleep at night.

Woohoos from the Fops and Phanatics.

LACY: Mrs. Forcible, if you will pardon me, you have the countenance of a grandmum.

FORCIBLE: You're an accomplished reader of the lines of the face, Ms. Undergarments. Each line represents a lesson learned by a child or a grandchild.

LOLs from the Fops.
OMGs from the Phanatics.

LACY: What about you, Miss Foggybottom? You didn't raise your hand.

FOGGYBOTTOM: A woman mustn't need to bear children to understand the joys and challenges of motherhood. I feel like mothering you right now, Lacy, by grounding you for impertinence.

A smattering of whistles from the Fops and Phanatics.

LACY: *Touché, Madame.* But we didn't invite you here for witty retorts. We invited you here to enlighten us.

FOGGYBOTTOM: Delightful!

LACY: Then, if you will, please regale us with your most salient observations about mums, as a marketeer.

Projected behind the panel are a series of illuminated images and charts.

FOGGYBOTTOM: As you can see from the images projected by yonder magick lantern, online enrichment by mums has increased 27 percent over the past two years. On our network, mum enrichment has increased 42 percent.

LACY: Do you mean to say, *engagement*?

FOGGYBOTTOM: I mean what I say, Ms. Undergarments.

WILDEHAMMER: (*aside*) Oh, dear. We appear to have gone through the looking glass!

Sniggers from the Fops and Phanatics.

LACY: What are the drivers of this increased...*enrichment*?

FOGGYBOTTOM: I'm glad you asked, Lacy. As the next slide clearly shows, the topics mums search for most include 'Victoria's Secret' and 'cranberry juice.'

LACY: Do you mean to suggest that the primary reason mums use the interconnected networks is to acquire lingerie that induces dads to join them in a familial activity that has been known to bestow upon mums an infection of the urinary tract, for which cranberry juice is a known home remedy?

FOGGYBOTTOM: Certainly not!

LACY: Do you mean to suggest that increased *enrichment* by mums is driven by the need to search for information?

FOGGYBOTTOM: You're putting words in my mouth.

LACY: I ask again, what are the drivers of the growth in enrichment among mums?

FOGGYBOTTOM: And I showed you popular search terms among mums!

LACY: Those terms are artifacts, not drivers!

FOGGYBOTTOM: Harumph!

Miss Foggybottom huffs and crosses her arms with a flourish, to jeers from the Fops and Phanatics.

LACY: Snort!

Lacy mockingly "huffs" and crosses her arms with a flourish, to ROFLs *from the Fops and Phanatics.*

FORCIBLE: This seems, Ms. Undergarments, to be a clear case of confusion between causation and correlation.

LACY: Right you are, Mrs. Forcible.

WATCHMEE: I always tell my students, "Do not speak of data in which you are not thoroughly enmeshed."

WILDEHAMMER: A cautionary tale for us all.

FOGGYBOTTOM: I will have you know, sir and madams, that I'm always thoroughly enmeshed in the data. I enmesh myself in it at work. I take it home with me and enmesh myself some more. I enmesh myself in it during my dreams as I sleep. I could not be more enmeshed in the data!

Cheers of derision from the Fops and Phanatics.

Lacy stands and, hands on hips, scoldingly glares the audience into restoring proper decorum. She sits, straightening the hem of her gown.

LACY: One final question, Miss Foggybottom. How do you think yonder magick lantern projects illuminations on the wall? Does it contain a little man with a little candle, casting shadows?

FOGGYBOTTOM: Certainly not!

Exeunt Miss Foggybottom, pursued by a Bear.

I said, "At least she didn't mention you by name."

"Several people identified me as Miss Foggybottom in the comments section."

"I still think your likeability is in the top quintile."

She tried to smile, but the muscles around her mouth didn't cooperate. We stared at each other across her desk. The sun had set within the past hour, but it seemed to rise and set and rise again. Set and rise and set again. It felt like eons passed, the time it takes for gravity to coalesce masses of spinning matter into a dense ball of hot gas that ignites into a sun that burns for billions of years before winking out as a cold cinder. Neither of us moved from our positions, but our pheromones seemed to fill the office with an animal mustiness.

Maryanne and I left work separately, but we met at the Dancing Palms Motel overlooking Highway 101. We worked out, through the flesh of our mortal bodies, the intangible anxieties of

- legions of frustrated Boing;) shareholders who wanted to sell their stock but continued to hold out hope it would make one last comeback;

- a generation of aging Boing;) users who used our website nostalgically, the way a grown man occasionally puts on a baseball glove and throws a ball in the air to himself before realizing he's got more important things to do;
- hundreds of major advertisers who wanted Boing;) to succeed and grow in order to give the dominant players some competition;
- thousands of Boing;) employees who wondered if Marian Sallowaskky was correct when she continually said, "Nothing but deadwood is left at Boing;)"; and
- the two of us—we'd been fighting the good fight, bleeding Boing;) Blue, and yet, we felt like we were failing.

Although Maryanne left early the next morning, I stayed at the Wild Palms for three more days. I called in sick and ordered room service. I used the motel's Wi-Fi to obsessively check the Boingstream data, watching usage conform to my prediction, declining with each passing day. I watched some cable TV, but that only reaffirmed my decision three years earlier to cut the cord. I found programming that suited my tastes better on Netflix, where I binged on the first three seasons, all 80 episodes, of the anime series *Naruto.*

At last I returned home. My newspapers—subscribed to as an act of charity toward an industry that my industry had disrupted—lay piled in the yard of my condominium like tiles fallen from a blue roof.

Maryanne and I continued to encounter each other at work—in the hallways, in meetings, at the gym, at Bytes. We both behaved as if our liaison hadn't occurred, but I'll never forget the night we set aside our challenges and embraced our opportunities at the Dancing Palms.

TRAINING

As a data analyst, I've been trained to notice outliers, points in a data set that are dramatically different from the rest of the data points. Sometimes outliers are anomalies. But sometimes they're meaningful.

I had a particular 1:1 meeting with Wilson during this period that was an outlier. We met in Integrity, the week after Boingstream launched. It was an outlier because we didn't talk about his incredibly beautiful and talented wife, children, and Weimaraner; we talked about me.

Wilson had just completed a leadership training course, "Being Your Best as a Boss at Boing;)," where he was taught managerial and coaching techniques. I knew he'd attended the course. And he knew I knew. So it was weird when he blatantly used the techniques on me. It was if he needed to achieve a personal goal to practice an assignment from the training.

He rose as I entered Integrity, and he offered me a seat. "How are you doing, Glenn?"

"No complaints." I sat, folding my arms and slouching in my chair. The reason I remember this is he mirrored me by folding his arms and slouching in his chair.

"So what I hear you saying, is, 'Things are normal.'"

"Pretty much."

"Good to hear. Is it okay, Glenn, if I provide you with some feedback?"

"Uh. Sure."

"When you say things like, 'Things are normal,' it makes me feel like you're not comfortable sharing with me."

"I didn't say, 'Things are normal.' You said that."

"You just said it. You just spoke the words, 'Things are normal.'"

"I was quoting you."

He consulted his notebook. "All right. When you avoid offering details about your daily work life, it makes me feel like you're not comfortable sharing with me."

"I'm *not* comfortable sharing with you."

"Why not?"

"Because we have conversations like this one."

"What's wrong with this conversation? I have conversations like this with other people, and they share with me. Why won't you share with me, Glenn?"

It felt like a trap. If I answered honestly, I expected him to use my own words against me. If I answered dishonestly, I expected the same, except the damage that can be inflicted by words I don't believe in can be wildly unpredictable. I inhaled, exhaled, did a little "Team Objective!" cheer in my mind, and gave him the difficult feedback he seemed to be seeking. "Wilson, I don't trust you."

"You don't trust me?" He looked at his notes. He looked at me. "You don't trust me?" A look of discovery washed over his face, as if realizing he intended to conduct a giving-feedback session but somehow ended up in a receiving-feedback session. He flipped through his notebook to a page near the end. He tapped it forcefully with his finger. He pushed the notebook away, disgustedly; it slid across the table and fell to the floor. He stared at me. He sat too straight in his chair. He seemed to be resisting an urge to remove his shirt.

"Why don't you trust me? I think I should've earned your trust by now, through my actions."

I shrugged.

"Actions speak louder than words, Glenn. That shrug. Louder than words!"

"I didn't—"

He interrupted me. "Don't I approve your vacation requests promptly, within twenty-four hours? Don't shrug!"

"I wasn't—" A look of discovery might have washed over my face as I realized that I thought I was in a two-way feedback session but had ended up in a one-way feedback session.

"You and I both know the answer: Yes. Oh, sure, there was that one time, when you had to remind me, after your vacation. I fixed the problem with HR. I *fixed* it. For *you*. I'm the one who ordered the cake for your last birthday party. *German Chocolate.* I'm the one who helped you craft your quarterly goals so they achieve the Three Ms: meaningful, manageable, and measurable. This is a data-driven company, Glenn. *Data driven!* Things need to be measurable, Glenn. *Numbers!* Remember the stretch goal you picked for Q3? 'Increase awareness of team internally.' How much? Does that mean making one more Boinger aware of the team? Or one thousand? You accused me of scoffing. I don't scoff. I *lead.* The sound that came out of my mouth, that, that *hwah!*, that was *leadership*, Glenn! Put a number on it. *Data driven*! We made it 'increase awareness by 50 percent.' Which is twice as much as you proposed. Stretch goal. *Twice as much.* That's why we set goals, Glenn. To *stretch.* I know it's uncomfortable. It's uncomfortable *for me. Hwah!* Leadership. You exceeded the goal. *Exceeded.* And what happened? You received your first-ever Exceeds quarterly rating. You'd been stuck at High Delivers. I got you to Exceeds. Me. I made that happen! And you don't *trust me*? I read all the emails you send me! Sometimes my inbox is nothing but Glenn! But I read them! Every word! Even when you go on and on and on! Which you do! A lot!"

I'd never seen Wilson become unhinged; needless to say, it was awkward. His face was red and puffy. He unbuttoned the top three buttons of his shirt and fanned himself with the collar. I watched him gain control over himself as he picked up his notebook from the floor and consulted his notes.

I had shifted my position so I was sitting at the edge of my chair with my hands folded on the table. My mouth was hanging open; I closed it. He assumed the same position, opened his mouth and then closed it.

My head had been cocked to one side; I cocked it to the other side. Wilson did the same.

I unfolded my hands and laid them flat on the table. He did the same.

I folded my arms tightly across my chest. He did the same.

I stared at him, then blinked three times. He did the same.

I rubbed my stomach circularly while at the same time patting my head up and down. He didn't do the same. He sighed. "I value you, Glenn, and the work you do for our team."

I assumed this 1:1 was an outlier because Wilson had just attended the training course, itself an outlier among Wilson's normal activities. The dual-outlierness prevented me from realizing this 1:1 was important. It wasn't an anomaly outlier; it was a meaningful outlier. The meaningful part was *Wilson had been closely reading all the emails I'd sent him.*

INITIATIVE

"Wassup, dawg?" That's how Darryl greeted me in his office for my second Coffee with Darryl, for my Boingstream Rockstar Award. He shook my hand in the normal way, not in the way he'd shaken Jocelyn's hand.

I sat across from him, and Felicious placed a steaming mug of tea before me. She cleared her throat extendedly before saying softly, "Hi Glenn-Glenn." She quickly walked away and closed the door behind her.

As he blew on his tea, I jumped right in. "Darryl, there's something you should know. Boingstream isn't performing well. In fact, it's doing quite poorly."

"Don't be Danny Downer, bro. I use it every day, and it's the bomb."

One of the amazing things about the internet is that you can be the only person experiencing something, and yet you assume everyone else is experiencing it, too. Or you can be experiencing something simultaneously with millions while feeling completely alone. It's difficult to tell whether you're in the midst of a global mosh pit or dancing alone in a barren wasteland.

There are indicators that tell you if the road you're on is well traveled or less traveled. When you watch a YouTube video, there's a views metric on the page that tells you how many times the video played. If it says: 237,441,317, then you know it's extremely popular. On the other hand, if the views are fewer than ten, you know you're watching something that probably only the uploader's relatives have watched; it's almost like being a member of their family.

I wanted Boingstream to prominently display a metric such as, "X million people are streaming music right now," but Joe Rupp was adamant about not including it. He claimed we didn't have access to the real-time data needed to do that, and he was probably right. But I later suspected he also was trying to avoid the embarrassment of someone like Darryl using Boingstream and seeing a message such as, "14 people are streaming music right now." A smart move by Joe Rupp, but it made it more difficult for me to convince Darryl that Boingstream was failing.

"Boingstream's total daily users have fallen to twenty thousand. The goal was two million. We're decisively off pace."

"I know, homie. I've been getting the data. And daily streams per user are whack, yo! We're up to fifty now. That's an average of almost three hours of streaming per user per day. Ridonculous!"

"Yes, but that's because we've shrunk down to a loyal core audience, and we're not bringing in new users. Daily streams per user isn't as important as total daily users and total daily streams, both which have fallen day after day since launch."

"I hear you, bro. But fifty streams per user is seriously bitchin'. And the users overindex among digital natives, like some smart dude I know said they would."

It took me a moment to realize he was talking about me. I registered the compliment with an awkward smile and then persisted. "Yes, but we need way more of them to have an impact on the network. Twenty thousand users isn't enough to succeed. It's simple math."

He looked at me sympathetically, as if I were incapable of seeing the big picture. "Fifty streams per user, yo. Three hours per day!"

It appeared somebody had convinced Darryl that streams per user was the most important metric. I'm not saying that person didn't Get It. It was probably the opposite. They Got It and had been spinning results in order to buy time for acquiring a higher-titled position at a digital technology company that was moving u&2tr.

I tried to think of a different approach to take, a different metaphor for Boingstream's slow death, a different way to convince Darryl. But he had something else top-of-mind. It caught me by surprise. "Switching gears. Apologies, dude. I'm taking you off the TTTT. But I want to thank you for your service. You rocked it."

"Can I ask, why?"

"Mission accomplished, bro."

"My mission, or the TTTT's mission?"

"Yours. The TTTT will continue to rock on, with a couple of fresh faces."

"So I'm being replaced."

"It's like this. The people on the TTTT are high-performance, high-maintenance, Type-A executives. Each of them needs to be the smartest person in the room. Especially Sousie, who needs to be the smartest person in all rooms that have ever existed. That doesn't always happen, especially at the TTTT, where everyone's smokin' smart. So the next-best alternative for people like them is to not be the dumbest person in the room. That's where you came in, Glenn."

I paused, awaiting further information.

"You're a smart dude, one of the best and brightest, but there are many kinds of smartness, yo. When they hear you go all in the weeds about data methodologies, they see it as proof that they're smarter than you. Because they're too smart to go all in the weeds about data methodologies. That's for losers and dumbasses, and they're genius executives who spend all their time focusing on the big picture. Any dumbass can be all in the weeds. It takes a genius to see the big picture. That's how they think. I'm just sayin'."

I managed to squeak out, "Yes."

"I'm sure you've noticed that after you speak at TTTT meetings, we get more stuff done, and conversations flow more smoothly."

"Yes."

"That's because before you speak, each of them is anxious about being the smartest in the room, so they bitch slap each other for dominance. But as soon as you speak, they realize they aren't the dumbest person in the room, making them more comfortable, more human, more able to work together to solve problems. And feel me, I don't think you're dumb. Nah, man. Screw dat, yo. You're probably a lot smarter than most of them. But your intelligence doesn't manifest in a way that threatens them. Instead, it manifests in a way that makes them feel superior—to you. Oh, dude! I'm bumming you out. You're not being fired. Just relieved of TTTT duty. It was fun while it lasted, cuz, so I wanted to make sure you got a parting gift, hence the second Rockstar Award."

I felt my twitchy eye twitching. I felt the back of my mouth go dry as dust, while the front of my mouth salivated so aggressively that I had to swallow rapidly to avoid drooling. The saliva hit the dry back of my mouth like a thunderstorm on a desert, running off into my throat like a torrent. I cleared my throat, Feliciously. My mind and salivary system were working in parallel. I objectified the situation. I was in control of how I interpreted it. This could be soul crushing, or it could be cathartic, depending on how I chose to see it. That might sound subjective, but it wasn't. It was a decision arrived at after objectively considering all the options.

I concluded that I was a catalyst whose presence made it possible for the TTTT to GSD. Without me, there was squabbling and gridlock. With me, the team accomplished its goals.

I swallowed and swallowed and swallowed again and was finally able to speak. "You've heard my motto."

Darryl nodded.

"'Being objective makes me effective.' If I had a sub-motto, which I don't, because sub-mottos are silly, it would be, 'I work harder so you feel smarter.' So, if the TTTT members felt smarter in my presence, I succeeded at something important to me, plus I helped the company."

He said, "All right!" except he said it in a stilted, urban way, removing the L's and R: "*Ah ight!*" He continued, "Sorry about this. Reality hits you hard, bro."

"Can I ask, who's replacing me?"

"Here's the thing. Two *problemos. Numero uno* is that Boingstream was your idea, and now it's been launched. So it's hard to just pass you off as a dumbass, because dumbasses don't launch products. *Numero* two is that you're only a senior manager, and it's just too easy to feel smarter than someone with a much lower title. So I needed to bring in a dumbass, no offense—"

"None taken."

"—with a higher title. You know him well, Wilson, your manager, who I'm also promoting to VP."

I stuttered as my mind skipped a beat. "You...you...you're promoting Wilson because the TTTT will function better if he's an executive? Not because he does excellent work?"

"The TTTT is the most important team in the whole damn company. I'm just doing what needs to be done to keep it running smoothly. Hate the game, not the player."

"Wilson isn't a good manager. I don't think he's ever come up with an original idea, and he takes credit for my work without attributing it to me."

Darryl sort of nodded and shrugged at the same time.

I continued, "Do you know what he does? He books a conference room every day for six months at a time, just so he has his own office. When other people try to use that room, he chases them out, claiming it's our market research war room. He thinks he deserves his own office, so he's taken one for himself, even though there's always a shortage of conference rooms for meetings. He has a cube he isn't even using!"

"I hear you, bro. Now he doesn't need to do that anymore. As a VP he gets his own office, officially. Plus, there's no denying that the dude looks great with his shirt off. *Amirite?*"

I nodded, reluctantly. But rather than ponder the injustice of torso-based discrimination, I did something unusual for me. I spoke without thinking first. "That's blatantly unfair. I deserve a promotion, too."

Darryl responded immediately. "True dat."

That's how I became Director of Marketing Insights. With those two words, Darryl increased my annual salary by twenty percent and doubled my target annual bonus, merely as artifacts of my promotion from Senior Manager to Director. The promotion also gave me privileges to use the fluffier towels in the company gym, a benny reserved for directors and above.

We shook hands one last time. And when I say last time, I really mean it. It was the final time Darryl and I were in a room together. As we said goodbye, in retrospect, his typically overly warm hand felt only normally warm, and his presence was unintimspirating.

CHANGE

I began my lunch alone, in Bytes, at the wobbly table, in the belly button of the known universe, a bit earlier than the twelve o'clock rush. After my second Coffee with Darryl, I felt simultaneously proud and humiliated. Proumiliated. As I objectively assessed the situation—I could accelerate mortgage payments for my condominium, and my Thursday afternoons were free to GSD—I realized my situation was net-positive. When you objectively assess a situation and realize things aren't as bad as they seem, you start to feel better.

Another Boinger came up to my table. "Mind if I join you?"

This was unusual, but not unprecedented. I myself made a point of sitting next to a Boinger I didn't know roughly once a month. That's how I became acquainted with Nathaniel in HR, who gave me a heads up about a new fringe benny—Boing;) tattoos, which the company would reimburse the expense of, if applied anywhere on the body except for the face, neck, or groinal areas. To be clear, you could get a Boing;) tattoo in those areas. The company just wouldn't reimburse you for it. I approved of lunching with unknown Boingers, so I gestured across the table. "Please have a seat."

He was tallish—more than average height—but he stooped slightly, making him seem shorter than he was. He had brown eyes, but they were flecked with shiny bits, so they looked somewhere in between light and dark. His brunette hair caught the light in such a way that it seemed to shimmer with a golden haze. As he sat, I caught a glimpse of the first name on his badge, Siddharth. Could this be the famous Sid Daturin, with the titanium card that granted him entry to any meeting?

He watched me as he slowly chewed a bite of veggie pizza. "You're Glenn."

"Have we met?"

"I've heard of you. Boingstream. Your motto. The direct report who was hospitalized."

"Are you in HR?"

"I work in the CEO's cabinet. My name is Sid." He slowly chewed another bite of veggie pizza. He pulled *the card* from the breast pocket of his shirt, and he handed it to me.

It did seem to be titanium, as rumored; it was dull gray, like a cloudy day, and it was heavier than it looked like it ought to be, about as heavy as a deck of cards or a dead mouse stuck in a trap. On it were engraved the words: "The bearer of this card is allowed to attend any meeting at Boing;) or to sit at any table in Bytes. If you got a problem with that, text me, yo." And it was etched with Darryl's signature and phone number.

I handed the card back to him. "What's the most interesting meeting you've attended with this card?"

He finished chewing before saying, "A meeting of the TTTT." He took another bite and watched me as he chewed.

I was unsure what to say. Should I have asked, "What is the TTTT?" even though I knew the answer? Should I have admitted I used to be a TTTT member? Should I have pointed out I never saw him at a TTTT meeting? I paused, awaiting further information, while slowly chewing my own food, *aloo gobi* with basmati rice.

"This was before you were on the TTTT."

"You seem to know a lot about me."

"It's my job to know about people."

"And what, exactly, is your job?"

"I'm a change agent."

"Ah." I thought I knew what a change agent was. I thought of myself as a change agent—working diligently to make beneficial change through illuminating insights. But I didn't want to sound clueless in front of someone who clearly knew more about change agenting than I did. So I took another tack. "What was special about that TTTT meeting?"

"Ted." He pushed the last bite of pizza into his mouth. It was a large bite. A double bite. He chewed it slowly and thoroughly, watching me the entire time. His expression was slightly self-amused and free of worry, like what the Mona Lisa's expression would have been if she'd been chewing a double bite of pizza. When he swallowed the last bit of food, he wiped his mouth with a napkin, pushed his tray aside, and leaned his elbows on the table. "Did you ever notice Ted's whiteboarding superpower?"

Although Sid clearly knew high-level information about personnel and the company, I was unsure how to respond. He responded to my hesitation by pulling out his titanium card and showing me the back. Etched on it were the words: "The bearer of this card has a Need to Know."

Relieved, I told him, "I noticed that nobody would let Ted near the whiteboard. Nearly every meeting he'd step toward the whiteboard, and the others would tell him to sit down. Sometimes they seemed frightened."

"That's because all of them have fallen prey to his whiteboarding skills before, like they did the time I attended the TTTT meeting. I don't even remember what he whiteboarded, but I remember it was perfect and brilliant, until the meeting was over, when whatever he whiteboarded disappeared, like a hallucination."

"I had the same experience while watching him whiteboard at a product demo. He's got charisma."

"Charisma, and more. The company's better off now that he's gone. He promised but never delivered. If you ever encounter that guy again, don't let him near a whiteboard. He'll mesmerize you, like a serpent, or a vampire."

"Or Charlie Sheen."

"That's right. His appeal is inexplicable. If you're arguing with Ted about a strategy, or a tactic, or politics, or the weather, you can hold your own, even convince him you're right. But if he's able to diagram his thoughts on a whiteboard, you will lose. You might not realize it at the time, but he'll bamboozle you with his brilliance, and you'll walk away thinking we're just weeks away from a three-hundred-dollar per share stock price, and unlimited power from cold fusion, and disease-free living through bio algorithms, and frictionless high-speed pneumatic travel that takes you from New York to Los Angeles in fifteen minutes, and a universal digital ledger of transactions that disrupts the entire financial system. But as soon as you're out of the conference room, down the hallway, you'll start thinking of exceptions. Details that don't make sense. Numbers that don't add up. You'll move out of the influence of Ted and his whiteboard. And you'll start wondering why his team hasn't launched a single successful product in years. And you'll remember that their biggest claim to fame was Marian Sallowaskky's 'glowing' review of the Boing;) Gas Finder app for iPhone, which she called, 'The best damn gas finder app for iPhone ever in the history of forever,' which everyone outside of Ted's team realized was sarcasm."

"If you know so much, why don't you change it? Isn't that what a change agent does?"

"The role of a change agent is frequently misunderstood. I can understand how you might think that."

"What does a change agent do?"

"Basically, I'm a storyteller and a consultant. I spot trends. I connect dots. I identify changes that need to be made, and then I suggest that other people make them."

"I thought a change agent inspired others to make change. Beneficial change."

"Yes, I do inspire. That's right."

"Do you GSD?"

"Of course. I GSD by pointing out what needs to be done."

"But do you GS actually D?"

He laughed. "I'm not the guy who makes sure things get done, if that's what you mean."

That didn't sound like actually GSDing to me. How can a person be an agent of change without actually GSDing?

He stood and picked up his tray. "You should try being a change agent, Glenn. You don't have to drink the Kool-Aid, and you can level up before the shit hits the fan."

That was the only time I ever saw Sid. Soon after, I learned he'd left Boing;) to work at Dobbler, Bueller, Spicoli & von Slonecker (DBSvS), a famous VC company in the Valley, where his title was Change Agent in Residence. It's worth noting that Ted subsequently joined DBSvS, where his title was Entrepreneur in Residence.

In retrospect, during our discussion, Sid displayed several of the signs and symptoms of a Boinger who was about to leave the company.

- Cynicism
- Lack of passion
- Quoting Marian Sallowaskky in a way that suggested she was right about an issue
- Overstuffing his mouth with food

POST

"Is that a new yoga pose?"

This question was asked eleven times in eleven BM windows on my computer screen. Co-workers had messaged it to me. This is something we did to each other when there was a new entry on TISATAASQ. And the newest question was, "Is that a new yoga pose?"

I began experiencing the symptoms of a full-blown anxiety attack. My mouth became dry. My tongue became numb. My heart pounded aggressively, and I could feel my pulse in my extremities—my fingers, my toes, the tip of my nose. I felt simultaneously nauseated and incontinent, as if a madman in my middle was waving a gun, and everything within my digestive tract was rushing for the exits. My field of vision grew darker, except for the fluorescent lights on the ceiling pulsing overly brightly.

I was having this reaction because when I'd found Jocelyn lying on the floor of her cube, I asked her, "Is that a new yoga pose?" The stupid question was mine!

Needless to say, my question was ridiculous. I'd known that as soon as I'd said it. Yoga is an ancient practice. It doesn't change with the seasons. They aren't inventing new poses every year in order to stimulate demand, are they? Clearly, yoga is trendy. More and more people seem to be doing it. I keep thinking I should do it to alleviate nagging lower back problems. Jocelyn did it. I think that's why I said what I said. Jocelyn on the floor equaled, in my mind, "She must be doing yoga."

It got worse. I also said, "You should try Downward-Facing Dog," a no-doubt strength-building, but also ill-suited for the workplace, position. As soon as I said it, I knew I'd crossed the line of appropriateness. Nevertheless, I continued to say over-the-line things. "You're so pretty. So full of life. And I'm sorry I crossed the line with my inappropriate comments," which, given the situation—Jocelyn unconscious and barely breathing—was ironic. She was much less full of life than normal.

As I pondered the question's appearance on TISATAASQ, the shadowy corner beneath my desk seemed to be beckoning as the safest place to be. If I'd lied down, and if anyone had found me and thought I was in a yoga pose, it would've been Knee-Biting Monkey. But I didn't lie down. I tried to think good thoughts, happy thoughts. I looked over at the "Resurrection, Yo" poster, but that didn't help. It made me imagine the Darryl in the poster pointing at me and saying, "You're a dumbass, yo." I closed my eyes while remaining in my chair. I thought about the ladybug and the Google Street View car. I thought about blue eyes and blue skies. I thought about Maryanne's crooked smile. I tried to breathe slowly and steadily, deliberately inhaling and exhaling. But my respiration system seemed to be spasming. My inhales were jerky. My exhales were interrupted by waves of muscular rebellion throughout my torso. I realized I was sobbing. Silently. Wetly.

I don't know how long I sat there crying. Eventually, my sobs grew further apart and then stopped. And my brain started working again. I re-read the IMs from co-workers. Some were informative. "There's a new TISATAASQ question." Some were inquisitive. "What does it mean?" Some were speculative. "It sounds like Darryl alpha-tested some new pickup lines at the Annual Sales Conference." None of them associated the question with me.

At least one person could associate me with the question. Obviously, Jocelyn must have been conscious when I asked it, and she must have heard me say those other things. And assuming Darryl was the person behind TISATAASQ, Jocelyn must have repeated it, perhaps during her Coffee with Darryl or during whatever time they spent together practicing their elaborate handshake. I PowerPointed the situation to help me assess it objectively.

TISATAASQ
Assumptions & Possible Scenarios

ASSUMPTIONS

- J. heard me ask the Q
- J. told the Q to D., who posted it on TISATAASQ

POSSIBLE SCENARIOS

- *D. doesn't know who asked the Q*
  - Stupidity of question doesn't affect D.'s opinion of me
- *D. knows I asked the Q and thinks…*
  - Q is stupid, but I'm a worthy Rockstar and not a dumbass
  - Q is stupid, and I must be a dumbass for asking it (*worst-case scenario*)

Boing;)

So, the worst-case scenario was that Darryl thought I was a dumbass. That's essentially what he told me during our recent coffee. It wasn't something I didn't already know, plus it was something I'd already accepted.

As I re-read TISATAASQ, I noticed that many questions on the list might be characterized as humorous.

- You want some meat to go with those buns?
- Where did you come from, you sexy thang?
- Do you know the way to San Jose?
- If I told you you had a beautiful body of work, would you hold it against me?
- Who needs the beat when the beat's too slow?

This meant some of the questions weren't necessarily stupid, as in the asker was unintelligent. They were stupid, as in silly and absurd, a state of being each of us is capable of entering occasionally. It seemed to me, "Is that a new yoga pose?" fell into the latter category. It was funny. A re-rereading of my BM messages corroborated this—many of my co-workers found this latest question to be funny.

It also was an accomplishment. I made TISATAASQ! It was the Boinger equivalent to having a post reach the home page of Digg or getting a cartoon published in *The New Yorker*. There had been Boingers who publicly announced their authorship of TISATAASQ questions. For example one Boinger friend posted on Facebook, "I admit it. The latest Stupid Question was mine," resulting in a round of Likes by his Boinger friends and a round of "Huh?"s by his non-Boinger friends. Wanda from B2B Marketing claimed to have been the source for thirteen questions, including, "Are Boing;) Days coming back?" in reference to special time off that everyone in the company was given a couple of years earlier in order to maintain morale after the stock price fell dramatically; she seemed to be proud of it. But I wasn't going to publicly own "Is that a new yoga pose?" because I didn't want to have to explain the circumstances behind it.

If this question sounds familiar to you, it's probably because you remember the meme it spawned. This occasionally happened to TISATAASQ questions; they went viral.

You might have seen the photos that spread virally of President Obama twisting his body to keep from dropping a squirming baby, or of Ryan Gosling and Eva Mendes pressing foreheads together, or of an Indian yogi in the Saturday Night Fever pose, each with the caption, "Is that a new yoga pose?" Or photos of cats in awkward and funny poses, with the caption, "Me haz yoga." Maybe you visited the newyogapose Tumblr, which was *NSFW* = not safe for work, which means content that is pornographic, gory, or thought provoking.

As I was concluding my analysis of the new TISATAASQ question, Jocelyn appeared at the threshold of my cube, holding her Rockstar Award. She looked taller and straighter than usual, as if she'd been doing a lot of yoga.

I closed all files on my desktop because they were NSFJ. I didn't want her to see that I'd been obsessing over the new TISATAASQ question. And she didn't bring up the topic. She offered me a pita chip; I declined it with a wave. Then she held out her Rockstar Award and a black Sharpie. "Will you sign it?"

"Sure." It had already been signed by Darryl and Wilson. Jocelyn had saved a place for my signature on the back side of the Rock. I signed it, "Glenn Cregg." There was no room for my title, Director of Marketing Insights, or for my motto. So I wrote beneath my signature BOMME, so that whenever Jocelyn looked at it, she would hear my motto in her mind.

"Thanks!" she returned to her cube.

It was a nice gesture. But it didn't change the way I'd come to feel about her behavior. If I'd been further along in my quest to become a truly great manager, I might've confronted her with a behavior-modifying statement, such as, "When you shared a personal and confidential statement with the CEO, I felt betrayed," or "When you criticized my analysis of the Project Melody results and also revealed that the WOS had been greenlighted, I felt ambushed and manipulated." If I had a real, tangible, Manila-folder file for Project Clarion Call open on my desk, I would've closed it and filed it away permanently.

Without thinking about it, I put on my headset and dialed the company conference call number and inputted eight random digits, followed by the pound sign (#). That placed me into a Sales conference call where a youthful-sounding woman was explaining a new audience targeting tool. I hung up and tried again and ended up in a B2B Marketing conference call where a man was shouting about one-pagers. When I joined the call, my presence was announced with an anonymous beep. The man yelled, "Who just joined the call? *Who just joined the call?*"

I hung up and gave it a third shot and got what I wanted—the onhold music, known as "The Boing;) Overture," an equal parts soothing and irritating wash of strings and woodwinds that rose and fell endlessly.

I must've listened for half an hour while trying to sort out my thoughts. It didn't work. I hung up, and I went to the parking lot and got in my car and drove until I found a secluded spot, the empty parking lot of the Shoreline Amphitheater, in the shade of an oak tree. I put on my Boingstream earbuds and plugged them into my iPhone. I dialed a number in my contacts list that I'd identified as belonging to ASDF. And I opened the kimono to Marion Sallowaskky.

METRICS

Marian Sallowaskky and I talked for a long time. When I called her, my car was fully in the oak tree's shade. When we ended our conversation, my car was fully in amber sunlight as the sun set in the west.

I told her everything. Well, almost. My motto. The TTTT. Darryl's weird youth-isms, which she'd noticed. Jocelyn's hospitalization. Project Clarion Call. TISATAASQ. The WOS. GSD. My Rockstar Awards and Coffees with Darryl. Project Melody. Boingstream. The research I might have manipulated without intending to be manipulative. How Jocelyn called me out on it. The Advanced Science guys. The wobbly table in Bytes. Wilson. Wheeezer. Sid. Ted. The ladybug.

She asked questions to keep me talking. "How did that make you feel?" and "What did you do next?" and "What was Darryl's reaction?"

After I'd talked myself hoarse and my iPhone had begun emitting complaining beeps signaling my battery was nearly dead, there was a long silence. She didn't fill it.

I asked, "How do you get all your inside information about Boing;)? Who's your mole?"

"You are, Glenn."

"No, I mean, who has been your mole? Who's been providing you with information all these years?"

"It's usually someone new. Boingers rarely give me information twice. They all get so infuriated by what goes on at your company that they want to unburden themselves to me, in the hope that I'll shine a spotlight on a particular madness and help them cure it. I'm sort of a confessor to

Boingers, from the lowest ranks to the highest. I have long-term, highly-placed sources at Google, Facebook, HP, Intel, Microsoft, LinkedIn, Twitter, Amazon, Apple, you name it. My sources at those companies provide me with all the intel I need. It's a problem, because when one of them moves to another company it can take months to find a new one. But at Boing;), I don't need to cultivate sources because everyone comes to me. My average tips per Googler, Microsoftie, or Tweep is greater than ten. My average tips per Boinger is 1.2."

Hearing her use those metrics impressed me. Even, dare I say, *aroused* me. There was one thing I needed to know. "Who told you we formed a White Tiger Team?"

"You know how it works, *Glenn-Glenn.* I don't divulge my sources." Then she cleared her throat in a dramatic, extended fashion. "Let's just say I have special ring tones for most of the people on the TTTT, and their assistants." Then she gave me some great feedback. "I can tell you're not made for this mole business, Glenn. Don't ever call me again."

The call terminated. I wasn't sure whether she hung up or whether my phone disconnected itself as the battery died. But it felt like as good a place as any for the conversation to end.

ACTIONABLE

"When the shit hits the fan" is a popular saying describing the moment when unpleasant private knowledge becomes public knowledge. I hadn't thought deeply about this saying until the shit hit the fan for me. When shit hits a fan, the rapidly rotating blade disperses the unpleasant material widely, flinging it onto everyone nearby. The fan that my shit hit was quite powerful, dispersing unpleasantness throughout Boing;). In my mind, I conflated the shit we were getting done with the shit hitting the fan, even though they were different shits—*When you're getting shit done, it's only a matter of time before it hits the fan.*

It all happened pretty quickly. Marian Sallowaskky published a blog post based on our conversation. She focused on Boingstream and how its development was predicated on "falsified"—her word—market research. She described how it was failing in the marketplace and how Boingers were ignoring evidence of its failure by not shutting it down. She didn't mention my name, but she referred to me as, "an *objective* source within Boing;)"—her italics.

I felt guilty. But I also felt relieved. It wasn't the most constructive way for Boing;) to finally believe me when I said Boingstream was failing, but it was effective.

The next day, the well-known financial services company that sponsored the Boingstream launch filed a lawsuit against Boing;), naming the executive team and the board of directors as defendants. I felt like I deserved to be on that list; after all, it was my actionable research results that turned out to be actionable.

The day after that, three Boingers visited me. They crammed into my cube and introduced themselves.

"Hi there, Glenn. Don't get up. I'm Donna, from HR." She was tall and wearing heels; she reached way down to shake my hand.

A short man in a sport coat didn't need to alter his posture to shake my hand. "I'm Jean-Claude, from Legal." He squinted as he smiled with his lips tightly sealed.

Donna gestured toward a well-built man in the corner of my cube; he seemed much too fit to be a typical desk-working Boinger. "This is Amir. He's a consultant." Amir kept his arms folded, and he nodded at me, with full, unbroken eye contact. Contractors and consultants had orange keycards; mysteriously hanging from Amir's belt was a blue keycard worn by true-blue Boingers. Donna said, "We need you to come with us."

"Is this about Project Melody?"

"We just need you to come with us."

"Should I bring my bag?"

She frowned slightly. "Bring your bag."

I packed a few things and hung my messenger bag over my shoulder. Donna and Jean-Claude led the way, and Amir followed me out of my cube, down the hall, to the elevators. We walked in a scrum across the street to the central campus, with me in the middle. I felt like I had my own Secret Service protection.

A crowd was gathered on the quad outside Bytes. We naturally drifted in that direction. Above Bytes was a floor of conference rooms and training rooms. Extending from beneath the windows of that floor, roughly 25 feet above the ground, was a metal grid—part balcony, part awning, but effective as neither. The windows didn't open, and there was no way outside from within the building, so it was a surprise to see a three year old boy toddling precariously on the grid.

A woman below—the mother—was calling out instructions frantically. "Just sit down, Aiden. Sit down and be still."

Aiden laughed and bounced, enjoying the moment.

I looked at Donna, and she nodded. We all pressed closer into the growing crowd of several dozen Boingers. At the front, next to the mother, stood Wilson. He called up, "Hey Aiden, buddy. I need you to sit down." He was as effective as the mother had been.

Wilson tested a lamp post nearby, wrapping his arms and legs around it. He turned toward the crowd looking anguished, as if he were imagining that child being his own beloved son, Jaryn. His expression quickly changed to one of amazement, as if he were realizing—there's a big crowd here! In retrospect, there was no doubt about what would happen next.

Wilson tore off his shirt, buttons flying. A choral gasp at the sight of Wilson's chiseled torso caught the child's attention—he giggled and sat, with his legs dangling. Wilson quickly scaled the pole until he was at the level of the grid—it was an impressive physical accomplishment, perhaps a result of his quadrathlon training. He reached for the child, who crawled over and climbed on Wilson's neck. It made me recall the monkey on my own back. Wilson slid down the pole gingerly. Based on the nauseating squealing sound, it's likely Wilson lost several layers of skin in the process. He weathered it stoically. As he handed the child to his mother, he pressed one hand against his scraped-and-bleeding six pack while smiling shyly at the crowd.

A big cheer erupted as we applauded Wilson. Wanda from B2B Marketing draped his now-buttonless shirt around his shoulders. I had to give it up for him; I clapped and shouted, "Bravo, Wilson!" I might also have been praising another of his impressive endeavors that I'd learn about soon.

LOOP

They escorted me to the first floor of Building Alpha, down a corridor I didn't know existed, to a conference room I'd never seen in the room scheduling system—Justice.

I sat at the table. Amir placed a beverage before me, again with the eye contact. It was a can of red Kool-Aid. He set it close enough to reach, but not intimidatingly close. Drinking it was optional. I abstained, congrastizing myself for not literally drinking the Kool-Aid just as I was experiencing the consequences of figuratively drinking the Kool-Aid.

Amir stood against the wall and remained there as Donna and Jean-Claude joined me at the table.

She started things off. "We spent some quality time yesterday with Wilson, your manager." She blushed and suppressed a smile, perhaps thinking of Wilson's brave act we'd just witnessed. "He had some interesting things to say that we'd like you to respond to."

"Okay."

Jean-Claude pulled a page from the top of a four-inch stack of papers. "These are printouts of every email you sent over the past year to Wilson." He, too, paused and blushed. I looked over at Amir, who wasn't blushing. Jean-Claude continued. "They're organized and annotated. They tell a compelling story of how you deliberately manipulated market research results to create fraudulent material that deceived key decision makers across the company into investing significant resources in the development of Boingstream. This allegedly fraudulent material was also used to convince a major advertiser to sponsor Boingstream."

"I think 'manipulated' is much too strong a word."

"Is there another word you prefer?"

"Not just one. I prefer to think I allowed myself to be blinded by subjectivity within the context of a struggling digital media and technology company moving in a poorly defined strategic direction."

He was taking notes. "Allowed yourself to be—"

"Blinded by subjectivity. I try at all times to be as objective as possible."

"—Within the context of a struggling?—"

"Boing;) is struggling, right?" Only Amir reacted, with a vigorous nod.

"A struggling technology company?—"

"Digital media and technology company."

"A digital media and technology company that you say is moving in an undefined—"

"A poorly defined strategic direction." At that moment I realized Wilson hadn't been ignoring my emails after all; he'd been studying them. Project Loop provided him with ammunition for an assault against me.

"Got it."

Jean-Claude glanced at Donna, who turned to me. "Why did this happen?"

"I don't know. I guess I got caught up in a deep desire to contribute to Boing;)'s resurrection. I guess I drank the Kool-Aid." I gestured toward the can of Kool-Aid.

Donna opened a folder full of papers. "Wilson has another theory. Is it possible that you're jealous of him and took these actions to sabotage his career?"

I laughed hard and fast, accidentally dislodging some upper-sinus phlegm and then choking on it. I could hardly breathe; I thought I was going to pass out. They watched me without reacting. Maybe they thought I was pretending.

I reached for the can of Kool-Aid. It was my only option. I drank it, and through its fruity sweetness, I washed down the phlegm and could breathe and speak again.

"I'm sorry. That's just ridiculous. I'm not at all jealous of Wilson. I pity him. And if I really wanted to sabotage him, I hope I'd do a better job of it." I coughed some more and took another swig of Kool-Aid. "In fact, it's largely through my actions that he got promoted to VP. Have you talked to Darryl about this?"

"There's no need to talk to Darryl about this." She handed a report to me. It summarized results of an analysis by a forensics lab showing that forty-seven different instances of my fingerprints were found on Wilson's Rockstar Award.

Needless to say, when I saw this evidence, my impression of the Magic 8 Ball improved dramatically. It led me to conclude that this Glenn guy was a criminal mastermind. It was Rockstar-worthy work.

I think I smiled. What else could I do? I also took a long, leisurely drink of Kool-Aid. It tasted pretty good, evoking some of the best parts of childhood: birthday parties, middle school assemblies, and the junk food binges after every sports game where my peers played on the field while I watched from the bench.

"There's an objective explanation for all of it, if you're willing to listen."

Donna sighed. "Of course. We'd like to hear your version."

I wasn't convinced, but I pointed toward the whiteboard anyway. "May I?"

She nodded. But before I mapped out my version of the story on the whiteboard, Amir frisked me. He placed the few possessions I carried on the table—two pens, a whiteboard marker, keys with a Boing;) keyring, thumb drive, wallet, sunglasses, iPhone, and a deck of cards. And then I opened the kimono once again.

I finished by drawing a little rock next to a little star, with a little "2" indicating "squared," to remind them they were dealing with the only two-time winner of the Rockstar Award.

When I was done, Donna took a picture of the whiteboard with her iPhone. "Thanks, Glenn. Duly noted."

I turned over my keycard and my laptop. I collected my possessions; they kept my thumb drive. Jean-Claude handed me a folder of papers that I refused to sign before consulting with an attorney. I was being placed on extended leave, pending the outcome of an internal investigation. And all three of them—Donna, Jean-Claude, and Amir—escorted me to the parking lot and watched me drive away. I waved. They didn't wave back.

ENGINE

Boingstream didn't die of natural causes; it was executed, in the nonbusiness sense of the word. It still had nearly half a million monthly unique users—much less than the two million daily users we had set as the goal—putting it in the top twenty among online streaming music services. It was killed because Boing;) was sued, and shutting it down was part of a settlement.

The sponsors had been doing their own market research and learned that sponsoring Boingstream was harming their brand. While it was increasing their awareness among young people, who had hardly been aware of them before, it was making an association in young people's minds between the brand and, in their words, "the lamest streaming music service ever." Even after it had been sampled and rejected by a mass audience, Boingstream remained somewhat popular among a niche cohort of young music lovers for the "asshattedness," a descriptor that emerged from their research, of the Boingstream recommendation engine.

The recommendation engine was the first in-product application of the WOS. After you selected songs to play, a feature in the product suggested other songs you might enjoy—this was the WOS p13n algorithm at work. Apparently, some young people found the recommendations to be so stunningly ludicrous they'd use it from time to time just for entertainment.

One example cited in the advertiser's research: If you played "Honey, I'm Home" by country pop singer-songwriter Shania Twain, Boingstream recommended "Ain't No Fun (If the Homies Can't Have None)," by rapper Snoop Dogg.

A Tumblr page (f**kyeahboingstream.tumblr.com) was created and devoted to cataloging "asshatted" Boingstream recommendations, along with guesses for why the recommendation was made. Here are some examples.

Song you played	**Song Boingstream recommended**	**How do you think the songs are related?**
"In Bloom" by Nirvana	"Rainy Days & Mondays" by The Carpenters	Depressing songs, depressing singers
"Gigolo" by Nick Cannon	"1812 Overture" by Tchaikovsky	The classical tune has cannons exploding at the end. Get it? Nick *Cannon. Cannons!*
"Bad Blood" by Taylor Swift	"Hot Blooded" by Foreigner	They're related by *blood*
"Dark Fantasy" by Kanye West	"Boris The Spider" by The Who	Both songs contain a whole lot of WTF
"Hey Ladies" by Beastie Boys	"Don't Fear The Reaper" by Blue Oyster Cult	Cowbell
"Pumped Up Kicks" by Foster The People	"Never Gonna Give You Up" by Rick Astley	Boingstream rickrolled me!

I admit I found some of Boingstream's recommendations charming, like the quirky advice of a self-educated, eccentric uncle who did too many drugs back in the seventies. But the sponsors weren't charmed, which just goes to show there's a fine line between charming and grounds for a lawsuit.

CLOUD

I became one of the defendants named in the lawsuit. Initially I'd been left out, so it felt like an oversight had been corrected. I was accused of fraudulent activities leading to large financial losses by the plaintiff, the financial services company. Boing;)'s legal department represented me, but I also had my own attorney who was recommended by a former coworker who'd once needed legal counsel for falsifying credentials on his résumé. I wasn't tried or found guilty of a crime. Instead, I agreed to an arbitrated settlement that required me to never speak the name of the sponsoring financial services company and to spend, at my own expense, two hundred days in a private detention facility called Washboard Acres, in California's Central Valley, that wasn't exactly jail and wasn't exactly camp, but somewhere in between.

Washboard Acres is where I attended Decision Hour Circles with recovering drug addicts like the Cocky Roach app developer, Stefan, and Bo, the large, hot-headed hockey fan. Surprisingly, it was a lot like Boing;)—they took care of our basic needs as long as we attended meetings—except that men who are incarcerated for doing petty crimes while high on drugs underindex in Getting It.

I wasn't allowed to bring my iPhone or other electronic devices, and I was denied internet access during my entire stay. I couldn't use email or PowerPoint. The only data I had access to was in the cloud storage of my own mind.

My time in detention was reduced to a hundred days, to alleviate overcrowding. Apparently there was a steady stream of nonviolent, yet incarceration-worthy people like me. I was informed this might be the case on day four, and it was confirmed on day fifteen. Despite the 50 percent reduction in time spent in incarceration, I had plenty of time to reflect on my actions. I also had time to reflect on why Washboard Acres disclosed it would keep my payment for the two-hundred-day stay even though I would only be there for one hundred days.

There's an old saying, "You can lead a horse to water, but you can't make it drink." The key disconnect is that you and the horse don't share the same language, so the horse doesn't know why you've led it to water, and you don't know why it won't drink. Yet, sometimes it does drink. It's sort of like casting dice, in that there are a limited number of possible outcomes—in the case of the horse drinking, there are two possible outcomes—but you don't know which outcome will occur.

I tried to lead Boing;) to water—a strategy for increasing audience and engagement among digital natives—and it drank. As a result of my attempt to do something good, key metrics—revenue, brand health, stock value—declined. So that was a case where it might've been better if the "horse" had been stubborn and refused to drink. I couldn't help but wonder what a horse would do if it attended meetings in inspirationally named conference rooms, or if it was instructed to block & tackle, or if it was led to a trough filled with Kool-Aid.

There's another saying, "It's darkest right before the dawn." That's just not true. It's darkest at the midpoint between dusk and dawn. At the darkest moment of any night, there are still hours and hours to go until dawn. By the time the sun is nearly up, you've been able to see pretty well and GSD. I know it's meant poetically. Troubles are "darkest," at the pit of desperation and bleakness, before "the dawn," the moment of realization that the worst has passed. But for poetry to work, it has to not completely defy what we know to be true.

And yet, things seemed darkest for me right before I was released from Washboard Acres. I knew when my release date would occur, but that didn't prevent sad Glenn from emerging in the final days before I returned home. I tried giving myself *attaboys* and negotiating extra, real cookies at mealtime—usually oatmeal raisin was the only option in the cafeteria—but they didn't prevent my mood from sinking into depression. I thought I knew how it felt to be depressed; during the course of my life, I'd experienced rejection, disappointment, bad luck, and deaths of friends, family members, and pets. Such events made me sad and, I thought, depressed. I thought I'd been in the pit of despair, but I realized at Washboard Acres that previously I'd merely visited the pit's reception area. True depression is like discovering a deep bottomless abyss is always nearby, just a step away. You might step forward safely, or you might fall.

The morning of my release, as I was packing my few items, I thought of Jocelyn and her pills and her overdose. I thought I could understand how she got there. It was just a matter of setting a stretch goal and working diligently toward achieving it—putting a pill into her mouth and swallowing it with a sip of water, and repeating the procedure until the medicine began to interfere with her motor skills. I couldn't relate to the goal, but I felt a new appreciation for the roadmap she created and followed in order to achieve it.

COMPLETION

In market research, a survey that's been completely filled out by a respondent is called a *completion*. By the time I returned to the world (aka Silicon Valley), many real-life completions had occurred. They were widely reported, not just in Marian Sallowaskky's blog, but in the mainstream media as well.

The Boing;) Board of Directors fired Darryl via text message. He quickly sent a company-wide Goodbye & Good Luck email before his username was disabled.

> To: Boingers-Worldwide
> From: Darryl
> Subject: G&GL
>
> The BOD just whacked me. It's been a pleasure.
> It's been real. Watch your backs, yo!
> Peace!
> d
> (Sent from my iPhone)

The entire board was in turn ousted by a group of shareholders led by Boing;)'s largest shareholder, the California State Employees Pension Fund, which, coincidentally, was a major investor in Washboard Acres. Paco and Stan sided with the shareholder rebellion, giving them the power to replace the board with a new slate of directors, who quickly appointed Stan ("the lucky one") to be the new CEO of Boing;). Paco also returned to the company, in the role of Advisor to the CEO.

You might think Paco ("the smart one") would have been the better choice for CEO, but he'd recently been embroiled in a scandal. He had an extramarital affair with a Boing;) intern that continued when she returned to Reed College to complete her double major in physics and philosophy. Paco split his time between Silicon Valley and the intern's dorm room, where she worked as a resident advisor and where he was granted the title Executive in Residence. Also, Paco's wife filed for divorce and sued for most of his fortune. If she were to win, she would become the number three Boing;) shareholder, behind the pension fund and Stan. So Stan became the CEO.

At his first all-hands meeting, Stan presented Boingers with his new strategy, dubbed The Digital Technology Ecosystem. He explained it by holding up a napkin sketch made during a reconciliation dinner with Paco that showed a three-way Venn diagram depicting an ecosystem of users, advertisers, and Boingers. Of course, I didn't witness this first-hand because I was no longer a Boing;) employee. Marian Sallowaskky somehow got a photo of that napkin and posted it on her blog.

Stan also presented a new logo that and he Paco designed during that reconciliation dinner. According to Stan, via Marian Sallowaskky, "After the seventh round of drinks, we realized—we need a new logo!" They sketched it out on another napkin. It was ALL CAPS, and it integrated the semicolon within the "g." Boingers were instructed to stop writing Boing;) and to start writing BOING) in all company correspondence. That logo napkin also made its way to Marian Sallowaskky's blog.

The day after Stan announced the new strategy and the new logo, BOING)'s stock price dropped dramatically, and within a month, it was below a dollar per share. It was unclear whether this was in response to a lousy strategy or in response to news that the CEO of Tsarevich had completed a transaction whereby all of the valuable parts of his company were "transferred" to another company he owned. This made BOING)'s 40 percent ownership of Tsarevich, previously valued at several billion dollars, nearly worthless. There was much talk in the tech media about whether this was legal, with the general conclusion being that the Russian legal system offered more opportunities for creative accounting than the American legal system did.

Many pundits and Boingers speculated that the extremely low market capitalization of BOING) would lead to an acquisition by one of the dominant players. Surely Microsoft or Google or Facebook or Apple or Amazon or Verizon or AT&T or Comcast or even USA Today would be willing to pay pennies on the dollar for the best damn digital company on the planet, which still reached hundreds of millions of unique users around the world. But as of this writing, such an acquisition hasn't occurred.

Maryanne was one of many BOING) executives who left the company or were fired. In Maryanne's case, she was fired because Stan wanted to "go in a new direction" by hiring a new marketing team. Stan announced the hiring of his new CMO in a video interview with *Business Insider.* The interview exposed one of Stan's personality traits that had the potential to cause his eventual firing—along the lines of Darryl's youth-isms and the excesses of previous Boing;) CEOs—his over appreciation of puns.

The reporter asked, "Why are you firing your entire marketing leadership and hiring a CMO from the retail industry?"

Stan enunciated distinctly, "Because we want to go in a *nude erection.*"

"Do you mean a *new direction*?"

"Yes, a *nude erection.*" Stan giggled uncontrollably. The video of that exchange spread virally throughout the tech industry.

I haven't seen or heard from Maryanne since then. She hasn't responded to any of my attempts to connect with her digitally. It's as if I no longer exist in her personal network; I've become an interstitial. I know she continues to engage digitally—I see her commenting on the posts of mutual friends on Facebook. Sometimes I like one of her posts, just to let her know I'm still here.

I was fired from my job at BOING). There were many minuses to this; I won't catalog them. There were few plusses, but they included a modest financial arrangement that I cannot discuss, per the settlement. Perhaps most importantly, I achieved my goal of no longer reporting to Wilson.

Soon after I was released from Washboard Acres, Jocelyn came to my home to deliver boxes of items from my cube. They included my Rockstar Awards and various Boing;) swag. Except for a mini replica of the orange Barcalounger in Darryl's office, all of it was Boing;) Blue: mugs, glasses, goblets, steins, water bottles, notebooks, ballpoint pens, fountain pens, Sharpies, pencils, bookmarks, business cards, note cards, playing cards, poker chips, challenge coins, key chains, lanyards, thumb drives, ruler, bottle openers, refrigerator magnets, sporks, coasters, stickers, bumper stickers, finger traps, headphones, sunglasses, candles, matches, flashlight, reflector, dog whistle, pennywhistle, "hater" whistle, earbuds, ear muffs, ear plugs, clip-on earrings, baseball caps, camouflage cap, stocking caps, bucket hat, beanies, visors, pith helmet, tam o'shanter, scarf, bandanas, headbands, wrist bands, watch, wall clock, alarm clock, clip board, white board, hand towel, beach towel, beach ball, beach chair, beach umbrella, golf umbrella, travel umbrella, travel plug adapter, travel mouse, wireless mouse, mousepad, apron, photo frame, banners, flags, mini flags, sunglasses, slippers, flip-flops, gloves, fingerless gloves, mittens, oven mitt, baseball mitt, baseball, minibaseball, minifootball, minibasketball, soccer ball, hockey puck, frisbee, thimble, ice scraper, box cutter, pocket knife, pocket watch, pocket sewing kit, pocket toolkit, tire pressure gauge, tape measure, license plate frame, potato chip bag clip, wrapping paper, phone holder, phone charger, phone case, hand sanitizer, mints, bubble gum, hot sauce, lip balm, nail polish, silly putty, guitar picks, class ring, lapel pins, gold medal, trophies, plaques, pet leash, stress ball, fidget spinner, hourglass, snow globe, action figures, plushies, reusable cotton sack, tote bag, backpack, duffel bag, mini duffel bag, Converse All-Stars, Boos Block, Beanie Babies, Snuggie, Pez dispensers, Patagonia fleece and puffy jackets and vests, Birkenstocks, tube socks, athletic socks, toe socks, soccer socks, knee-high socks, boxers, briefs, boxer briefs, raincoat, hoodies, coveralls, jujitsu belt, sweatshirts, tank tops, polo shirts, tuxedo shirt, muscle shirt, long sleeve T-shirts, short sleeve T-shirts, raglan shirts, several different name plates with my name on them, a framed photo of a group of a dozen people at a graffiti art team building workshop in San Francisco that included Jocelyn, Wilson, Maryanne, and me smiling in front of our street-art depiction of the word "Delightful," and a big blue button that when pressed chimed, "Boing;)!"

Jocelyn stood on the threshold of my condominium, holding one of the open-topped boxes of my belongings in front of her. I opened the door wider. "Would you like to come in?"

She declined. "I need to be going."

While I was away, Jocelyn had received and recovered from Lasik surgery. She no longer wore glasses. Even so, she looked at me while tilting her head, as if she were looking over the rims of the glasses she wasn't wearing, seeming to imply something, fidgeting with the box, until I realized she wanted me to take it from her, which I did.

She said, "I will—"

At the same time I said, "I've got—" We both smiled self-consciously. "You go ahead."

"I'll always be grateful to you for hiring me and making me a Boinger."

"Once a Boinger, always a Boinger." I meant it, but it sounded hollow at that moment, as I'd recently entered the ranks of former employees not allowed on campus without signing in, wearing a guest badge, and being personally escorted by a current Boinger.

I'd been referring to myself, but Jocelyn seemed to apply it to herself. "I'm still a Boinger," she said apologetically.

"Of course you are." The meaning of her apologetic tone would become clear several weeks later, when Jocelyn, Joe Rupp, and the

Advanced Science guys would leave BOING) to create a startup called WOSsup, where Jocelyn would be CEO, Joe Rupp would be chief product officer, and the board of directors would include Darryl. Over time, after a few rounds of VC funding, WOSsup would widely be considered a prime acquisition target for the major players, expecting to sell for billions of dollars, making Jocelyn and the others helicopters-and-house-staff rich. In the process, Jocelyn would speak regularly at prominent tech industry conferences. She'd become known for popularizing the codepunk style of fashion that incorporates wearable technology into everyday street clothes. She'd be mentioned regularly in tech industry publications as one of the top young females in the industry—in some, for her brains, and in others, for her looks and fashion. She'd appear to achieve her #lifegoal, creating a platform for inspiration, one that would spawn countless fawning stories in *TechNomNom*, *Business Insider*, *Wired*, and other publications.

All of this was yet to happen. Future Jocelyn would be gracious enough to endorse my skills on LinkedIn and give me a recommendation that would help me acquire a position at another declining internet company that had failed to keep up with the technology and the times, a company with fluffy towels in the gym for everyone and with excellent Chinese and Indian food in the lunch room. In that recommendation, she would generously note that I was "the only two-time winner of the prestigious Boing;) Rockstar Award," so I wouldn't have to be braggy in listing that accomplishment myself.

I still don't see the stunning potential of the WOS. Its promise still hasn't been realized. Like nuclear fusion, peace in the Middle East, or a pill that cures obesity, the disruptive potential of the WOS is always just beyond the horizon. And yet the smartest people at the world's most important digital companies continue investing heavily in WOS-like ideas. So, either the WOS is a truly transformative idea that eventually will get worked out, or it's a seductive fantasy, like the communist idea that people will altruistically give according to ability and take according to need, or like the capitalist idea that unregulated free markets will distribute resources efficiently and fairly, or like the Rastafarian idea that all of society's problems will disappear if everyone smokes marijuana.

If the first of these options is true, then people like me who don't understand or deeply believe in the WOS just need to be patient. I just have to trust that people smarter than me are going to make this work and aren't simply on antidepressant medication that makes them more susceptible to believing in fantasies and taking unreasonable risks.

If the second of these options is true, then it means *everyone*—Jocelyn and the Advanced Science guys, the executives at major digital media/technology companies, the tech industry journalists, the venture capitalists, the stock market analysts and investors, the Big Data researchers, the B&B, the janitors who share stock tips while waiting in the microkitchens to use the microwave—the entire Silicon Valley!—doesn't Get It. And that's just not possible. LOL! *Amirite?*

On my doorstep, Jocelyn went to hug me. I shifted the box to one hip, but not sufficiently for a proper hug, so we sort of bumped shoulders. "Good luck, Glenn. Stay in touch. I'll connect with you on LinkedIn."

"Thanks. Same to you. Let me know if there's ever anything I can do for you."

As she turned to go, I blurted out, "Jocelyn! Please don't ever again try to take your own life. You have so much to live for!"

She looked at me, confused. She tilted her head. Her pupils dilated. A realization washed across her face as she gasped and raised her hand to her mouth. "Oh, Glenn! I have hypoglycemia. I thought you knew that. It's why I'm always snacking on things. When my blood sugar level drops too low, I get depressed and disoriented. If I'm not careful, my blood pressure drops, and I can pass out. That day I wasn't paying attention to my blood sugar level because I was distracted by that stupid Boingmail user-feedback deck."

"But the pills—"

"Glucose. I should have taken one when I felt myself getting wiggly. I was able to open the bottle and shake some out, but I must've passed out before I could take one. I don't remember much after opening the bottle."

My mind raced through the dots I'd connected. Happy Jocelyn. Sad Jocelyn. The plastic guilt. The pills. The new yoga pose. The personal leave. Project Clarion Call. The #lifegoal. The antidepressants. The WOS. Project Melody. The White Tiger Team. The handshake with Darryl. The backstabbing insurrection. Clearly, I hadn't collected and connected the dots objectively, and as a result I'd painted a false portrait.

Jocelyn had a horrified, slack-jaw look that made me realize I was standing there with my mouth hanging open. I closed it. She closed hers.

"I wasn't trying to kill myself. But I do think of you as a lifesaver. If I'd stayed there the rest of the afternoon, I might have slipped into a coma." She looked out into the sunlight, toward the street. Then she turned back to me. "Wait a second. You thought all this time that I tried to kill myself." It wasn't a question. It wasn't an exclamation. It was a conclusion she made from connecting the dots. She chuckled sympathetically. "That explains a lot."

"Like what?"

"Like why you were so nervous the day I came back from my personal leave. It was endearing."

"I thought you were mentally ill and had taken time off to get better."

"That's not far from the truth. I was burned out and hadn't been taking proper care of myself. I spent that time eating right, exercising, and getting plenty of sleep."

"And you started taking antidepressant medication."

"And then I stopped when I no longer needed it. Some people benefit from it long term, but it helped me get through a rough patch. If you're a smart, sentient person and you haven't ever taken antidepressant medication, there might be something wrong with you."

"I've never taken antidepressant medication."

Her eyes filled with empathetic wetness. She put her hand on my shoulder and squeezed gently. "Goodbye, Glenn."

"Goodbye, Jocelyn."

As she walked to her electric car parked on the street in front of my condominium, I stood there holding the box filled with Boing;) Blue swag. With so much blueness in the lower portion of my field of vision, I felt like I was standing in water—perhaps a warm, shallow, tropical ocean bay, or a serene, scenic lake. She got into her car, without looking up, without waving, and she drove soundlessly away, out of the blueness, into the brightness of the day.

ACKNOWLEDGMENTS

Thanks to

- August and Theo. I'm proud to be the dad of the people you've become.
- My dad Gary, mom Barbara (RIP), brother Dave, and hometown friends for letting me be that weird kid in our small town.
- Elizabeth for being the first reader.
- My Peace Corps friends. *Para sa iyo, mga pare ko!*
- The people of Sitio Ibad for teaching me to speak Ilocano, play guitar, make rice over a fire, and wield a machete.
- My Hampf bandmates and friends in The Seattle Scene, where I learned to express myself.
- My Seattle Slam and poetry slam friends for teaching me that creative people are all the same age.
- My friends and mentors at Yale School of Drama for expanding my horizons.
- Smith and Geiger of SmithGeiger for teaching me about the media research business.
- Work friends and colleagues at Yahoo! for inspiring this book.
- Work friends and colleagues at Meta (formerly known as Facebook). We'll always have Live Lockdown, Teh Best Practices, The Cavalcade of Insights, and an old deck that can easily be refreshed for the latest creator incentive program.
- Jen Charat for editing my messy manuscript and teaching me to write a book.
- Suji for making life delicious.

A NOTE ABOUT THE AUTHOR

Brian W. Robinson received a master's degree in playwriting from Yale School of Drama and a bachelor's degree in engineering from UC Davis. He works in the tech industry, analyzing data to understand how and why people find and consume video and other content. He built and led analytics teams for more than eight years each at Meta (Facebook and Instagram) and at Yahoo. He lives in San Francisco.

Manufactured by Amazon.ca
Bolton, ON

39276090R00122